HOME FIRES

HOME FIRES

SUSAN JOHNSON CAMERON

IGUANA

Publisher: Greg Ioannou
Editor: Jess Shulman
Cover design: Jess Sheridan
Interior design: Caitlin Stewart

Library and Archives Canada Cataloguing in Publication

Cameron, Susan Johnson, 1949-, author
    Home fires / Susan Johnson Cameron.

Issued in print and electronic formats.
ISBN 978-1-77180-154-6 (bound).--ISBN 978-1-77180-146-1 (paperback).--
ISBN 978-1-77180-147-8 (epub).--ISBN 978-1-77180-148-5 (kindle).--
ISBN 978-1-77180-149-2 (pdf)

    I. Title.

PS8605.A484H64 2015   C813'.6   C2015-906269-1

                                              C2015-906270-5

This is the original print edition of *Home Fires*.

This story is dedicated to the Johnson clan – past, present and future. You are my sunshine.

Dense clouds of smoke and debris whirled past Annie's tiny kitchen window. She jumped at the deafening boom of an explosion somewhere in the forest beyond. Fingers of fear snaked up her back as she watched flames pounce frantically from tree to tree. A sudden gunshot blast of boiling sap launched chunks of burning bark into the sky. The flying sparks hit the surrounding tinder-dry field. It ignited in an instant.

"The field! God help us!" She grabbed the baby from the cradle and turned to the others. "Run to the tracks!"

Tightly clasping her wailing infant, she snatched a biscuit tin – her few precious family photos and meagre savings – from a high shelf and ran for the door behind her panicked, crying sons.

Hot cinders rained down, pricking her arms. She pulled the baby's blanket tightly around his face. Her eldest son hoisted up his screaming two-year-old brother and bolted down the well-worn path towards the railroad tracks. The other two boys sprinted after him, bawling loudly. Annie was close behind, her lungs burning. The half-mile to the railway seemed insurmountable. Finally they reached the water-filled trench beside the tracks. Annie ordered the children to jump in and clumsily followed them. Her voice was hoarse; she was desperately thirsty. She brought a handful of gritty ditch water to her face and drank. Panting, Annie clutched the terrified children tightly against her. The family watched helplessly as a wall of fire galloped towards their home. In minutes, the house was completely engulfed. Her vision blurred with tears.

"It's gone!" She grabbed her middle son by the shoulder to steady herself. "Our house is gone."

A gust of hot wind brushed across her face. The powerful stench of burnt flesh hit her suddenly and she gagged. She covered her nose and mouth, and the baby's head, with her water-drenched apron. All around her were frantic voices calling for help.

Was that a train she heard in the distance, whistling over the roar of the flame? Or was she was hallucinating in the last minutes of her life?

PART ONE

Chapter One

Cardiff, Wales
1890

Annie heard a scuffle behind her, followed by a child's wail. She turned and saw her little brother Georgie running towards her, tears streaming down his face. The six-year old nearly knocked her over as he flung his arms around her waist.

She had considered leaving without her three younger brothers after they left her waiting fifteen minutes by the school's iron fence, but that earlier irritation was quickly forgotten as she knelt down to inspect Georgie's skinned knee and elbow. She brushed away his tears. Hearing angry, shouted expletives, she looked past her brother to where some boys were fighting.

"You dirty bastards," someone yelled. Annie realized it was her brother, Alfie. He and her brother James stood at the corner of the red-brick building, holding their fists up in fighter stance, ready to defend themselves against the three bullying Jones brothers. "Why would you knock down a little boy?"

"Ah, the little shit was just in my way. I was aimin' for you! Think you're so great, yous don't even have a Pa, do ya?" taunted the biggest of the Jones boys.

"Do so!" shouted Alfie. "You take that back!"

"He must be invisible then!"

Annie shouted, "Stop fighting this instant or I'll report all of you to Mr. Morgan!" It was an inconsequential threat, but the boys stopped and looked at her.

"Aw, Annie, we was just playin," said one of the Jones brothers. "No harm done."

Annie glared at him. The eldest boy had greasy, brown hair and a face covered in pimples. She felt her own face grow hot with anger and impulsively shouted the coarsest Norwegian curse words she could think of. Her insults bounced harmlessly off the bullies; they didn't understand the language. But the Larsen boys did. They gaped at their sister with eyes wide, shocked.

I should have told them off in Welsh, she thought, kicking herself. *My brothers wouldn't have understood, and the Joneses sure would have.*

She could feel the bullies watching her. She felt conspicuous with her new blue satin ribbons in her braids and her clean, pressed indigo dress. She glared at the oldest boy as he wiped his nose on his filthy sleeve and gave one his brothers a malicious whack on the head. "Come on," he said. "Let's go."

Annie turned her attention again to her youngest brother, who was still sniffling. "Don't cry, Georgie. We'll clean you up." The other two had escaped without injury, but they were filthy.

"I need to get you boys washed up before Mamma sees you. Thank goodness you didn't tear your good school clothes!"

They stopped at a creek near the school playground and Annie used her petticoat to wipe away most of the boys' dirt and grime. On their way home the cobbled street was crowded with men on bicycles, horses pulling carriages and various delivery carts. Annie held Georgie's hand tightly as they dodged business men, shopping ladies, shoeshine boys and newspaper carriers shouting out the latest headline. The warm spring breeze soon dried her wet petticoat. They turned down the street towards the docks. She could see the tops of the ships' masts gently bobbing above the city buildings.

Annie's anger evaporated as she took a deep breath and inhaled the briny sea air. She skipped home, tugging Georgie along. A few steps from the house, the children spotted a pair of large, heavy boots neatly aligned on the doorstep.

Georgie squealed, "Pappa's here!" He dropped Annie's hand and raced towards the house.

The front door flew open and there stood their father with arms wide. Henrik Larsen was a tall, handsome man with a fair Nordic complexion, light blue eyes and short dark hair. His job as a ship's carpenter kept him away for several months at a time, and he now sported a trim moustache and goatee, to the children's delight. He had once explained to Annie that the small gold earring in his left ear proved that he had crossed the equator, and it also ensured him of a proper burial should he die in a foreign port.

In the doorway, Annie's mother beamed as she watched the family reunion, but said in her Norwegian-English lilt, "Come inside and stop that racket! The neighbours are going to think there are banshees invading the street."

They all crowded in, Georgie on their father's shoulders, Alfie on his back and James and Annie under his arms. They all hung on as he leaned down to kiss his wife.

Annie saw that her mother's cheeks were bright pink from working in the kitchen. Her hair was pinned up into a neat arrangement, with a few light brown strays framing her face. The spring weather was pleasantly warm, but she had had to keep a fire going in the stove to prepare a special meal. Her figure was matronly now that she was in her mid-forties, but she was still attractive. Tiny smile lines were etched in the corners of her eyes. Annie knew that her mother's one vanity was the small pearl earrings she wore every day. They had been a gift from her husband on their wedding day twenty years ago.

As Annie's father gently lifted his young son from his shoulders, their mother asked how Georgie scraped his elbow and knee. The little boy burst into tears and blubbered the whole story, ending with what Annie had said to the Jones boys. Both parents turned to Annie, astonished.

"Where did you ever hear such language, Annie Larsen?" cried her mother. Now everyone was looking at Annie.

"I was just so angry with the Jones boys for hurting Georgie." She felt tears threatening to surface, but she was determined not to cry. "Honestly, I've never said those words before. I didn't even know they were in my head. They just came out!"

"But where did you hear such language? We are the only Norwegian family in a neighbourhood filled with Welsh and English." Then the realization hit. "Oh no, it was Jack, wasn't it?" Her mother looked sharply at her father and Annie saw him quickly hide a grin.

"Well, young lady," she snapped, turning back to Annie, "that kind of language will earn you extra chores." To her husband she added, "Jack is going to get a piece of my mind when he comes home. He should be more responsible around his brothers and sister!" She looked around at her children. "Oh, for heaven's sake, go change out of your school clothes. Annie, I want you to peel the potatoes. And, I never want to hear of you using such language again! Annie felt her face grow warm. She was ashamed to have caused such an upset on her father's first day home.

The small, hot kitchen was filled with the pungent aromas of their mother's Norwegian cooking. Hearty fish soup was simmering on the stove and fresh rye bread was cooling on the table next to baby carrots, potatoes, pickled beets and lingonberry preserves. A large bowl of fresh prawns sat on the counter. Annie wrinkled her nose at her father's favourite treat, an aged, odoriferous cheese that her parents called *gammel ost*.

Later, as the family sat around the table, Annie saw her father smile as he looked at her mother.

"I have some good news, Mary. I've been hired on the *Cowrie*. We set sail in two months." Her mother began to speak but he continued. "The ship leaves from South Shields. Two months will give us plenty of time to move back to County Durham and find a place to rent."

Jack had stopped eating. He looked at their father. "Do you think I could get hired on a ship when we move? You know I've always wanted to sail."

Nineteen-year-old Jack was just over six feet tall and well-muscled from his heavy manual work at the brick factory and the odd jobs he picked up on the docks. He resembled his father, with his fair complexion and dark hair. Unlike Annie and their youngest brother, Georgie, Jack was not a scholar and had been earning a wage for a few years now.

"Well, son, as a matter of fact, I have found you a position with me on the *Cowrie!*" Jack jumped up and whooped for joy. Their father laughed. "This way you'll be too far away to teach your sister and brothers any more salty words!"

"Pappa, thank you! And, Ma," he added, grabbing her in a hug, "I didn't teach those words on purpose. They spy on me and my friends!" Their mother begrudgingly gave him a smile. "Pappa," Jack went on, "I'll make you proud of me, I will. I'll work hard and prove that I belong on the ship."

"I know you will, Jack." replied his father, giving his son a playful punch in the arm.

Annie felt a lump in her throat as she looked around the familiar kitchen. She was happy here in Cardiff. She liked the school and she'd certainly miss her best friends, Gwynneth and Bronwen, when the family moved. But at least they were returning to South Shields, a place she knew, and she was grateful that her father would be home for two months. Her little brothers wouldn't mind the change because they were young, and she was pleased for Jack's good fortune.

Annie's mother smiled as she got up from the table. "We have so much to celebrate tonight!"

Alfie, James and Georgie shouted with delight as their mother handed each of them a large portion of pudding. The younger boys barely understood what was being discussed; they were just happy to have a treat. Jack sat back with a wide grin. *Dreaming of his coming adventures,* Annie guessed. She rose from her chair to hug her father. He returned her hug and planted a kiss on her forehead.

"I'm so happy you're home, Pappa," she whispered.

Chapter Two

The children had all been born in the north-east of England, and South Shields had been the home port for Annie's father's ship for many years. He had no difficulty finding a place for the family to rent that spring; he knew many people in the area. Their mother soon turned their newly rented house into a home, with familiar furnishings and favourite smells filling the kitchen.

Summer passed and once again her father was gone, this time taking Jack with him. Annie found the house oddly quiet without them. She missed Jack's gentle teasing and his kind ways, like how he would sometimes bring home sweets for the boys or pretty ribbons for her. Annie knew that he and her father would be away for many long months. They would eventually return home for a short respite, only to leave again on another voyage. She vowed to herself that although she loved living close to the ocean and walking along the shore in the cool, salty breeze, she would never marry a man of the sea. The goodbyes were too painful and the long absences too solitary. She dreamed of living in a home that she owned, in one place, and never having to move from rental to rental again.

Over the next few years, while her father and Jack travelled the world with only brief stops at home, Annie, her mother and younger brothers lived comfortably in South Shields. When Annie finished her schooling, she found a sales position in a clothing and hat store. After a couple of years in the shop she applied for a position with an insurance company. *It would be wonderful to work in an office and earn more money,* she thought. She wore her long, light brown hair pinned up fashionably and people often complimented her on her looks. She admitted to herself that she was a little vain about her appearance but felt that she had to make more of an effort than others; she knew that she looked younger than her eighteen years. She remained petite while all four of her brothers now towered over her.

Alfie and James had jobs in the shipyards; Georgie was still attending school. Annie and her brothers gave most of their earnings to their mother. Annie often spent quiet evenings with her when the boys were out, Alfie and James working late and Georgie off with his friends. The house seemed small when her brothers were home; they were big, loud young men. Annie was happy to sit in the warmth of the hearth fire with her mother and enjoy a simple meal of hearty vegetable soup and warm wheat bread.

"Mother," said Annie one night as she cleared away their dishes. "I have a little gift for you. I bought some lovely Nottingham lace curtains for the parlour window." She slipped into her bedroom and brought a brown paper package back to her mother. "Moore's had a sale. They're absolutely perfect!"

Her mother protested as she unwrapped the parcel. "Annie, you shouldn't be spending on such things for me. Oh my, but they're lovely."

"They really were inexpensive. The clerk said that it was a special order that was never picked up. Come, let's take down these old curtains and brighten up the room."

After they'd hung the new lace over the windows, they stood back to admire them. "Thank you, love. They make the room look grand."

They tidied up, banked the fire and retired to their bedrooms. But Annie was asleep for only a couple of hours, until she awoke with a start from a nightmare. Her heart was racing and she was wet with perspiration despite the chill in the room. In the dream, she'd been on the deck of a ship when a monstrous ocean wave rushed towards her. The wall of sea-water crashed onto the deck, and just as she was heaved overboard, she woke up.

Knowing that she would not get back to sleep easily, she got out of her bed and tiptoed into the kitchen, wrapping her shawl around her shoulders. Bringing the fire back to life, she replaced the filled kettle to make herself a cup of tea. As she quietly took a cup from the cupboard, her mother shuffled into the room.

"Did you have that same nightmare again, love?"

Annie nodded. "I'm sorry if I woke you. Would you like a cup of tea, too?"

"Ah, you didn't wake me, dear. I was just tossing and turning in my bed. A cup of tea would be wonderful."

They sipped their hot drinks and talked quietly at the kitchen table. Suddenly, her mother covered her mouth with her fingers. She leapt up from her chair to reach for a letter pinned on the wall.

"I don't know where my head was tonight. I forgot to give you this! It came in the mail this morning." She placed it on the table beside Annie's cup.

Annie tore open the letter with a thrill of anticipation. "It's from the insurance office! Listen to this! 'Dear Miss Larsen, please call and see Mrs. Swales at 2 o'clock on Thursday. Your character is very satisfactory. Yours respectfully, P.T. Smith.' I think I've been hired!"

Annie danced around the room and hugged her mother. Smiling, her mother asked her what she would wear for her new job.

"The outfits I've bought in the shop should do," Annie replied, "but I will buy a new hat and gloves." She was ecstatic at the prospect of working in an office building and earning a higher salary.

Annie stifled a yawn. "Go back to bed," said her mother. "You'll want to be bright-eyed and fresh for tomorrow."

Annie kissed her cheek, wished her a good night, and returned to bed with thoughts of the following day swirling in her head. She felt a little foolish for having been so anxious over a silly dream. Talking to her mother always made things better.

Pulling her covers over her shoulders, Annie heard the creak of the old rocker in the kitchen. She smiled; her mother was humming an old song.

I wish I could banish that nightmare from my head, she thought. As she drifted off to sleep, she tried to focus on her mother's soft tune to keep the dream at bay.

Chapter Three

It happened on a cold, drizzly grey day late in November. The news arrived in an official letter delivered to the house. Annie's mother held her composure long enough to take the envelope from the young delivery boy and give him a small tip, but tore it open as soon as he turned to leave. Reading the single sheet of paper, her face grew ashen with shock. She collapsed on a kitchen chair as the note slipped from her hand.

"What's wrong, Mother? What has happened?"

Annie slowly picked up the note from the floor and read the terrible words. The captain of the *Cowrie* "regrets to inform Mrs. Larsen that her husband, Henry Larsen, 51, of 52 Morton Street, South Shields, England, ship's carpenter on the vessel *Cowrie*, drowned August 29 1898, 25.55 North 120.58 East." *Had Pappa been swept overboard by a rogue wave?*

She dropped the letter as if it was burning her hand, ran to her bedroom and muffled her sobs with a blanket. She tried to remember her last minutes with her father before he left, but couldn't. She cursed her nightmare for tempting fate; she felt a surge of anger and punched her pillow. It was an hour before she could calm herself enough to return to the kitchen and try to comfort her mother.

Annie was heartsore with grief. Her eyes were puffy and she seemed to have a permanent lump in her throat. Alfie and James held their feelings in and kept themselves occupied with their work at the shipyard. Georgie wandered through the house aimlessly for several days and was visibly relieved when Annie suggested he go back to school. Annie herself had stayed home three days to be with her mother, but had returned to work for fear of losing her new position at the insurance office. Her mother was so quiet, it alarmed her.

The Master Mariner's Annuity Society along with many local seamen who knew Annie's father, donated to a fund for the family. Neighbourhood women brought prepared food, and some made tea for her mother and sat with her. But she just stayed in her old rocker, not talking, not eating.

Annie often replaced her mother's cold tea with a fresh cup, knowing it would not be touched, but at least she was doing something. Annie watched her became a ghost of her old self; she grew thin and pale. Annie was at a loss for how to help her.

Several months later, on a cool, rainy April day, Jack returned. He looked like he had aged ten years since he was last home, although he'd only been away ten months this time. There were a few strands of grey in his dark hair. He carried their father's weather-beaten chest into the house. The appearance of the old battered trunk made the death real; the family mourned him anew. They now knew for certain that he would never return.

The trunk sat unopened for a week. Annie's mother stared at it but didn't move from her rocker, while it grew harder and harder to ignore. Finally Annie decided to sort through it herself, to save her mother from the sad task. She gave James a few of their father's carpentry tools and they decided to sell the rest. At the bottom of the trunk, under some shirts, Annie found a small, red silk bag with a gold tassel. She gently picked it up and handed it to her mother. At first, her mother just held the pouch for several minutes. She sat for so long that Annie began to wonder if her mother had forgotten it, lost once again in her despair. But then, as if she had summoned all her strength, she finally spilled the contents onto her lap. Annie gasped at the sight of an exquisite pearl necklace.

Before her mother could suggest something practical like selling it, Annie gathered the string of pearls and said, "Pappa held these in his hands. Wear them and you will feel him close to your heart." Her mother shook her head, but Annie continued. "You can tuck the necklace under your jumper and nobody but you and I will know that it's there. They will give you comfort. Pappa bought them for you." Before her mother could object, Annie placed the necklace around her neck and closed the clasp. The pearls were lustrous against her pale skin and for the first time in months, she smiled. She placed her hands over the necklace, and tears streaked down her mother's cheeks.

The day before Jack had to return to his ship, Annie impulsively suggested, "Let's have a family party!" She spent a week's salary on food and treats. Their mother even agreed to help Annie prepare the farewell dinner.

That evening, everyone but Georgie was in the kitchen. The other three brothers were noisily teasing each other and their mother seemed at ease while preparing the food, more content than she'd been in a long time. Since finding the necklace from her husband, she had slowly begun to come back to life. Her kitchen was filled with the tantalizing aromas of fresh baked bread and roast beef sizzling in the oven. She looked at her sons and said, "Would you boys stop horsing around! Dinner's almost ready. I just have to pop the Yorkshire pudding in the oven." Annie laughed; it was reassuring to hear her mother scolding her brothers like old times. "Annie, be a dear and run over to the Kidds' house to get Georgie, he's there with Charlie."

As she left the house, Annie glanced back at her family in their bright welcoming kitchen; she was happy that the heavy sorrow seemed to have lifted, if only a little. She took a short-cut through their small backyard vegetable garden, which was bordered by flowers. Her favourite was the showy, fragrant lilac bush growing near the kitchen door. She had picked a large bouquet earlier for the table but couldn't resist stopping again a minute to bury her nose in the aromatic blossoms.

The Kidd's home was just one street away, a sooty red-brick row house similar to the Larsen's home. Annie knocked at the kitchen door and walked in to the delightful scent of mutton stew and rhubarb pie. Jane Kidd stood by the stove, stirring the pot. She was a portly woman, worn out before her time after giving birth to nine children, but she had a comely face. Jane was her mother's friend, and Annie was fond of her. Since Annie's father's death, Jane had often sent over a fresh loaf of bread or a pot of soup and had regularly sat with her mother while Annie was at work.

"Hello, Mrs. Kidd. It smells wonderful! I've come for our Georgie."

"Oh Annie!" said the woman, wiping her hands on her apron. "It's lovely to see ya, dear. Georgie's out back. How's your poor mother?"

"She's slowly getting back to her old self. I can't thank you enough for sitting with her while I'm at work."

Annie had the sense that she was being watched. Looking around, she realized that Charlie's older brother, Jim, had been sitting at the kitchen table the whole time, quietly studying her. Annie felt her face grow warm and she quickly looked away.

"You're jist starin' at a bonny lass, Jim!" Jane teased him. Jim's face turned scarlet. "Go on, get Annie's brother."

He left, but not before Annie snuck another look at his handsome face. His eyes were as blue as a warm summer sky. She had known who he was but had only glimpsed him occasionally. She'd heard that he had been working in Newcastle until recently. She wondered if he had a female friend and resolved to casually ask Georgie about that later.

As Annie left, Jane reminded her, "I'm here if ever Mary needs owt."

"Thank you, Mrs. Kidd. And please tell Georgie he's to come straight home for Jack's going away tea."

That night, the Larsen family enjoyed the hearty meal and treats that Annie had splurged on. The brothers joked, teased and laughed just like when they were young. Annie looked at her siblings, and then at her mother, and realized what a difference it made to have their mother joining in daily chores and conversation again. *Mother may never again be the same but I do believe she is enjoying herself tonight.* She watched her mother unconsciously place her left hand over the hidden pearl necklace.

Jack was excited about returning to the Orient. "There are amazing sights in the Far East," he told them. "The weather is warm and the countryside is lush with green mountains and bamboo forests. There are acres of rice and tea and temples older that you could possibly imagine."

"I long to see the world, too," Georgie added as he loaded his fork with a large slice of beef. "One day I'm going to join the merchant marine or maybe the Royal Navy."

Bloody Larsen men and the sea, Annie thought. *I'll have none of that in my life. What's wrong with wanting a permanent home?*

She chided herself to lighten up and enjoy her family while they were together. Her mother looked happier than she'd been in a long time, surrounded by all of her children. It warmed Annie's heart to see her smile. She even heard her mother chuckle at her brothers' antics. There was a lump in Annie's throat whenever she looked at Jack; he looked so much like Pappa. She wished that this moment could freeze in time.

Chapter Four

Annie saw Jim occasionally while walking home from work; she would nod and smile in reply to his greeting. He seemed to like her. She knew from Georgie that Jim wasn't seeing another girl and she nursed a small hope that he might consider courting her. She worked long hours at the office and sometimes went out with her friends on Sundays to walk in the park or the beach. Sometimes they'd treat themselves to a tea and pastry in the hotel restaurant. But still she longed for something more. Just when she decided that Jim must not be interested in her, he surprised her.

She was walking home after work, accompanied by a young man from the insurance office, and saw Jim coming towards them with his head down. "Hello, Jim," she called out.

He looked up at the sound of Annie's voice, and his initial smile was replaced by a downtrodden look. At first, Annie was confused, but then it dawned on her. *He does care for me! He's upset that I'm with another man.* She pretended to adjust her hat, ducking her head to hide her smile.

The following Sunday, Jim arrived unexpectedly at Annie's door and asked, in his Northumberland Geordie accent, "Would ye like ta come fo' a walk to the beach?"

Jim had made a considerable effort in his appeal. His short dark hair was freshly washed and his face clean-shaven, emphasizing his blue eyes. He was wearing what was likely his best shirt and trousers in his effort to make a good impression. There was a small wicker basket by his feet. Annie smiled at Jim and said, "I'd love to walk with you." She quickly wrote a note with her regrets to the friend she had planned to have lunch with, and asked Georgie to deliver it. Lifting her summer bonnet from the coat hook, she turned to Jim and said, "Shall we?"

Annie boldly slipped her arm through Jim's as they strolled down the cobbled lane, past the shops and busy streets on their way to the sandy beach near the pier. Cool breezes blew briskly in from the coastline and she had to hold her hat with her other hand. Jim appeared to enjoy the approving nods from some of his mates as they strolled through town. When they stopped to cross a crowded intersection, Jim turned to look into Annie's eyes.

"Yer a bonny lass, Annie Larsen," he said. "Ye must hev many admirers. Ah... are ye a good friend wi' that bloke who walked ye home last week?"

Annie blushed at the compliment. "Andrew is not a special friend. We just work in the same building and he was walking my way." She laughed. "Having four over-protective brothers seems to scare any admirers away!"

"Well, I'm happy te hear that!" Jim grinned. "And yer brothers aren't so scary!"

At the shoreline they took off their shoes and stockings to walk through the cool lapping waves. Later they spread a blanket over the sand and unpacked their lunch from Jim's wicker basket. They ate in silence as the ocean breeze dried their cold feet. Annie saw Jim surreptitiously admiring her slim ankles below her skirt. She made no move to cover them. Annie asked him what he had been doing in Newcastle. "Ah served two years in the militia," he said, "in the Durham Light Infantry. Right now, ahm workin' in the docks but ah hear that the copper works are hiring."

Annie couldn't resist. "Have you ever thought of working on a ship?" she asked.

"Lord no! I need to feel firm ground under me. Ma stomach does flip-flops just thinkin' about spending months on the waves."

A handsome man with his feet on the ground!

She smiled and said, "My dream is to own a house one day. I don't want to move every few years to rented flats in different cities and towns. That's all my family ever did."

Jim looked into her eyes, placed his hand on her cheek and boldly kissed her on the lips. She knew she should be shocked, or at least act it. She felt her face grow warm as her heart skipped a beat. But today was not an ordinary day. She placed her hand on his upper arm and kissed him back, right there in the middle of the public beach.

After that day at the beach, Jim met Annie at the insurance building every day that he was not working at the shipyard, and walked her home. Sometimes he stayed at the Larsens' for tea and other times Annie ate with the Kidds.

Jim's father, Charles, was a serious, stern man. He had a full head of thick white hair and the same summer-sky eyes as Jim. He worked as a train engineer at the copper works and had not known Annie's father. He was a religious man; every night before the family dinner began, he would read a passage from the Bible, and then say grace. "For what we are about to receive may the Lord make us truly thankful." Annie could see that he was proud of his large family and that it was important to him to be a good provider. At first she had a hard time placing his peculiar, quaint manner of speech; he was originally from Norfolk, she discovered. As she came to know him better, she found he had a wonderful sense of humour, and he soon treated her as one of his own daughters (unlike many men who favoured their sons over their daughters, Charles treated his children equally). Annie enjoyed the time she spent at the Kidd's and as the months went on, she grew to love Jane and Charles as well as Jim's brother and his seven sisters.

One evening when Jim walked Annie home, nearly two years into their courtship, she invited him in for a cup of tea. As they entered the house, Annie spotted a note on the table. She picked it up and read aloud.

Annie dear,

I had to go to the Brown's for the evening as the granny is feeling poorly and they needed someone to stay with her while the family was in Newcastle. The boys are working late shifts tonight and Georgie's out, too, so I hope you don't mind being on your own. I'll see you in the morning.

Love, Mama

"Well, it looks like there's just the two of us. Come, I'll find you a sweet to go with your tea."

Jim wrapped his arms around her and said, "Annie hinny, you're all the sweets I want." He kissed her.

She punched his arm playfully and he pulled her close and kissed her once again. This time she put her arms around his neck and kissed him back. He took her hand in his and led her to the sofa in the parlour, where he lay down and pulled her down on top of him. He gasped with pleasure as she pressed her body into his.

Running his hands over her back, Jim kissed her deeply and looked into her eyes. "Annie, will ye marry me?"

She smiled and kissed him back. She teased, "I'll have to think about that." Then she laughed and kissed him again. "Yes, yes, a thousand times, yes!"

"Ah, Annie me love, you've made me a happy man."

The families were thrilled. The couple planned to marry the following year, and Jim promised Annie he would find a better job so they could furnish their home properly. He applied for a position as a fireman at the copper works. "There's stiff competition," he told her, "but I think I have a good chance."

Annie planned to quit her job once they were married, but until then she was enjoying the independence that came with supporting herself, and she was also glad to be helping her mother. She had already earned a raise and was carefully saving her money.

One sunny October day, Jim handed Annie a small package. She was curious and carefully opened the blue velvet circular box. Inside was nestled a gold ring with six tiny red stones.

"Oh Jim, it's beautiful, but we can't afford this."

Jim gently took it out of the box and placed it on her left ring finger. "I want ye ta have a proper engagement. I've worked extra shifts on the docks, an' borrowed a bit from me brother. I didn't touch our house savings." He pulled her into his arms and kissed her. "Besides, we have months ta save for our life together."

But their plans were about to change.

Chapter Five

"What will I do? I'll have to quit my job. There will surely be a scandal. Oh, I cannot bear Mother's disappointment in me. God, why did this happen to me now?"

Jim gently brushed away her tears with his fingers and replied, "It happened tuh us, Annie. You aren't alone. I dinna regret that it happened." He kissed her softly. "It just happened sooner than we were ready. I love ye an' I want ye to be me wife. I've been savin' me money. You'll see. Everythin' will work out."

"We're not ready for a baby yet. We just can't afford it!"

Jim held her close to him and whispered, "Dinna fret. I'll take care of ye an' our bairn."

Annie sobbed. "My brothers will not be forgiving. They've been so protective of me since Pappa died." She couldn't begin to imagine how she would tell them. "Your mother will likely accept it but your Da will be furious."

"Everythin' will work out, Annie." Jim reassured her, holding her tightly in his arms. "We'll have our own bairn, just sooner than we planned. But I'll be the happiest man around, wi' you for me wife."

Both mothers were shocked and disappointed when first told, but were eventually supportive. Charles, on the other hand, was mortified. He had threatened to disown "a son who would cause such shame to the family."

Annie's brothers, for their part, took matters into their own hands. Annie was walking home from work one day, when she came across Jim on the walkway. He was staggering and grasping his sides. She ran to him. "What happened?" She looked him over frantically. "My God, you're bleeding!"

"Ah'm fine, Annie," he slurred through swollen lips. "I had a bad fall in the shipyard and jus' need to lie down for a bit."

She put her hands on her hips and cried, "This is more than a fall, Jim! Just look at you!"

Jim leaned against a brick wall and gasped with pain. He forced a grin and said, "Dinna fash, Annie. It's no matter and was worth it."

Annie frowned as the realization dawned on her. "This was my brothers' doing, wasn't it? The bloody idiots were likely drinking again, weren't they?" She seethed with anger. "I ought to report them to the police. Here, lean on me a bit."

When they reached her house, she helped him peel off his shirt. As she wrapped a bandage - improvised from an old, clean sheet torn to strips - around his ribs, she discreetly admired his muscular build, marvelling at how white and smooth his skin was. When she was done, she rested her hands for a moment on his shoulders and gently kissed a corner of his lacerated mouth.

Annie learned the full story from Jim's sister Maggie. George and James had waited for Jim after his shift at the shipyard, after quaffing several drinks the local pub. Jim had been warned that Annie's brothers were planning to ambush him, but he offered little resistance to their kicks and blows. Annie knew that most onlookers must have known the beating had to do with her pregnancy, but thankfully a couple of older, more level-headed men had stepped up to stop it. Jim was fortunate to have suffered just a few bruises, a black eye and a cracked rib, but Annie was so angry at her brothers that she did not speak to them for a week.

On April thirtieth, she and Jim were quietly married at St. Michael and All Angels Church in South Westhoe in the presence of Maggie and Alfie. Jim had found a flat for them to rent; it was dark and dreary with just two rooms and a shared water tap in the back lane, but it was affordable. He bought a new mattress and a second-hand bed, dresser, couch and chair. Against Charles' wishes, Jane gave them a sturdy wooden kitchen table and two matching chairs. Annie's mother gave them her good set of dishes from her own wedding and helped sew new curtains and bed linens.

Annie was pleased that, at first, her figure hardly changed with her pregnancy. People said that from the back she did not appear to be expecting at all, and that the little, round bump that soon had replaced her once-flat stomach was endearingly small. As the months passed though, she began to feel heavy and uncomfortable. She was lonely while Jim was at work and frightened of giving birth. As her time approached, she told Jim that she had made a decision.

"I'm so frightened. I want to be with Mother when the baby comes." She sniffled and wiped away her tears. "I want to move back home until our baby arrives. You could come after work and have your dinner with us each evening."

Jim kissed away her tears, then tenderly touched Annie's distended belly. "I'm worried meself if ye should go into labour while I'm at work," he admitted. "I would be relieved to know your mother was takin' care of ye." He placed his hand on her cheek and kissed her.

Annie moved to her mother's house the following day. Her mother was happy to be useful and soon found an experienced midwife with a good reputation. Jane and her daughters were often over and they busily collected or knitted everything the baby could need, while Annie anxiously awaited the arrival of her child.

On a warm July morning, Annie complained of an uncomfortable pain in her back, which then radiated down her legs. By early afternoon she noticed her abdomen tightening regularly and she felt an increasingly painful cramping. Her mother remained calm and stayed by her side throughout the day. By dinner time Annie's contractions were becoming more intense, so as soon as Jim arrived, her mother asked him to fetch the midwife, Mrs. Mitchell. Jim froze for a moment then bolted out the door.

When he returned ten minutes later, with the short, plump midwife who bustled into the bedroom, Annie caught a brief glimpse of how anxious and bewildered Jim looked as the bedroom door was closed, leaving him standing alone in the kitchen. She wished he was allowed in, but knew it would be scandalous to suggest it.

At eleven o'clock that evening Annie gave birth to a tiny baby girl. Exhausted but ecstatic, she watched from the bed as her mother handed Jim the little swaddled bundle.

"You and Annie have a bonny daughter. Congratulations! What will you name your wee one?"

Jim's eyes moistened as he kissed his daughter's forehead. "Annie and ah decided that she'll be Margaret Mary Jane," he said in a broken voice. "Mary Jane is fo' the two grannies. And don't tell me other sisters, but Maggie's me favourite."

Annie had never known that she could love a child more than life itself. Maggie was a small miracle, a tiny version of Annie herself, but with her father's blue eyes and hints of blond fuzz on her head. As Annie and Jim had both grown up with younger siblings, they were confident young parents. Little Maggie thrived. The tiny baby healed all wounds, imagined and real, in both the Kidd and Larsen families.

Annie's mother and Jane loved their new granddaughter before she was born. Charles' anger dissolved the second he held her in his arms. And little Maggie's many aunts and uncles cherished her and spoiled her with little gifts. This unexpected baby was blessed.

Annie took Maggie out every day, proudly pushing the pram, a gift from her brothers, down the cobbled walkways. She would pick up a few items at the greengrocer's shop, stop in at her mother's, and then at the Kidd's. Annie was often delayed by neighbours, who fussed over her happy baby. Maggie always rewarded everyone with a toothless smile. Annie could not believe how her life had changed so, over just a few months.

Jim stepped through their doorway, and greeted Annie as he usually did with a hug as she was preparing their meal. Maggie was in a basket on the floor, playing with her toes and cooing sweetly. Jim picked her up and nuzzled her neck until she giggled.

"Who's this bonny bairn here?" he teased and tickled, making her giggle.

Annie turned from her work and said, "If you get her any more excited, she'll not go down to sleep."

Jim kissed Annie's cheek and said, "Divvint worry, I'll have her fast asleep afore dinner's ready."

He carried his squirming daughter to the bedroom. While Annie was filling their plates, she heard Jim singing.

Go to sleep my baby, close your big blue eyes.
The Lady Moon is watching, from out beneath the skies.
The little stars are peeping, to see if you are sleeping.
So, go to sleep my baby, go to sleep, good night.

When Jim came back to the kitchen, having laid the sleeping Maggie in her crib, Annie said, "That lullaby was lovely. How do you know it?"

"Ma used to sing it to my younger sisters and brother, every night at bedtime. Ah even remember her singing it to me."

"Well, it certainly did the trick for Maggie. Sing it again so I can learn it."

As Jim sang, Annie laid her head on the table and pretended to snore. He groaned at her silliness.

"Ah have somethin' grand to tell you!" he said as they started to eat. "First of all, ah got the job at the copper works and start next week." When Annie jumped up from her chair to congratulate him, he held up his hand. "And . . . ah've found us a bonny new flat on Catherine Street!"

"Ah, Jim! A good job and a new home! I'm a lucky woman."

His timing could not have been better, as Annie had some news, too. She was expecting their second child.

Chapter Six

Jim was thrilled that they were expecting another baby. Annie's easy pregnancy seemed to fly by quickly as she was busy with Maggie, packing up their old flat and settling into their new one. This time, when Annie was near her time, her mother moved in with them to help out.

It was lucky she did, because the baby arrived quickly one day while Jim was at work. When he came home that night, he was surprised to see Annie sitting comfortably in bed with a small swaddled bundle resting on her chest. Tears came to his eyes and he stammered, "You should have sent someone to get me! I'd ah come home."

Annie's mother patted his arm. "Ah, Jim, this baby was in a hurry to come into the world. Annie and I managed on our own."

"Where's Maggie?" he asked, looking around for her.

"I ran her over to the neighbours'," said Annie's mother. "I'll just go now and bring her home. Poor little girl doesn't know what the fuss was all about." As she was about to slip out the door, she turned to Jim and said, "You have a wee son, by the way."

Jim crushed his mother-in-law to in a tight embrace. "Thank you!" he whispered.

He knelt by the bed and gently stroked Annie's forehead. She unfolded the blanket to show Jim their baby boy. He gathered his new son into his arms.

"Welcome, my little man. You were in a rush to meet the world, weren't you? Imagine surprisin' yer Da. What a wee bonny boy ye are."

He carefully wrapped the blanket around the baby and placed him back in Annie's arms, then lay down beside her. He put his forehead against hers and her cheeks soon grew wet with his tears. After a minute, he wiped his face with his shirt sleeve, and got up before Maggie and Annie's mother returned.

"I love ye, Annie Kidd. We are so wealthy with a daughter and a son!"

Maggie, now almost two years old, pouted at first when her mother's attention strayed from her, but she soon discovered that her baby brother, Bobby, couldn't walk, dance or sing as she could. Playing to her rapidly growing reputation for heart-warming quips, she said, "Baby jus' seep and thit!"

"Maggie!" Annie scolded. "That's not a nice word to say."

The little girl hung her head. "Da thays thit," she replied, then quickly added, "I won't thay thit anymore, Mummy. Thit ith a bad word."

Annie had to bite her cheek so she wouldn't laugh.

Later, while Annie was nursing Bobby in the rocking chair, Maggie ran into the bedroom and returned with her dolly. She sat down on the floor, lifted her top and put her dolly to her chest. "I'm feeding my baby, too, Mummy."

Annie smiled and shook her head at the little girl's antics. She couldn't wait to tell Jim and Mother.

In April, Annie and Jim celebrated their second anniversary with a night out at the pub, while Mary watched the children. They walked hand in hand in the warm spring air. A couple of neighbours on the street called out that they looked like they were courting and not the old married couple that they really were. Jim guffawed and opened the pub door for Annie. The overheated room was crowded and noisy with loud conversation. They jostled their way to a small table and Annie sat down while Jim pushed his way up to the bar to order two pints of ale and their fish and chips. It was a lovely time. They agreed they pitied everyone else who couldn't possibly be as happy as they were.

After Bobby's baptismal service, Annie and Jim waited for Jane, Charles, and Annie's mother outside the church. Her mother promptly took the crying infant from Annie's arms and gently soothed him. Charles reached down and scooped up a giggling Maggie.

Jane laughed and said, "We filled the church wi' all the Larsens an' Kidds. And what a lovely service even though Bobby bawled through th' whole thing!"

Jim's parents' little house was soon overflowing with all the aunts, uncles, and cousins. The men sat outside to enjoy the warm spring weather and to escape the chaos inside. Maggie entertained her aunts and uncles, twirling in her new frock. She was thrilled to be the centre of attention once her baby brother had fallen asleep. Annie picked up her daughter and hugged her. "Aren't we lucky to have both a boy and a girl in our family? I love you, poppet."

Maggie put her arms around Annie's neck and gave her a wet kiss on the cheek, then squirmed to get down. The little girl ran back into the kitchen and called out, "Granny Jane, I want another lolly."

"Maggie! That's not polite," Annie scolded.

Maggie looked at Annie, then ran to hug her grandmother. She asked, "Granny, I want another lolly, *please*?"

Annie caught her mother-in-law's eye and had to smile.

A few hours later, Maggie was sound asleep on her grandfather's lap and everyone was saying their goodbyes to Jane and Charles. Jim gathered his daughter into his arms as Annie got her sleeping son from the bedroom. They walked home slowly in the mild evening breeze, neither of them wanting the evening to end.

Jim wiped his daughter's red, flushed forehead with his fingers. "Our Maggie's danced herself inta a sweat! She's fast asleep."

At their new rented house on Catherine Street, Jim tucked Maggie into her bed while Annie fed and changed the baby. After Annie put Bobby in his crib, she returned to the kitchen and sank into chair. Jim placed a cup of hot tea in front of her and sat down with his own mug.

Just as they were finishing their tea, they heard Maggie crying in her sleep. They both rushed into the bedroom to calm her and prevent her cries from waking the baby. Jim reached Maggie first and as he placed his hand on her forehead, he gasped. "She's burnin' up!" Annie looked at Jim in alarm. He gently picked up Maggie's hot little body, carried the little girl to the kitchen and sat down with her in the rocking chair. She was limp and listless.

Maggie woke up and whimpered, "Dada, hot."

Annie brought a cool cloth to Maggie's forehead. "She's had a bit of a cough these last few days. I'm sure she'll bounce back in no time," she said, trying to suppress her growing fears.

Jim stayed in the rocker with Maggie for a few hours, but Annie finally sent him to bed while she took a turn. Maggie whined and covered her eyes, complaining, "Eyes hurt, Mummy." Annie patted her back. She leaned over to extinguish the candle and continued to rock her through the night.

When the full moon shone through the window and lit up the room, Annie covered Maggie's eyes with a flannel. Examining her daughter in the moonlight, she was shocked to see small, red spots inside the girl's mouth. She called for Jim. When he saw Maggie's spots and felt how fevered she still was, he quickly dressed and left to find a doctor. Within a half-hour he returned with Dr. Bootiman.

After the doctor examined Maggie, he declared, "Margaret has the measles."

Annie felt faint with fear. "What does that mean?"

"Every child goes through this illness," Dr. Bootiman assured her. "Just keep the room dark and ease her fever with a cool bath."

"But what about the baby, can he catch measles, too?" Annie asked, her voice trembling.

"You must have someone else watch the baby. He's too young to be exposed to the disease."

Annie looked at Jim, "My mother will help. Can you take Bobby to her before you go to work?"

Dr. Bootiman interrupted, "I can give your message to Mrs. Larsen. It's on my way."

As he left, Annie and Jim held on to each other for a moment in the doorway.

Even before Jim left for the copper works in the morning, Annie's mother was at their door. She bustled in, handed Jim a knotted handkerchief of hot scones with a large hunk of cheese for his lunch and reassured them that all children get the measles; little Maggie would be fine in no time, she said. Looking content to be needed, she made a cup of tea for Annie. She gathered her granddaughter into her arms and held her for a while, humming softly. Though her mother was putting on a brave face, Annie could tell she was distressed at how ill Maggie was. She gently placed her sleeping granddaughter back into bed and then carried little Bobby over and set him on Annie's lap. Annie barely looked at her little son. Her mother whispered, "Give him a good feed as this will be his last. We'll have to wean him now."

Annie mechanically put the infant to her breast and let him suckle. Her cheeks were wet with tears. Her mother packed up all of the baby's clothing and supplies, and placed them in the pram.

"Don't you worry," she said to Annie, patting her hand as she took the baby from her. "I'll take good care of little Bobby."

After they left, Annie went to the bedroom. Maggie was still fevered, so Annie brought her to the rocking chair and bathed her with a cool cloth. Annie held her daughter for several hours, whispering stories to her and trying to get her to drink some water. She paced the house, gently bouncing Maggie to try to comfort her. By late afternoon there was an angry rash on the little girl's head, neck and upper chest.

When Jim got home from work, Maggie was asleep in Annie's arms, so he set about frying some eggs and bacon for their dinner – the only thing he knew how to cook. After dinner, he wandered around the small kitchen, rocking Maggie and singing his lullaby. He told her fairy tales and nursery rhymes he remembered from his own childhood. That night, Annie and Jim slept with Maggie between them in their bed.

The next morning the angry rash covered Maggie from head to toe. There was a rattle in her chest and she was still burning with fever. Jim reluctantly packed his lunch and left for work, his brow furrowed with worry. He ducked back a minute later to give Maggie another kiss. "Feel better soon, poppet. Da loves you."

Annie spent the morning bathing Maggie with a cool, damp cloth. At some point, the little girl started to shiver, and then she convulsed. Annie tried to quell her own panic, by rocking her child and repeatedly singing Jim's lullaby.

Late that morning, as the midday sun beat down on the little flat, Maggie cried out, "Momma." She stiffened, and then was still.

Annie froze. She pulled her daughter closer to her chest, brushed the fine blonde hair off Maggie's forehead, kissed her eye lids closed and carried her to the bedroom. She wrapped the tiny, cooling body in several blankets, and brought it back to the rocker. Annie's throat was raw with unshed tears.

"Wake up, baby," she whispered. "Wake up! Come back to Mummy, Maggie."

She rocked Maggie's cold body all afternoon. She sang and told stories, just as Jim had done the night before. And she rocked. And rocked. She was only vaguely aware of Jim arriving home from work. He cried out and cursed as he rushed towards her. Annie numbly allowed him to gather Maggie into his arms. He laid the small body tenderly on the bed and covered it with a sheet. He then came back to the kitchen, picked Annie up as if she were a child and sat with her in the rocking chair, embracing her tightly. His body heaved with sobs, but she could do nothing but stare at the floor, numb. They stayed in the rocker throughout the night.

Annie was paralyzed with grief. On his own, Jim arranged for the church funeral service, chose a small coffin and bought a plot in the church cemetery. Annie was dimly aware of Jim's own sorrow, but she couldn't console him. Her own pain devoured her.

Annie's mother visited with Bobby but told Jim she'd keep the baby a little longer. She was quite happy to care for her little grandson and enjoyed his company, she said, but she could also see that Annie needed her own mother. Annie dully watched Jim fend for himself. He made their meals and urged her to eat, with little success. He stopped by Mary's every day after his shift to play with Bobby. Annie was aware that he was trying to engage her but she could not feel anything but pain.

After three weeks however, Annie's mother strutted into Annie's kitchen and set Bobby on her daughter's lap. "This baby needs his own mother, Annie. For heaven's sake, stop wallowing in your grief." She went to the window and flung open the curtains, which had been drawn since Maggie's passing. "You are not the only one who has lost Maggie. And you are certainly not the only mother to have ever lost a child." Her left hand went to her throat to feel the pearls. She took a deep breath and said, "You need to care for your living baby, now." Mother wiped away a tear and left the house. Annie stared at the closed door a moment then mechanically placed Bobby in his crib.

Annie went about her days in a fog. Jim cared for Bobby each day after his long shift at the copper works. He said he was happy to bathe and change his little son but was worried about her coldness towards the baby. "Snap out of this, Annie! Bobby needs you!" She just shrugged woodenly. When he passed the baby to her so he could prepare his dinner, Annie took him but promptly placed him in his crib. Bobby cried pitiful sobs. Jim swore and picked the baby up again, patting his back to soothe him. He looked at Annie with incredulous incomprehension. She knew she was getting too thin and her skin had lost its glow, but she didn't care.

One day Jim arrived home earlier than usual. Annie was weeping in the rocking chair and Bobby's voice was hoarse from crying in his crib. "For God's sake, Annie, d'ya not hear your own bairn?" Jim swore as he gently picked up the screaming child. Bobby's face was dirty with dried mucous and trails of tears streaking his cheeks, and he had a sopping wet nappy. Jim bathed his son and dressed him with a clean flannel shirt. He held the baby close to him and softly whispered, "Da's home, wee Bobby. Dinna fret." He left Annie where she was and took the baby outside, slamming the door as he left. Some small part of her knew that she was detached and neglectful, but she felt dead inside.

After another week of preparing his own meals and caring for the baby following a full day of work, Jim confronted Annie. "Annie, I know that you're mournin' for Maggie. I never knew that I could love a bairn so much, an' I can't understan' how God could take a wee lass. I miss Maggie too, but ye have to take better care of yersel' an' our baby." Tears streamed down Jim's face. "I'm tired of puttin' in a full day's work, preparin' all of me meals, and findin' our son desperate for any attention when I get home. Ye have to pull yoursel' together. Do you want to lose this child, too?"

Annie looked at Jim, silent and unresponsive. Jim threw up his arms in disgust and stomped out. Annie paced around the kitchen for an hour, then checked on Bobby and went to bed. She lay there replaying the evening in her thoughts and could not sleep.

Jim did not return home until after midnight, with whiskey on his breath. He crawled into bed but turned his back to Annie.

That night Annie had a vivid dream. Her father appeared to her. He was still the handsome man she remembered, with his thick black hair parted to one side, a smart moustache and a goatee. He was wearing his good dark jacket and vest with a white shirt and bowtie. His familiar light blue eyes gave her comfort. She realized he was trying to say something to her. As she looked harder, she saw he was holding Maggie in his arms. He told Annie that he found her and that she was bonny. He said Maggie looked like Annie had when she was little. Maggie wiggled free from his arms and sang, twirled and danced around her grandfather. Her father smiled and said, "Thank you, Annie," and then faded away.

Annie woke up with a start and got up to check on Bobby. He was sleeping soundly, so she went back to bed, but she could not get her dream out of her head. In the morning, she picked the baby up and felt warmth towards him that she hadn't felt in weeks. As she cuddled him, he reached up to touch her face with his tiny fingers. She realized then that she had been afraid to cherish this child as she had Maggie. She kissed her baby's chubby cheek and whispered, "Bobby, my sweet little boy, I'm so sorry to have neglected you. I do love you." She cried remorseful tears as she held him close.

When Jim woke up, he found his breakfast ready and his lunch packed. Annie was singing to Bobby while she rocked him. He quietly approached his wife and son, and gently kissed the top of the baby's head. She placed the sleeping baby in a wicker basket and took Jim's hands in hers.

She had planned to tell him about her dream, but in that moment she decided to keep her precious dream to herself. Instead, she said, "I know I've been bloody selfish. I'm ashamed to have made everything harder for you. I promise I will make it up to you both."

He didn't reply. He gave her a weak smile and left for work. She looked at his untouched breakfast and wondered if he would ever forgive her, or love her as much as he once did.

Chapter Seven

Annie worked hard to prove to Jim that she wasn't sliding back as she tried to be to her old self again. It was much simpler to win Bobby's affections, which made her feel even guiltier about her neglect of their baby boy. She knew that she had withdrawn from everyone after losing Maggie, but she couldn't bear to have Jim withdraw from her. She did love him and was so sorry to have caused him more pain.

Jim's celebration of the birth of their second son finally assured Annie that he had fully forgiven her. The baby looked identical to Bobby, both children chubby-cheeked and blessed with their father's blue eyes. They christened him John, but were soon calling him Jack. Mother visited almost daily, often finding time to play with Bobby or go for walks with him while Annie was nursing Jack.

Annie's brother Alfie was skilled in woodcarving and made beautifully crafted toy boats and horses for his nephews. Her mother often took Bobby to the seashore so he could play with one of his miniature sailing ships. He had become a quiet, introspective child and could amuse himself for hours. Annie noticed that the summer sun had bleached Bobby's hair. He was losing his baby fat, and growing taller.

Although they were happy, Annie and Jim struggled with money. One day, after her mother and Bobby returned from another walk by the seaside, Annie resolved to seek Mother's advice. She made a pot of tea and gave Bobby a biscuit to eat while he was playing on the floor. Jack was asleep in his crib, content with a full belly. Annie studied her mother. She was heavier now but she was still an attractive woman. Although a couple of widowers had asked her to marry, she had told them all she was not interested. She maintained that she would never love another man as much as she had loved Annie's father. "Jim works so hard at the copper works," Annie began, "but we barely have enough money to live on. I've offered to find a job, but he got angry at the suggestion and he absolutely forbade it." She looked down at her tea. "He's never spoken to me like that before."

"Now Annie, you know that a man would be frowned upon if his wife worked. It would hurt his pride." Mother patted Annie's shoulder. "Besides he's a good man, Annie, and doesn't waste his wages on drink as some husbands do, or some sons," she added with a sardonic smile.

"Yesterday he came home with a government pamphlet, advertising cheap farmland in New Ontario, in Canada. He thinks it would be a way to make a better life for us." Annie knelt to wipe the crumbs from Bobby's hands and face. "I know that he's always wanted property and we both dream of owning a house, but I don't want to move so far away."

"It's not so frightening to move to a new country. Remember, Pappa and I moved from Norway to make a better life." Annie shook her head. Norway wasn't nearly as far away as Canada. "But don't fret, love," continued Mother. "Jim may just be dreaming out loud."

"You're right, Mother. I'm likely worrying about nothing. The children are healthy and we've enough to eat. I should count my blessings. Did you and Bobby enjoy your walk?"

"Well, poppet, he's such a quiet, serious little boy. I find that I have patience with him that I never had with you or your brothers. We've had a special bond ever since I cared for him that month."

Annie felt the familiar guilt burn through her as she remembered how she had neglected Bobby. Mother glanced at her and patted her hand.

"Bobby's a wonderful, clever boy, Annie. You're doing a fine job raising your children."

Annie knew it would take a lifetime to make it up to Bobby. She feared the family would never get ahead. Every day was such a struggle and she just wanted to give their sons a chance at a better life. But fate had handed her another concern that compounded her money worries, one she would have to share with Jim before she confided to Mother. She once again found herself pregnant. She didn't know how she would tell him.

Chapter Eight

Annie sat with her elbows on the kitchen table, resting her forehead on her clasped hands. She sniffled and reached into an apron pocket for her handkerchief. When she heard Jim's voice and the children's laughter through the outside door, she stood up and briskly brushed away her tears. Bobby exploded through the entrance, letting in the cool spring breeze. Jim held Jack's small pudgy hand - he was just starting to walk - as they followed Bobby inside. The children's cheeks were rosy and Jim's hair was windblown.

"Well Annie, ah think that ah've tired them out with all that fresh air. They'll be ready for a good snooze." Annie gave Jim a quick kiss on the cheek and turned to fetch some biscuits from a tin on the counter.

"There you go, boys," she said. "You can have one each with your milk, then off to bed for your nap."

"Is your headache any better?" Jim asked.

She forced a smile. "I'm fine." But she heard the false tone in her own voice. She hadn't yet told Jim about the baby; the time had never seemed right to add to his financial worries.

Later, when the boys were sleeping and Jim was reading in his favourite chair, Annie picked up her mending basket and sat down in her rocking chair, mindlessly sorting through the clothing. Looking at Jim, she thought, *He's reading that damned pamphlet again and likely dreaming of New Ontario. How are we going to manage?* She was at least five months along now; she couldn't hide it much longer. *I will have to tell him today.*

She studied her husband. He was so engrossed in his reading that he didn't notice her gaze. He was thirty years old now and wore his thick, brown hair short, but he still looked youthful with his slim, muscular build. She noticed a new frown line between his brows. *Oh Lord, give me strength.* She steeled herself to deliver the news.

Jim held out his ragged pamphlet towards Annie. "Listen to this! Ye can buy land fo' fifty cents an acre and just pay a quarter of the price in cash an' the remainder within three years. We could buy a farm property wi' just twenty dollars. Your dream of owning a house could actually come true!"

Annie sighed. They had been having this conversation for many months. "But we'd be so far away from our families, Jim! We might never see them again. I do want to own our own house some day but why can't we do it here?"

"Annie, we could never in a lifetime afford property here, but it's possible in New Ontario." He leaned back in his chair. "Just think about it, love. We could build a better future for our boys." He looked at her and frowned. "There's something else bothering you, isn't there?"

She felt her throat constrict. Her eyes welled with tears and her voice broke. "We're going to have another child."

Annie watched Jim's face grow pale, but then he quickly rose from his chair and pulled her up into his arms, knocking the mending to the floor.

"Divent fash yousel', Annie. A bairn is a blessin'! We'll manage just fine."

Annie shook her head. She knew he was trying to hide his concern from her and she wondered how they'd ever get ahead.

She suffered with heartburn and nausea over the following month, then her legs and feet ballooned. She didn't recall having such discomfort in her other pregnancies and she took it as her punishment. She shamefully admitted to herself that she didn't want this unexpected baby.

Annie had to rest in bed more often than not, but her mother came over regularly to help care for Bobby and Jack. Sometimes she took them to visit the cemetery. Once, Annie overheard them talking as they left the house.

"Your sister Maggie was a little tinker. She would just have to smile at her granddad Kidd to get a treat. She looked very much like your own Mamma when she was a little girl."

Annie heard Bobby's high-pitched voice. "I thought only old people died. Why did she have to die?"

Annie wiped a sudden tear from her eye as she heard her mother answer, "I don't know, poppet. We still love her very much and will never forget her."

The following week, Annie felt more energized, so she sent the boys outside to play as she caught up on household chores. She was surprised to hear a sharp rap at her door and recognized the tall, skeletal vicar from their church.

"Mrs. Kidd," he sputtered in a rage, "your children have done damage in the church cemetery. You must come with me immediately."

She had not forgotten how the vicar had treated her when she and Jim got married – he'd been a condescending toad. She blushed at the irony that she was once again very pregnant.

Annie frowned and forced herself to reply calmly. "Vicar Brown, my sons are only little boys. How do you know it was Bobby and Jack?"

He puffed out his thin chest. "My dear Mrs. Kidd, my good wife caught them in the act!"

That old busybody, Annie thought. The vicar's wife was known for seeking faults in everyone. *Now she's picking on children?*

She followed the vicar as quickly as she could. It was only a ten minute walk, but she was almost nine months pregnant and moving was difficult. Her hips hurt with all the extra weight, and she was tired of sharing her body. *This baby needs to arrive soon!* she thought miserably.

When she finally reached the cemetery, she paused for a moment, pressing her hands to the small of her back to ease the pressure. She looked around as she stretched, and burst into peals of laughter. There, on Maggie's little gravesite, was a small mountain of flowers. The boys had gathered every bouquet and floral arrangement from all of the other graves and piled them on Maggie's plot.

Annie saw the colour rise in the vicar's face, so she stifled her laughter. In as serious a voice as she could muster, she said, "I'm very sorry, Vicar Brown. I will bring my boys back to apologize to you and we will place all the flowers back where they belong." She waddled away, her suppressed laughter erupting as soon as she was out of sight.

Annie laughingly recounted the story to her mother the following day.

Her mother's face reddened. "Oh Annie, I'm dreadfully sorry. It's my fault for taking them there and filling their heads with stories about Maggie."

"It is nobody's fault. They're just little boys who wanted to show their love for their sister. It was a beautiful tribute." She laughed again. "I just hope their recollection of where they got all the flowers was accurate!"

As Annie walked the half-mile distance home from Mother's, with Bobby and Jack in tow, she felt a sharp pain in her abdomen. A few minutes later, she felt another. Mrs. Clinton, the midwife, lived in a tidy cottage near the church, so Annie decided to stop there on her way. Before Annie could knock, Mrs. Clinton swung the door wide. The kindly midwife greeted Annie, "I saw you coming, love." She quickly picked up her birthing basket, her small, compact body braced for action. "I've everything I need here and I'll go with you."

She reached into a pocket and gave each of Annie's boys a peppermint sweet. The children looked at Annie for her consent, thanked the woman and ran on ahead. Mrs. Clinton held Annie's elbow and chatted nonstop as they slowly walked the rest of the way home, stopping every few minutes to help Annie breathe through her contractions.

When Jim came home from work, he took his sons to a neighbour's house. He returned in minutes and sat beside Annie to offer what comfort he could. She was in great pain. Every so often Mrs. Clinton shooed Jim out of the bedroom so she could check Annie's progress, but each time she called him back; it wasn't yet time. As the hours passed, the pains grew harder and harder to bear. Annie crushed Jim's hand and clawed at his arm, screaming in agony. He brought her a cool cloth, a drink of water, but she pushed everything away. She could only think about the pain.

After six long, agonizing hours, the midwife told Jim to go and get a doctor. Jim looked at Annie, the fear plain on his face. Within fifteen minutes, Jim came back with Dr. Bootiman, the same doctor who had cared for Maggie.

Dr. Bootiman closed the bedroom door, and kindly asked Annie how she was feeling.

Like I'm being drawn and quartered, she thought, but replied, "I'm managing, doctor. Mrs. Clinton and Jim are helping me through the worst."

After the doctor spoke to Mrs. Clinton and examined Annie, he called Jim into the bedroom. "This is going to be a long night, I'm afraid. It appears that we have a large baby, and your wife is a small woman, Mr. Kidd."

Jim looked tenderly into Annie's eyes, brushed her damp hair back with his hand and said, "Ah'll fetch the boys and take them to Ma's." She could tell he was making a great effort to appear unworried. "The bairns will be fine there. Ah won't be long, love."

The doctor stayed overnight with Annie and the midwife, which was a small comfort. Annie could hear Jim pacing back and forth in the kitchen. Hang tradition, she wanted him with her to help her bear the agony. She knew she could be stronger with him beside her, and she insisted that he come in.

In the early hours of the morning, Dr. Bootiman left the bedroom with Jim. Annie overheard him.

"This is one of the most difficult births I have seen. I will have to deliver by forceps. This will be very hard on your wife but if I don't do it, we may lose both mother and child."

The doctor and Jim returned to the bedroom. Through her tears, Annie saw Jim look at her helplessly and mouth, "I love you, Annie." He wiped his eyes with his shirt sleeve.

Annie had never known such fear. *I may never see Bobby and Jack again.* Had she kissed them them before Jim took them to Jane's? She couldn't remember. Another contraction slammed through her. *I cannot take this pain any longer!*

Jim took both of Annie's hands in a strong grip and looked deep into her eyes. "Stay strong. You're almost done, love. You can do this!"

Annie tried to be stoic but the pain of the forceps was so intense that she couldn't help but scream. Just when she thought she couldn't endure the torture any longer, she felt a massive pulling sensation, heard the mewling cries of a baby, and the doctor's warm, relieved congratulations.

Mrs. Clinton beamed at Annie. "You've been brilliant, dear. You have a healthy baby, and what a handsome boy, too. I declare if there isn't some Viking in him."

Annie felt groggy as the midwife placed the baby on her chest, but it didn't keep her from seeing what a beautiful child he was. He had white blond fuzz on his head and was perfectly formed. Amazing to think how just minutes ago she had been so afraid for this child, and for herself. She kissed his head and guided him to her breast. Jim gently stroked her hair off her brow. His face was pale and tear-streaked. His voice cracked. "Oh Annie, I thought I was going to lose you." He leaned over to kiss Annie's forehead and looked down at his new son.

"Well, little man, you've given us all a good scare. Let me look at you." He gently touched the top of the baby's head as he nursed. "Ah, Annie, you've given us a bonnie bairn. Wait 'til the grannies see him."

That evening, when Annie's mother saw the new baby, she said he was "the spitting image" of Annie's brother George.

Annie looked up at Jim. "Shall we call him George, then?"

While Annie recuperated, her mother once again moved in to care for the children and make meals for the family. Annie healed very slowly and was in constant pain for over a week. It hurt to move and she spent most of her days in bed. But by the second week she was feeling a little stronger, and ventured into the kitchen to nurse the baby in her rocking chair. The first time Jim came home from work to find her out of bed, relief washed over his face. She knew that she had battled death and won, but these last two weeks had been awful, and she knew Jim had continued to worry about her health.

Annie loved her mother's company, and Jim and the children enjoyed being spoiled with Norwegian meals and treats. By the fourth week after Georgie's birth Annie was finally feeling well. Her body was healing, her baby was thriving and her house was in order, so her mother returned to her own home.

One evening, several weeks later, when the children were asleep, Jim brought out the tattered pamphlet about New Ontario and looked seriously at Annie.

"Annie, I know that ye aren't keen on moving to Canada. But there we could have our own house built on our own land." He ran his hand through his hair. "We'd have a fresh start wi' better opportunities fo' our sons. Can ye even imagine ownin' one hundred and sixty acres?"

Annie stared at her husband and smiled. He was still the handsome man she had married. She even loved that new worry line between his eyes.

"It *is* my dream to own a house and land and I *do* want a better future for our boys, but I've always pictured our house where our families are – where we grew up." She sighed. Maybe it was time she considered Jim's dream. "If moving to Canada were the way, how could we ever save enough money to make it happen?"

"Just think about the opportunities for us in Canada, Annie. Don't say no yet. Think about it and dinna fash about money. We'll manage someha and save bit by bit."

Months later, when the January cold had set in, Annie and the children were visiting her mother. The small house was warm and cozy and filled with the teasing odour of sweet buns hot from the oven. Bobby and Jack played on the floor with an old wooden toy horse and cart and Georgie was asleep in the bedroom. The women were drinking tea and talking about Annie's future.

"Jim's still talking about a new start in Canada," she was saying as she sipped her tea. "But it feels like it will take forever to save enough." She was suddenly interrupted by loud pounding at the door and a panicked shout. The women rushed to answer the door together. She recognized Alfie's friend Don from the glass factory.

The young man was red-faced and sweating in spite of the raw weather. "Alfie's been hurt real bad." He gasped to catch his breath. "There was an explosion and he's lost a lot of blood. You've got to come quick!"

"Oh lord, Alfie!" Mother cried, and, not even bothering to grab her coat, followed the man back down the road to the factory.

Annie picked up Georgie and hurried Bobby and Jack out the door, and then ran all the way to Jane and Charles' home.

"My brother Alfie's been hurt at the factory!" she explained breathlessly. "Can you watch the children? I'll be back as soon as I can."

Jane took Georgie from Annie's arms and patted his back.

"Oh, me! Ah pray he's not too bad. Go - take all the time ye need, hinny."

Annie left without saying thank you or goodbye and ran the half-mile to the factory. As she approached the brick building, she saw Alfie being carried out on a wooden door by two burly men. They carefully rested the improvised stretcher on two sawhorses in the yard. Alfie's face was contorted in pain. His left arm was wrapped in a thick layer of bloodied towels. Annie saw her mother push through the crowd of men and tread right through the sticky trail of blood on the ground, to reach Alfie's side.

Annie watched her mother calmly whisper to Alfie and tenderly stroke his forehead. She began to tentatively approach but was stopped by a large hand on her shoulder. She turned to see Alfie's supervisor, a big gruff-looking man. He was visibly shaken.

"I'm so sorry about Alfred's injuries. I don't know yet what caused the explosion, but I'll make sure the company pays for the best medical care."

Annie nodded woodenly at the man, and slowly walked to her brother. When she reached him, she leaned over and pressed her cheek to his. She whispered, "Don't you dare give up, Alfie Larsen. If I could fight and survive, so can you!"

Alfie was deathly ill for a long month. His left hand had been mangled so badly that it soon became infected. Finally the doctor pronounced that Alfie had to choose between his hand or his life. He was in no condition to make a decision so their mother tearfully agreed to the amputation. After the operation, he would have to endure several long months of healing.

Annie's mother became despondent. Several times Annie found her quietly weeping while clutching the pearls at her neck. She was barely eating and had lost weight. She was able to hide her mood when she was with Alfie, but she couldn't keep it from Annie. Annie suspected that almost losing Alfie had brought back the pain of Pappa's death. She resolved to bring the boys by every day, to help liven the mood and give her mother something else to focus on. Maybe having little ones around would remind her of happier times when Annie and her brothers were small, and help snap her out of her doldrums.

After one of his visits during Alfie's long convalescence, Don, his friend from the factory, confided to Annie. He said that management had moved Alfie off the factory property after the explosion in case he died, so they wouldn't be taken to court. Rumour was that the factory owners were afraid of negative publicity, so to reduce the chance of a walkout or strike, Alfie was going to receive a large settlement.

Annie was furious. "How can the factory owners get away with that, if everyone knows?" She paced up and down the front walk, her face red with anger. "Bloody hell! No amount of money will get my brother's hand back!"

"There could be some good in it, Annie," said Don. "Everyone is afraid of losing jobs, and a walkout or strike would be devastating when so many are struggling from pay to pay."

"I'm sorry, Don. You're right." Annie pushed a strand of hair back and composed her face, although inside she was still fuming. "My mother and I do thank you for visiting Alfie so often. You lift his spirits."

"Perhaps the settlement will help him sort out what to do next," said Don. Annie nodded but she was doubtful. How could anything good come from such a terrible accident?

Alfie's natural good humour slowly returned as he healed. "No limit to what I'd do to get out of work!" he joked.

Annie rolled her eyes and groaned, but she was very thankful that he was recuperating. She was there every day visiting with her brother. With Alfie's good humour came their mother's, another thing for Annie to be thankful for. Knowing Alfie was on the mend, her mother was happier helping with the care of Georgie and his busy brothers. Meanwhile, Annie talked and joked with her brother for hours at a time. Their mother would regularly pop into Alfie's room and scold Annie.

"Let your poor brother rest!"

"Ah Ma," Alfie protested on one such occasion, "I've been resting for almost a year! I can rest more when I'm dead and gone." He quickly apologized when he saw the flustered look of shock on their mother's face.

She admonished him. "You shouldn't jest like that! We almost did lose you."

Annie told her brother about Jim's dream to move to Canada, and she brought out the tattered pamphlet. Alfie thoughtfully fingered the worn paper with his good hand. He grew quiet and thoughtful. "Can I keep this for a day or two?"

One evening months later, when Annie, Jim and the children were visiting Alfie, he handed Jim a sealed envelope. Jim looked at him, eyebrows raised.

"Go ahead, open it." Alfie said.

Jim shrugged, and tore open the seal. He pulled out a thick piece of printed paper. Jim looked back at his brother-in-law in confusion. "This is a ticket fo' ship's passage to... Canada? Are you goin' to Canada, Alfie? You lucky bugger!"

Alfie laughed. "The ticket is for you, Jim. I bought it with some of my settlement money."

Annie sat up, alert. Jim looked astounded. "Ah canna take that, Alfie. It's your money."

"I've been lying here doing nothing but a lot of thinking these past months," said Alfie. "Here's my plan. You go over first, and get set up in New Ontario. When you've found work and a place to live, and I've healed enough to travel, I'll sail to Canada with Annie and the boys."

Annie felt a lump in her throat. Jim looked at her with a silent question. She slowly nodded her head, her eyes bright with tears.

"Well, that's a grand plan and vera generous, Alfie," said Jim, finally. "But I'll only accept on the terms that it is a loan, no' a gift."

"Oh, fine. You're a stubborn old Geordie!"

Jim laughed and shook Alfie's good hand affectionately. "Ah canna believe this! You're a good and generous man!"

"As for me, I'm afraid, I will not be able to join you in settling in New Ontario," said Alfie. "Apparently you need two hands to clear land or work in the mines." He chuckled at his own joke then grew serious again. "There are other jobs that I can do though. I already have letters of reference and a few leads for a job in Toronto."

Annie smiled at her brother and hugged him. "Oh, Alfie, you have been busy!"

"Well, I've had plenty of time to think. I have dreams, too – and I'm ready for a new life."

Annie kissed her brother's cheek. "I am so happy that you plan to travel with me and the children. I had wondered how I would manage to travel alone, if the time ever came."

"Don't get all soft on me now, sis. Besides, you don't know what I'll be like as a travel companion," Alfie teased.

"Oh, Alfie, you've always been an annoying brother, so I'd expect nothing less from you on the voyage!" she laughed as she teased back.

By August, after tearful goodbyes, Annie and the children were on their own and Jim was on a ship somewhere in the Atlantic. After a couple of days alone, Annie felt a red haze envelop her. She was angry that things had happened so quickly. She was angry at Alfie for buying Jim's ticket, even for having the accident that had given him the means. She avoided Alfie and her mother for a week in case a comment slipped out. It was hard enough to stay civil around her boys. She was angry with Jim, too. Maybe Jim just wanted to escape, to have an adventure and enjoy some freedom. Maybe he didn't love her enough to stay.

And through it all, she was angry with herself. *Bloody hell, woman! It's your dream to own a house and Jim is working hard to make it happen.* Besides, hadn't she given her consent when Alfie handed him that ticket? Finally, she managed to calm her anger. But still, she was lonely for Jim.

There was an agonizing three-week wait until Jim's first letter. She read and reread it so often that she memorized every word.

August 15, 1911
Dearest Annie,
I hope this letter finds you and the children well. I enjoyed the train trip to Glasgow and all went well until I boarded the ship. Let's just say a life at sea is not for me. I'm thankful though that it only took a week to cross the Atlantic. I don't know how your Da and brothers could work on ships for so many years!

The good news is that I qualified for the British Bonus. That should smooth the way to get our own property. I didn't have a chance to see much of Montreal because I had to make my connection to Toronto right away. I've been in Toronto for a couple of days and plan to take the train north tomorrow morning. Yesterday, I met some men who had just returned from New Ontario and they say that there are plenty of jobs with the railroad or building roads. The newspapers are filled with news about more gold deposits found up north, too.

I hope that I'm doing the right thing for us. Well, I'm in Canada now and will work hard so that we can be together again soon. I miss you and the boys.

Love, Jim

She didn't receive another letter for several weeks. Finally, Jim wrote that he had found temporary work on the railway the day he arrived in North Bay. After that job he had travelled by train further north, to Mile 225, the end of the line, and found some rough accommodation for himself, in a government camp. He described miles and miles of forest. She had difficulty imagining such a sight. She sighed and wished she was with him, wherever he was.

God knows how long it'll be before we'll see each other, she thought, *or even if we ever will be together as a family again.* She hoped they hadn't made the wrong decision.

Chapter Nine

The kitchen was cozy and warm from the oven heat despite the damp, cold wintery day outside. The table was covered with a small mountain of clothing that Annie had been folding and sorting. She looked at the half-filled steamer trunk on the floor and felt overwhelmed by the number of chores she had yet to complete. She could hardly believe that she, Alfie and her boys would leave for Glasgow tomorrow, and go aboard a ship the following day.

Sinking down in a chair, she reached into her apron pocket and took out Jim's latest letter to read again.

December 30, 1911
Dearest Annie,
At last! It's time for you and the boys to join me in our new home on our own property at Mile 225! I have almost finished building a small timber home for us. It will be done by the time you arrive. Best of all, we own it! I had all the wood I needed right here on our property! You couldn't guess how many trees we own.

Sell all of our furniture for the best price you can get and we'll buy or build what we need here. I have tables and benches, beds and two good wood stoves already. The cabin is comfortably warm, even on the coldest nights.

Alfie wrote to say that your passage has already been purchased. I'm counting the days until I see you and the bairns again. It's been so lonely without you.

Send me a telegraph when you arrive in St. John, to let me know when your train will arrive in Toronto. I'll head south in time to

*meet you at Union Station. I can barely believe that we'll be together
again so soon. I miss you.*
  Love, Jim

Annie refolded the letter and tucked it back into her pocket.
Sighing, she got up to finish the packing and glanced out the
window to check on her children. The boys were playing a
boisterous game with sticks and a ball, shouting and giggling. She
watched them for a moment. Ten-year-old Bobby was a serious,
responsible boy whom she relied on heavily, especially with Jim so
far away. Both Bobby and seven-year-old Jack were small boys
with light brown hair and chubby cheeks. Georgie, however, was
already tall for a four-year-old, and his hair was still white-blonde.
He would likely tower over his brothers when he was fully grown.
She recalled shamefully how she hadn't wanted that pregnancy.
Now, she couldn't imagine her life without that precious child. He
was so like his namesake, her brother.

Annie continued packing the large trunk, which she'd bought at a
second-hand store. She wanted to make sure that there was enough
room for the lace tablecloth and the good set of dishes. As she
worked, and listened to the boys' laughter, she remembered playing
the same games with her brothers. It didn't seem so long ago. She
wondered how her children would react to this huge change in their
lives. Of course, they'd miss their grandparents. She had to blink
away tears thinking of living so far away from her mother. She knew
Canada would give the boys more opportunities than they had here.
They didn't even know their family was poor; everyone they knew
was in a similar circumstance. She chuckled to herself, recalling a
neighbour who often cooked fat at dinnertime to make the rest of the
street think they were eating meat. No one was fooled.

Jim had laboured for long hours and little pay in South Shields.
He still worked hard in Canada, but at least now he chose when and
where to work. He was well paid, he told her, and had the luxury of
accepting or refusing a job. Best of all, he had fulfilled their dream of
owning a place of their own.

She scolded herself for daydreaming. She moved to the kitchen, which was filled with mouth-watering odours; she had decided to make their last dinner in South Shields a special one and had made the boys' favourite foods.

She removed a roasted chicken from the oven. Gravy simmered on the stove and a large pot of mashed potatoes sat on the counter. There was a freshly baked loaf of bread on the table. The boys cheered when they came in and spotted a chocolate cake on the shelf. They were noisy with chatter while they ate, excited about their adventures to come.

Before Annie could take a bite of her own meal, she heard a timid *hello* and a knock. She opened the door to a wizened, painfully thin woman, dressed in several layers of tattered clothing. The children were suddenly silent; they stopped eating and stared at the strange visitor.

"Do ye have anythin' to spare afore ye sail to the new country? I'd be grateful for anythin', good lady."

Annie felt pity for the poor old woman. "The house is all but empty now, but I can give you an old pot you can keep and I'll fill it with a good meal that will hold you over for a bit."

The crone bowed and mumbled, "Thank ye. Thank ye, kind lady. I wish you many blessings."

Annie retrieved her oldest and smallest pot from her trunk and filled it with the remains of the roast chicken. She scooped potatoes and carrots from her own plate to top it off. As she handed over the pot of food, the old woman snatched Annie's hand in a papery, claw-like grip. Annie tried to pull away but the woman held her fast. The ancient woman then leaned in to whisper to Annie so the children wouldn't hear.

"Brave lass, ye'll conquer water, fire, disease and death. Sky lights will give ye comfort. God bless."

She dropped Annie's hand, thanked her once again for the food and shuffled down the lane. Annie closed the door and sat down at the table, puzzled by the odd message. It sent a shiver up her back. She picked up her fork, and said, "Well, that certainly was strange. Eat up boys. It'll be early to bed tonight. We'll be up before the sun tomorrow."

Annie tucked her younger sons into bed and told Bobby she was going out for a bit of air. She put on her warm boots and coat and walked briskly to the church. She breathed in the familiar coastal air and clutched her coat at her neck to keep out the chill, wondering if she would miss the rich salty scent of the sea.

She continued past the church to the cemetery. The iron-gate squeaked in protest as she opened it. Her feet imprinted the frost-covered grass as she crunched her way past rows of stones. Some grave markers looked elaborate but most were frugally plain; a few tombstones were so old that only rough indentations were visible where the letters and dates had eroded over the years. She located the tiny cross engraved with Maggie's name. Kneeling on the frozen ground, she gently touched the grass over her daughter's grave and the familiar pain of loss coursed through her. As tears spilled down her cheeks, she said her farewells to her little girl. She didn't know if she would ever see this place again.

She was annoyed to hear footsteps approaching; she had hoped to spend these last moments with Maggie alone. But looking up, she saw the familiar shape of her mother walking slowly towards her. She hesitated when she saw Annie, and then smiled.

"Ah, I'm sorry love," she said. "I should have known you would be here tonight. I come here every evening to say good night to Maggie."

Annie wiped away her tears and said, "I didn't know that."

"You'll think me a daft old woman, but I often dream of your Pappa holding Maggie in his arms. She is always singing and laughing. It gives me a lot of peace."

Annie remembered how that same image had pulled her back from her own private hell after Maggie died. She had never spoken of it to anyone. The hairs stood up on the back of her neck.

"Oh Mother," she cried, "I may never come back here, and feel like I'm abandoning Maggie."

"Don't worry about this little plot, pet," said Mother, reaching her arms towards Annie. "I'll continue to visit every night for as long as I am able." Annie leaned into her mother's warm embrace. "I'll see you off tomorrow morning, Annie."

She tried to compose herself on the walk home, but as she came in the door, the worried expression on Bobby's face told her she hadn't succeeded.

"It's okay," she said. "I've just been to see Maggie. I'm a bit sad, that's all."

"Will we be all right, Ma," he asked, "in Canada?"

"Oh, yes, Bobby, I have no doubts." She patted his arm.

"Good night, Ma," he said, and pecked her on the cheek. "I'm off to bed."

"Good night, son. Sleep well."

Her thoughts went back to the old woman's ominous message. "Brave lass, ye'll conquer water, fire, disease and death. Sky lights will give ye comfort." *Likely the poor old granny was daft. Of course I'm crossing water. Wouldn't Jim and Alfie tease me if I believed such nonsense?*

Chapter Ten

A gust of frigid January wind blew in from the coast in the early morning hours of their moving day. Frosty fingers of cold air crept under the door and into the kitchen. Shivering, Annie used her few remaining bits of coal to light a fire in the stove before waking the children. They had a hot breakfast of porridge and tea, and she washed the dishes one last time before packing them away in the trunk.

She heard a horse clop over the cobblestones and stop outside her doorway. Opening the door, she saw Alfie, Mother, and Jim's parents climb down from a horse-drawn wagon. Her boys squeezed past her with squeals of excitement.

Alfie and Charles came inside to haul her heavy trunk out the door and hoist it onto the wagon. Neighbours peeked curiously out windows of dreary brick buildings or came out to the street to gawk. Annie's boys were loud and boisterous as they helped load the rest of their baggage, but she didn't scold them. She gazed wistfully down the familiar street. The adjoining streets were dark and quiet. She thought of the large, destitute families living in just one room in many of these houses, and silently wished them good luck and goodbye. Annie sighed with both relief and regret.

She went back inside to take one last look at their rooms, closed and locked the door, and then tearfully gave Mary, Jane and Charles one more hug goodbye. "I'll write often and I'll have the boys write as well," she promised, and she climbed aboard to sit beside Alfie.

Before she knew it, she was waving from the cart and she, Alfie and the boys were on their way to the railway station. Annie continued to wave until they turned a corner and Mother, Jane and Charles were out of her sight. She looked up at Alfie.

"This makes me realize how much easier it is being the one leaving than the one left behind," she said. "Do you remember how it felt, the many times Pappa left us for a sea voyage?" Alfie nodded. "And it was so difficult to say goodbye to Jim. I didn't know when I'd see him again."

"Well, you'll see him in less than two weeks now. Tomorrow you'll get to test whether you have proper Norwegian sea legs or not!"

I'll be with Jim in two weeks! Annie could hardly believe they owned their own land and house, thanks to Jim's hard work and perseverance. She could only hope that fate would be kind and allow them never to be separated again.

Chapter Eleven

Annie gazed out the train window and watched the landscape outside whip by at a furious pace. It was her first rail excursion. Travelling at such speed gave her a pang of fear and, inexplicably, a tingle of excitement. The children were unusually quiet on the trip to Glasgow. She imagined that they felt the same trepidation and thrill that she was feeling. Their eyes were huge and their mouths agape as they stared out the windows. Annie rested her head affectionately on Alfie's shoulder.

A smartly dressed, elderly woman stopped in the aisle beside their seats, and remarked in a Glaswegian accent, "Whit well-behaved wee jimmies. Ye must be sae proud o' yer sons, sir."

Georgie piped up, "Oh, he's not my Da!"

The scandalized woman muttered to herself and huffed off. Annie bubbled over with laughter, giggling until she had hiccups. Georgie looked bewildered.

Alfie gathered the little boy to his lap. "Aw, Georgie," he said in a loud whisper, "don't you worry one little bit. Women can be a little peculiar sometimes."

Annie laughed, and muttered to her brother, "Peculiar, is it? I'd say that's the pot calling the kettle black!" She gave Georgie a reassuring pat. She was enjoying her first experience of train travel and was surprised at how quickly the time had passed.

When they arrived at the Glasgow station, Alfie found a buggy for hire which would take them to the port, and the men loaded

Annie's trunk while she settled the children on the bench seat of the cab. The driver clicked at the horse and shook the reins. Annie hung on to the seat as they jerked ahead. She spotted a multitude of ship masts in the distance, standing at attention like soldiers. Cold, briny breezes blew in from the harbour.

"There's our hotel over there."

Annie peered in the direction Alfie was pointing and saw a long three-story sooty-grey building. She had never stayed in a hotel before. "I feel as if I'm one of the gentry, travelling by rail and staying in a hotel. I'm as excited as the children."

"Well, don't make your expectations too lofty," said her brother. "The hotel is not first class, and by the time you get to New Ontario, you may well be sick of train travel."

Alfie had reserved two rooms at the hotel. He shared a room with Bobby, and Annie was with her two younger boys. She unlocked the door and peeked curiously into her room. Jack and Georgie squeezed past her to goggle at their night's lodgings. The space was sparsely furnished with two narrow beds and one small dresser. There was a detectable musty odour and the floor was grimy, but the bed sheets appeared to be freshly laundered. The boys were tired from the day's excitement and fell asleep soon after she tucked them into their bed.

Annie stayed up a little longer gazing out the dusty window. Grey buildings were crammed together and she couldn't see a single tree anywhere. She looked over the horizon and her eyes welled up with tears. She was torn between grief over leaving her mother, and joy at the prospect of seeing Jim again. She thought again of little Maggie and turned to gaze at her sleeping children. She tiptoed over to straighten the blanket and gave each boy a kiss.

"Sleep tight. We're going to see your Da soon."

Finally she lay down in her own bed and closed her eyes.

The next morning they carried their bags to the dock and identified Annie's large trunk, which would be placed in storage on the ship until they arrived in Canada. There was a strong fishy odour in the cold, salt-filled air, and a brisk winter wind blew in from the sea.

Alfie explained that their actual embarkation on the *Cassandra* should be quick because they were British subjects and were travelling to British territory. But there was a lot of pushing and shoving until a man in uniform took charge and bellowed out an order to line up.

Annie heard many different languages and even recognized some Norwegian. She tugged anxiously at her children's sleeves and cautioned them, "Stay close to each other. It's too easy to get lost in this crowd." She was thankful that her brother was a head taller than most people on the dock so she could keep him in sight.

While waiting their turn to board, Annie scrutinized the *Cassandra*. The steel-hulled ship was about five hundred feet long and had two masts and a large white horizontal stripe, painted along the funnel. The company flag, with vertical red, white and blue stripes, flapped in the brisk wind. There was a large blue letter "*D*" on the flag, for the owners, the Donaldson Brothers. She knew from a pamphlet she had read that they would be among nine hundred steerage passengers.

The *Cassandra* was gently rocking as they approached the gangway. Just as Annie was about to step onto the platform, Georgie burst into tears.

"Come along, Georgie. We're holding people up. What's the matter?" People pushed and shoved around them.

"I'm too scared, Mummy!" he sputtered. "We'll go under the water, like my toy boat at the seashore."

Annie picked up her youngest boy. "This is a real boat, son, not like your toy. We'll be perfectly safe." *I hope!* She couldn't deny that the whole endeavor seemed implausible for a ship of its size.

Georgie wiped away his tears. "But Mummy, what makes the ship float?"

Annie paused to consider how to explain flotation to a four-year-old, but then Georgie asked, "Could it be buoyancy?"

Annie laughed. "Yes, my clever little boy, it is buoyancy."

Once on the ship, she was confused by the veritable maze inside. She was so concerned about keeping her children beside her that she lost sight of her brother. He would be sharing accommodation with three other unmarried men, while she and her boys had their own sleeping quarters. Reading the nametag of one of the crew members and realizing he was Welsh, she greeted him in his mother tongue. The man beamed with pleasure and offered to carry her bags.

He led Annie and the children to their steerage cabin, assuring her that they were better off than the second-class passengers, as they would be much more comfortable down there when they hit rough seas. Annie groaned inwardly, and tried not to think about nasty weather.

Not knowing what to expect, she was pleasantly surprised with their enclosed cabin. There were four beds, one bed over another, against two walls. Each bed had a mattress, pillow, two clean sheets and a blanket. There was a water basin for washing, a jug of cold sea water and four towels on hooks. Just as she was wondering where her brother had disappeared to, Alfie knocked on the door jamb.

"Ah, I found you!" he said. "Come on. Let's go up to the promenade deck and watch as the ship pulls out."

They slowly climbed the crowded stairs and found a spot near the railing at the stern of the boat. Annie tearfully gazed at the shoreline, while the ship gracefully sailed away from the harbour. She felt her throat constrict as they moved further out to sea. Alfie looked at her with concern and put his arm around her, and together they watched the disappearing shore.

Just then a brass band on the deck above began to play a lively, happy tune. The music instantly lifted Annie's spirits. After taking one last look at the country she was leaving behind, and agreeing to meet Alfie in the dining saloon in an hour, she guided her boys back down to their quarters.

She set out in search of the lavatory, but when she located it a last, there was a long queue of passengers waiting their turn. Finally, after a long delay, with the boys pushing and poking at each other the whole time, it was their turn. Inside, there were private stalls with china commodes, and these flushed with seawater. There were four basins with hot and cold salt water on tap and a jug of fresh water for rinsing. She soon discovered the reason for the jug of extra water; as hard as she tried, soap would not lather in the salt water. Annie was impressed with how clean everything was.

The dining room was spacious and well-lit with wall sconces, and it ran the width of the ship. Looking around the crowded room, Annie spotted Alfie. He was saving chairs for them at one of the long tables.

"Oh, Alfie, it's just grand," she told him. "Our cabin is wonderful and the boys are excited to have beds all to themselves. Even the lavatories are splendid."

Alfie smiled at his sister's exuberance and then guided her and the children to the buffet. Their first dinner on the ship was another delight. The tables groaned with the weight of barley broth, beef and oyster pies, boiled cabbage, baked, fried and mashed potatoes and fruit, cheese or rice pudding for dessert.

Stuffed after a huge dinner and double desserts, the boys ran off to explore the dining room. There were other children in steerage and they quickly made new friends. Annie and Alfie played cards while the boys were occupied. At eight o'clock, Annie stood up to find her sons.

When she located them across the room, she overheard Jack boasting to a much bigger boy, "My Uncle Alfie is a pirate so you better watch out!" The older child scoffed at Jack's threat, but his eyes widened when Alfie walked over, and he saw the hook where Alfie's hand had been. The boy howled and ran back to his family. Annie stifled her smile before scolding Jack about telling fibs.

When she told her brother what Jack had said, Alfie laughed. "Well, that's always an option if I can't find work in Canada."

Chapter Twelve

Annie tossed and turned that first night. As she envisioned the ship ploughing through the ocean waves, she could hear the water slapping against its sides. The throb of the engines finally lulled her to sleep.

The next morning, there was a lengthy file of passengers awaiting turns in the lavatory. Annie and the boys joined in at the end and by the time they got in, Georgie was jumping up and down with urgency. After they all finally used the toilets and washed up, Annie and her boys climbed the stairs to the dining saloon for breakfast. They had a choice of fresh apples or oranges, hot oatmeal porridge, hard-boiled eggs, soda scones and oatcakes. Annie quite liked the notion of not cooking for a whole week.

But soon, the novelty of the voyage began to wear off. The food was plentiful, but getting monotonous with the same meals offered every day. The boys quickly found their sea legs but after a few days, the journey began to grow tedious for them and they started picking fights with each other and arguing with Annie.

On the fourth day, the weather turned wild and the boys turned green. High waves rolled the boat constantly making many passengers seasick. Bobby, Jack and Georgie skipped meals and grew quiet; they stayed close to Annie. She and her brother were two of very few passengers who didn't become ill, and she blessed their

Nordic blood. She tended her children through the worst of the storm and was thankful when, after a couple of calmer days, the boys began to feel better.

While she didn't mind the movement of the ship, she hated the way it creaked and groaned as it travelled through the ocean. The air in the third-class area was vile because of all the seasick passengers, but on the fifth day she was permitted to go up to the promenade deck. She cleared her lungs with bitingly cold fresh sea air. Looking out over the waves, she saw what appeared to be a huge white mountain in the distance. She asked one of the crew what it was.

"That's an iceberg ma'am. The cap'n is taking great care to give it wide berth. They say that we only see twenty per cent of an iceberg. The rest is hidden under the waves."

Annie saw something even more exciting two days later; flocks of puffins and gulls. *Where there are birds,* she thought, *there has to be land.* She was more than ready to disembark in New Brunswick; she had had enough of the ship. They had one more day of sailing and then would finally step ashore. She spent their last day at sea sorting out their belongings and repacking.

At lunch that day she complained to Alfie, "I hope that somehow, somewhere, we will be able to wash off the stink of the voyage. Salt water is not cleansing at all. How I long to wash my hair." She lowered her voice to a whisper. "Our deck stinks of dirty bodies and vomit, and the smell in the lavatory is truly unbearable. The end of this voyage cannot come soon enough!"

"We'll be off this ship soon," Alfie replied. "Just think how much closer you are to Jim now."

Jim! It would be just a few days until Annie saw Jim and their new home. After such a long, lonely separation it seemed almost unreal that they would be together again. *Have I changed much? Will he have changed?*

"Now, why not take a break from packing?" said Alfie. "I need to regain some manly pride and beat you in a card game!"

PART TWO

Chapter Thirteen

Annie sympathized with the new immigrants who fell to their knees and kissed the snow-covered ground. She would have done the same, but didn't want to give Alfie the teasing ammunition.

The harbour at Saint John was a beehive of activity. Thankfully, being British citizens, they cleared customs quickly. Alfie left Annie and the boys outside, guarding their possessions, while he searched for a buggy and driver and looked for a decent place to stay the night. Before they left South Shields, his friend Angus had asked if he would deliver a parcel to his aunt while he was in Saint John.

"Angus told me that his widowed aunt, a Mrs. Murray, offers room and board for families passing through on their way west. I'll see what I can find out."

Georgie whimpered and complained that he was cold, so Annie took him inside to wait. Georgie's little fingers were turning white and she tried to warm them inside her coat. Bobby and Jack stayed outside to play in the snow, but soon joined her, stomping their feet and shaking their fingers for warmth.

Annie kept checking out the window for Alfie. Finally, after nearly an hour, she saw her brother directing the driver of a horse and wagon to stop in front of the building. Annie called Bobby and Jack over and guided the children outside. As the men lifted her heavy trunk onto the cart, she settled her sons on the bench.

"Angus' aunt's house looks like a fine place so I've arranged for us to stay there tonight. I've reserved two rooms. She lives on the outskirts of the city but it's not far."

As the sway-backed horse slowly pulled them along a snow packed road, they passed colourful clapboard homes. Annie's nose tingled and she could see the condensation of her breath, but the seaside air felt cleansing. She was happy to be away from the foul-smelling ship. Just when the children were beginning to grumble about the cold, they came to a stop in front of a tidy, white two-story house with a wide welcoming veranda facing the street.

Annie and the children walked up the steps to the entrance while Alfie and the driver pulled her steamer trunk down from the wagon. She knocked on the heavy oak door and was greeted by a tall, stout woman, with frizzy brown hair and untamed eyebrows.

"Come in, come in," said the landlady, speaking with a burr right out of the Scottish highlands. "Ye must be Mrs. Kidd. I'm Christine Murray." She ushered Annie into her warm, spacious kitchen. "Ye must be starving. Ah ken how bad th' meals on ships can be. Och, what bonnie bairns!"

The room was filled with rich, succulent odours that made Annie's mouth water. When Alfie came in, Mrs. Murray ordered them all to sit down at a long dining table. She served them generous bowls of thick fish chowder and light wheat bread, hot from the oven. Mrs. Murray chatted nonstop as she refilled bowls.

"What a braw man ye are, Mr. Larsen. But a big man's appetite has nae defeated me yet!"

Annie looked down at her lap. She was afraid that if she looked at her brother, she would burst out laughing. Mrs. Murray continued without stopping, looking from Annie to Alfie.

"This bonnie wee hen cannae be your ain sister!"

Alfie smiled and shot Annie a glance. "Yes, this wee hen is my sister all right. Don't misjudge her, she may be small but she squawks quite a bit."

Annie scowled at him and supressed a grin, while her little boys giggled.

When everyone's stomachs were filled to bursting, the brusque Scottish woman frowned. "Ah have one rule for mah guests," she said, "an' it is tae have a bath, affore ye lie on my clean linens!"

Mrs. Murray had converted her summer kitchen to a wash house, complete with a wood stove to heat water. In the room off the kitchen, Annie could see a large tin bath and huge tubs of water simmering on a stove. The boys groaned but were quickly led into the laundry room by the officious woman, and ordered to wash each other thoroughly. Then she sent Annie to get clean clothes for them.

"I have a surprise for you!" Annie said when she returned with the children's change of clothes. In her hand was a new bar of lilac scented soap. She had been saving two precious bars, a Christmas gift from Jim the year before. In unison, the boys complained they did not want to smell like girls.

"Well, you can use Mrs. Murray's homemade yellow laundry soap or my lilac bar. You decide. Make sure you wash your hair thoroughly, and that you are squeaky clean!"

Twenty minutes later, the boys emerged from the laundry room scrubbed pink and perfumed with lilac. Alfie raised his eyebrows and smiled, but before he could say a word, Annie froze him with a shake of her head.

While Alfie took his turn in the bath, having dumped the boys' water outside and refilled the tub. Annie followed the children upstairs to her bedroom. The large room was decorated with a feminine pink-flowered paper. There was an upright wardrobe in one corner, a maple dresser against one wall and each bed had a soft feather mattress and several warm blankets. The little boys snuggled into the fresh sheets and Annie tucked their top quilt around them. Georgie was sound asleep in minutes.

She peeked into Alfie's bedroom and saw a single quilt-covered bed and small dresser crowded into the tiny space.

Oh, the poor man, she thought. *His long legs will hang over the end of the mattress!* She resolved to offer to trade beds with him.

Annie tiptoed downstairs and had a cup of tea at the kitchen table while she waited for her brother. Mrs. Murray showed Annie the contents of the package from her nephew – two Scottish newspapers, a stack of letters from family and a small novel.

"I dinna know how to thank ye for delivering my mail from away." Annie tilted her head towards the laundry room and said, "We thank you, Mrs. Murray! I can't tell you how long I've been dreaming of having a lovely bath and washing my hair."

When Alfie finally entered the kitchen, he too had a strong lilac scent about him. He helped Annie empty the bath water and refill the tin tub with fresh hot water. *What luxury!* Annie thought, as she gathered her change of clothes and closed the door.

The next morning, after a hearty Scottish breakfast of porridge, fried eggs, bacon and hot scones, they reluctantly prepared to leave Mrs. Murray's boarding house. While Alfie paid for their rooms and meals, Annie discreetly placed her last bar of lilac soap on a dresser to thank the generous woman.

At the train station, Annie sent a telegram to Jim to let him know when they would arrive in Toronto. While they waited for their train, she became lost in thought. She wished they could have stayed an extra day at Mrs. Murray's and be pampered.

She was weary of travelling and freezing in the bitter cold. *The boys aren't properly dressed for this dreadful weather and neither am I. Are we really prepared to live in this climate?*

Chapter Fourteen

Annie had purchased bread, cheese, a couple of cooked chickens and a few other items so they could avoid paying for some of their meals on the train. She was anxious to see Jim and the boys were excited to be on another adventure. She paid for one sleeper for them to share but did not want to spend the money for another bed. She planned to try to sleep in her seat.

Because the boys had full stomachs and were able to sleep comfortably in berths on the train, the first night quickly passed. For a few hours in the early evening, Annie sat quietly beside her dozing brother and gazed out the train windows as cleared farmer's fields and homesteads flew by, interspersed with thick forests. She had never imagined that there could be so many trees in this new country. She stared out the window until it was dark and all she saw was her own reflection. Then she closed her eyes to try to sleep.

The next morning and over the following two days, Annie doled out food from her stash whenever they were hungry. While the boys were sleeping, she and Alfie played several games of cards. She was surprised how quickly the time had passed when a conductor came through their car on their third day of travel and announced that the next stop would be Toronto Union Station.

The train wheezed and squealed to a stop, and they disembarked. Alfie went back to the baggage car to claim the trunk while Annie gathered all their bags. While scanning the platform for Jim, she found a free bench for the children and their belongings. She searched for Jim in the bustling crowd for what seemed an eternity, and she began to worry that he might not have received her telegram. But just as she was retracing her steps to check on the boys, she got the sense that she was being watched. She turned and her heart skipped. Those familiar blue eyes!

Annie called out to the children, "Here's your Da!" as she opened her arms and threw them around Jim. Bobby and Jack ran to their father, but Georgie walked over slowly and clung to Annie's skirts.

Jim held Annie close and sighed, "I didn't think this day would ever come!"

He ruffled his children's hair affectionately. "Look how much our bairns have grown since I saw them last."

Annie was shocked by how wiry and thin Jim felt, even through his winter coat. A few grey strands were showing in his thick brown hair, and he had grown a moustache. *I'll soon feed him a proper meal,* she thought, *and then shave off that awful thing!* There was something else that was different. She started when she figured it out.

"Why, you've lost your Geordie accent!"

"Well, I got tired of repeating myself so many times to be understood around here," he said, laughing. "I've been reading anything I can get my hands on." He explained that the local school principal had teased him for dropping his *g*'s, and had lent Jim books from his personal collection as well as the school library. "Now I feel that I need to read as much as I need to eat!"

Alfie suddenly appeared beside them and thumped his brother-in-law on the back, teasing, "It looks as if you've been reading more than eating, Jim! Annie's going to have to fatten you up."

They put their things into a storage locker and walked the short distance to a small hotel where Jim had reserved rooms for Alfie and the family. There was an icy wind blowing between the tall brick buildings. Annie felt the bitter cold in her bones and was painfully aware, once again, that her supply of warm clothes for the children was completely inadequate. The sidewalks and roads were covered in grey slush and her feet soon grew numb in her sodden boots. They arrived at the hotel and she welcomed the warmth from the dining room fireplace. Jim guided them to a large table close to the fire and then ordered a hearty lamb and potato stew for everyone.

With her hunger satisfied and her body warm again, Annie took the children up to their hotel room and, after warning them about expected behaviour, placed Bobby in charge. Annie, Jim and Alfie walked to a large department store to buy warm winter coats for the boys and some supplies to bring north, including two new wooden chairs and a few heavy blankets. Jim arranged for the chairs and blankets to be delivered to the hotel.

Alfie bought himself a smart winter coat and coaxed Annie to try on a long black wool coat trimmed with a soft fur collar. She playfully modelled the coat. When she began to take it off, Alfie said, "Keep it on, Annie. I bought it for you."

Annie blushed, then reached up and kissed her brother's cheek. "That's very generous. Thank you, Alfie. It's beautiful." As they walked back to the hotel, Annie decided that Jim must be exaggerating about the weather up north. New Ontario could not possibly be colder than Toronto.

The next morning, they said their goodbyes to Alfie before heading back to Union Station. Alfie was going to remain in Toronto; he had an interview for a desk job at a fire station.

"I promise to write, and when I can, I'll take the train up north and visit you."

He shook Jim's hand and gave his sister a long hug. Then he knelt down to his nephews and pressed some candy into their hands. He patted Annie's arm and turned to leave. He waved one last time, and walked back into the hotel.

Annie fumbled for her handkerchief and wiped away her tears. *Another goodbye.*

Chapter Fifteen

As the train pulled out of the station, Annie was pleased to see that the children were feeling more comfortable around their father already, despite their separation. She had seen the hurt in Jim's eyes the day before, when they had been so shy around him, especially Georgie. The family was seated together on the northbound train and their possessions were safely stored in the baggage car. Annie smiled as the boys peppered Jim with questions.

"Are there cowboys and Indians up north?" asked Jack.

"What about man-eating bears?" asked a worried Georgie.

Jim laughed. "If you ever see a bear, Georgie, it will likely be more afraid of you! Don't you worry, son. No cowboys but there are Indians. I bought my *mukluks* and snowshoes from an Abitibi Cree trapper."

"*Mukluks!*" giggled Georgie. "That's a funny word, Da. What are they?"

"Well, they are toasty warm, comfortable boots made from caribou hide. My feet never get cold when I wear my *mukluks*."

Annie felt a pang of guilt as all three boys looked down at their unsuitable English shoes. While Jim was talking, Georgie, who she knew was used to his uncle's easy affection, climbed onto his father's lap and stayed there until he drifted off to sleep. Jim looked pleased to have his youngest son curled up against him.

"Are there lots of big wild animals up north, Da?" asked Jack, looking concerned.

"Well, the black bears can be a nuisance if food or garbage is left close to settlements. But they're usually timid and run away when they see people. A moose might wander close to town, once in a while."

He smiled at the boys' wide-eyed reaction. "What's a moose?" they asked in unison.

"You'll soon see, that and a lot of other amazing things. You won't believe the stars - there are a million of them in the night sky. And the most amazing sight is the Northern Lights. They are a spectacular miracle in the evening sky, with beautiful colours waving all about. I can hardly wait to show you."

Jim told them that almost everyone up north had at least one dog to protect their homes from wild animals.

Jack perked up and Bobby asked wistfully, "Do you think that we might have a dog someday, Da?"

"Well, Bobby, we already have a dog."

The boys both gasped and fired questions. "What's his name?" "What kind of dog is he?" "Is he big?"

Jim laughed. "He's a big black mixed-breed dog. I think he has a little Newfoundland in him because he is so large and muscular and has a thick double coat that keeps him warm. And his name is Mike."

"Can we play with him?" asked Jack.

"Not yet. We'll have to give him a little time to get used to you."

As the train chugged north, more and more passengers disembarked at their stations. Soon there was plenty of room for the family to spread out. There were so many stops breaking up their journey that Annie wondered if they would ever reach their destination.

She saw that the boys were fighting to stay awake, so she improvised overcoat beds on the benches so that they could lie down to sleep. *Likely dreaming about their dog,* she thought. Jim gently laid Georgie, down near his brothers and covered him with his coat.

When the children were finally settled and sleeping, Annie leaned into Jim. "How hard has your time been here? I feel so guilty. Although I've been on my own with the children, I've had my mother and brothers and your family, too."

Jim put his arm around her. "I won't lie to you, Annie. It has been a long, difficult and lonely time."

"What was it really like? Your descriptions in your letters were so brief."

"I stayed in a government barracks at first. It was basic, with a communal kitchen, but I spent little time there. There have been plenty of opportunities for good-paying jobs since my first day in the North, though." He explained that the government had started a town site at Mile 225 and named it Jackpine Junction, which was where their property was. Soon after arriving, Jim had found steady work with the railway when they extended the track to a gold mine, a few miles west of the new town site.

"What's our land like?" Annie asked.

"We own acres of trees like spruce, poplar and pine. There are masses of wild raspberry and blueberry bushes and in the summer the woods are filled with wild lilies, irises, orchids and many more flowers that I don't recognize. I sold some of our timber for a good price. With that money and my wages, I was able to hire carpenters to help me build our house."

Jim gently kissed Annie's forehead, then pulled away and looked at her solemnly.

"At first life was so hard, I wondered if I was crazy to have come here. I often felt like giving up." He took a deep breath. "And I have something to confess to you Annie. I needed to wait to tell you in person."

Annie's heart missed a beat and she couldn't disguise the sudden anxiety she felt. "What is it, Jim?"

"That promise of rich agricultural farmland was a bloody lie," said Jim. "The land is suitable only for root crops or hay, and the growing season is too short. I was a fool to dream of farming our own land."

Oh, Lord. "What are we going to do?" She heard her voice waver. *The die has been cast. We're committed to this life now.*

He pulled her hands into his and kissed her fingers.

"Dinna fash, love. I've cleared enough land for a field of hay and I'll clear more over the year. Hay is a good crop to sell for horse feed and there are plenty of work horses around. We still have acres of timber that can be sold for cash, and I'll keep working for the railway to guarantee a steady income. We'll manage."

Annie didn't speak. She was afraid her voice would betray her misgivings. Despite his reassurances, she thought, *My God, what have we done?*

Chapter Sixteen

After twelve long hours, just as Annie started to wonder if they would ever reach their destination, Jim glanced out the window and said, "We'll soon be at our stop. I've arranged with our neighbour Pierre to meet us with his horse and sleigh."

The train slowly chugged, and then hissed to a stop. Annie woke the children and gathered all their bags. She hoisted Georgie, still groggy and half-asleep, into her arms and followed Jim, Bobby and Jack down the steps to the platform.

She stopped and gasped when she inhaled the sub-arctic winter air. It was pitch black outside and bone-chillingly cold. *Bloody hell! It actually hurts to breathe!*

She put Georgie down and adjusted the children's caps and scarves, while Jim waited near the baggage car for the trunk and supplies. Bobby and Jack squealed with delight at the sight of so much snow and soon were throwing handfuls at each other, until Annie grumpily cautioned them to behave. When Jim returned with the baggage, he led Annie and the children to a tall, bundled-up man, standing in front of an enormous workhorse hitched up to a sleigh. The stranger was holding the collar of a huge black dog.

"Pierre," said Jim, shaking the man's hand, "may I introduce my wife, Anna, and children, Robert, John and George. Pierre has the next farm to us, Annie. And this overgrown animal is our dog, Mike."

Jim gave the dog an affectionate pat on his big black head, and motioned for the boys to do the same. Mike eagerly wagged his long tail and barked a welcome, as Jack and Bobby happily patted him. Annie put out her hand to greet Pierre. He was wearing a thick brown fur coat and a brightly striped knitted hat and long scarf. Annie couldn't see much of his face, as it was hidden in a huge bushy black beard.

"I'm pleased to meet you, Pierre."

Pierre took her hand in his own large mitt and bowed gallantly. "My pleasure, madame. Welcome 'ome."

Pierre's hulking workhorse stomped its massive hooves and snorted a cloud of condensation around its head. Giving the Clydesdale a wide berth, Annie and the children climbed up onto the sleigh and settled themselves on hay bales.

Georgie whispered in Annie's ear, "Mummy, I'm freezing!"

"I know poppet. Shush." Annie shivered as she pulled Georgie onto her lap. Bobby and Jack snuggled close to her. She reached down and lifted a heavy brown rug made from some kind of animal hide. It was lined on the underside with a red plaid wool blanket. As she tucked it around herself and the children, she discovered that Pierre had thoughtfully placed heated rocks on the floor of the sleigh. Jim and Pierre loaded her heavy trunk, the new chairs and their other supplies onto the sleigh. The two men and the dog climbed up front.

Pierre clicked a signal to his horse and the powerful animal pulled the sleigh with a jerk and then slowly plodded through the hard-packed snow.

Jim turned around and reassured Annie. "We don't have far to go, just a ten minute ride. That rug should keep you all warm. It's a buffalo hide from out west. Pierre won it in a card game. Lord knows how it ended up here."

It was a pitch-dark, starless night. The sleigh's lanterns dimly illuminated mountains of snow framing each side of the narrow lane, and the forest of evergreen trees hugging the road. Huge snowflakes began to fall from the sky, covering them in a soft white blanket. The only sounds were the sleigh's blades cutting through the snow and the horse's laboured breathing. Annie felt ice crystals form around her nose and mouth. She had pulled off her earrings minutes into the sleigh ride; they'd been freezing her ear lobes. At long last, the horse stopped near a small log cabin.

Annie could barely make out a narrow footpath leading to the cottage. Colossal mounds of snow confined the tapered walkway. A faint glimmer of light struggled to flicker in a tiny frosted window at the end of the path. The boys, forgetting their discomfort, climbed boisterously over the baggage and off the sleigh and climbed a snow bank. Jack and Georgie laughed as Bobby sank up to his waist and struggled to free himself.

Pierre had a fire going in their stove to warm the cabin and his wife had sent over a pot of stew for their dinner. Annie and Jim thanked him profusely for his generosity and invited him inside but he declined. He said that he had to get home, but Annie suspected he was purposely giving them some privacy as a family. He patted his horse, climbed back up on his sleigh and waved goodbye as he drove off to his own farm.

Jim lit an oil lantern and hooked it on the ceiling. The light gave the room a warm orange glow. Annie surveyed her new home as Jim gathered all the coats, caps and scarves and hung them up on wall hooks by the doorway. The humble cabin was divided into two rooms. The front room had an iron cook stove, and some cupboards and shelving. A pine dining table with a long bench rested against a wall. In the back, there was a smaller wood heater sandwiched between two wide beds.

Annie fought tears of disappointment. She was cold, hungry and disillusioned with this bare accommodation and freezing weather. She felt instantly contrite, knowing how difficult it had been for Jim. And she did have to admit to herself that the cabin was comfortably warm. A mouth-watering aroma reached her. Annie lifted the lid of a large cast-iron pot on the stove and was amazed at what she saw bubbling away.

"How could a neighbour ever afford to welcome us with a beef stew?"

Jim grinned and replied, "Well, it's not really beef stew. It's moose."

Annie raised her eyebrows, but her empty stomach rumbled. Jim chuckled as he placed the two new chairs at the table. Annie rummaged through her trunk to find five bowls and spoons and the children scrambled to sit on the long bench.

Annie filled the bowls with generous portions and carried the steaming dishes to the table. She found a tin plate of warm bannock on the back of the stove and she carried that over too, and then she sat down to tentatively taste her own dinner. The meat wasn't as gamey as she had imagined and the savoury dish had generous portions of moose meat, with potatoes, carrots and turnip floating in a thick flavourful sauce. She sighed contentedly. The hot meal was filling and it warmed her chilled body.

When they had finished their dinner and cleared the table, Jim announced, "Boys, I have gifts for you and your mother!"

He leaned over and picked up a cotton flour sack, and tipped it onto the table. Out tumbled four pairs of *mukluks* and four pairs of moose-hide mittens. The boys squealed with delight and promptly sat on the floor to try them on. "Thank you, Da," all three boys called out together.

Jack added, "Now we'll have warm feet like you, Da! I can hardly wait to try them in the snow!"

The boys stomped around the cabin and clapped their mittened hands, asking their father endless questions, until Annie announced that it was time for bed. She indulged them and let them go to sleep in their shared bed wearing their gifts, then she unwrapped two of their newly purchased wool blankets and covered them. The exhausted children quickly fell asleep.

Jim grinned at Annie and said, "I hope that you don't plan to wear your *mukluks* and mittens to bed too!"

Annie laughed and she gave Jim a tight hug. "I certainly would have, if Pierre hadn't warmed the cabin for us." Then she turned serious. "It's wonderful to have the family together again! I missed you so."

He replied soberly, "Aye, not as much as I missed you and the boys, Annie. Every long night that I was here alone, I worried that you might just give up on me and not come."

"Oh Jim, of course I would come. Home is where you are."

Jim pulled Annie close to him and softly sang his own words to an old Geordie folk tune she recognized.

Aa've land in the New North
Will but both hose an shone
Aa've land in the New North
Wi' hosen in tha toun
Why should ah not love my love
Why should not my love love me?
Why should ah love not my love?
Because my love loves me.

Chapter Seventeen

Annie woke up to the sound of Jim adding wood to the fire in the kitchen. She quietly got out of bed and took a quick peek at her sleeping children. She tiptoed to the kitchen and whispered, "You're up early!"

He turned and said, "I've to go to work today."

"But Jim, I thought we'd spend the day together. We haven't seen each other for so long. Can't you spare me a day?"

"Aw, Annie, I've missed three days already and this job at the junction is a good one. I'm hoping to get a full-time position at the station."

She swallowed her disappointment and went over to the stove to make a pot of tea and the breakfast porridge. Jim came up behind her, and hugged her and kissed her neck.

"I'd rather stay here with you and the boys but I need to work to keep this job. I'll be home by six." Annie sat at the table and sipped her tea while Jim ate his breakfast. She was grateful that they had some quiet time together at least before he had to leave.

"I suppose I'd better take the dog with me," he said. "Mike isn't used to the boys yet." Annie was relieved - she wasn't used to that huge malodorous animal just yet. She was glad that the beast had his own shed to sleep in.

She watched Jim dress in several layers of clothing and lace his thick knee-high boots. Then he kissed her goodbye and headed outside; a blast of frigid air rushed into the cabin before he quickly closed the door behind him. Annie heard him talking to the dog and went to the window to look out, but was surprised to find the window completely frosted over - she couldn't see a thing.

Annie poured herself another cup of tea and sat down again at the table. The house was quiet while the children were sleeping and she thought she would enjoy a few minutes of peace. She surveyed the cabin with a critical eye. The walls and floors were constructed from rough timber. The windows and doors, however, were factory made, so Jim had to have ordered them. The two wood stoves would have been purchased as well. Jim or one of the carpenters must have built the serviceable table, the bench and the shelving.

What a fool I was to think that I could use a lace tablecloth here! she chided herself. Maybe she could cut it up and make curtains for the windows.

She walked over to the cupboards, curious about what kind of storage space they had. She opened the first door and a small mouse darted out, over her shoe and ran towards the bedroom. Annie squealed and jumped up onto a chair, wrapping her skirt tightly around her legs. Her three boys popped up in unison and scampered out of their bed. Trying to appear calm, Annie pointed at the rodent diving under the stove. The children sprang into action, chasing the mouse all over the cabin until they finally cornered it by the door. Jack grabbed his cap and placed it over the mouse, closing his hand around the brim so it could not escape. He opened the door to toss it out. When the door shut after it, they all cheered, but Jack did not smile. He looked down at his cap and cried out in disgust.

"It messed in my cap!"

Ignoring her other sons' laughter, Annie took the offending cap and stepped outside, shaking the mouse pellets onto the snow. She declared it "good as new," but as she placed it back on a hook she realized that it was Jim's cap, not Jack's.

"Oh, Jack, it's not even your cap. It's your Da's. Don't be upset." The boys laughed even harder but agreed not to tell their father.

After breakfast, the boys bundled up to play outside. She heard them laugh with delight at the sight of so much snow. They piled up a huge mound and took turns climbing it and jumping off.

Annie tidied up the cabin and started a bread batter with the flour and yeast Jim had bought in Toronto. She realized she needed to return Pierre's stew pot. There would be enough of his stew left over for dinner if she added the carrots and potatoes she had found in the vegetable bin, so she poured the remainder of the stew into one of her own pots.

She knew she should register the children in school soon. Jim would know where the school was. She also thought she'd like to meet Pierre's wife and perhaps bring a pie to thank her for last night's meal. If Pierre's farm was on the next property, maybe it wouldn't be too far to walk, she reasoned.

Jim came home that evening as she was taking her bread from the oven, bringing a solid wall of cold air in with him. The boys greeted their father excitedly. Georgie interrupted his brothers to tell Jim about their day.

"We had so much fun playing outside! We made a snow hill to jump off of, and Bobby fell right on his face!"

Jim smiled as he removed his coat and boots. He looked at Annie. "Did you play in the snow, too?"

Annie rolled her eyes at him. "No, but I'm happy that the boys enjoyed their first day here. I think I'll go tomorrow and register them for school, and I'd like to meet Pierre's wife. I'll need you to give me some directions."

"You have ambitious plans for tomorrow," said Jim, sitting down at the table. "Both are easy to find. The school is about a mile away, just past the railway station. Follow the same route we took last night. But Pierre's house is a good two miles the other direction." Then he smacked his hand on the table, remembering.

"I got some good news today! My name is at the top of the list for full-time work at the railway junction. I think when management heard that my family had arrived, they knew that we'd be staying. Most men come for a short time to make some money, then leave."

"That's wonderful news. I'll be happy to have you working nearby instead of off in the woods, miles away."

After dinner, Jim put his warm things back on, to get more wood for the fire and feed the dog. Just as he placed his cap on his head, all three boys exploded with laughter. He looked at his children in bewilderment.

Georgie shouted, "Daddy, a mouse messed in your cap!"

"Well how did a moose get into the house?" Jim teased his youngest.

"No, Daddy," Georgie giggled. "A *mouse*, not a moose!"

"Oh, thank goodness! A few little mouse pellets should make my hair grow." Jim winked at the children and went out the door.

Annie shook her head as she cleared the table. She knew she was in for some teasing when the story came out about her waking the children with a scream over a little field mouse. She knew that she wasn't doing much of a job of being brave. She felt a lump in her throat and her eyes moistened. She was glad to finally be with Jim but she missed her family back home. Until now, she had always been surrounded by people. She wasn't afraid of hard work, but still she wondered how she'd manage in this new life.

Chapter Eighteen

I'll never get used to this cold! Annie thought. The walk to the school had taken longer than she had expected. It was difficult trudging through the ankle-high snow on the road, so she and the children had walked single file along the sleigh tracks. She was relieved that her boys had new coats, boots and mittens for protection against such brutal elements. She felt well-dressed in the woollen coat Alfie had bought for her. On impulse, she added her Sunday hat and her good leather gloves to her outfit, but she now regretted her vanity. Her ears burned and her fingers tingled. She pulled up the fur collar of her coat and tucked her hands in her pockets. She almost hadn't worn her own pair of *mukluks*, but she had changed her mind and pulled them on just before they left the house. *Thank goodness.*

She carried a small canvas bag holding the children's lunch of bread, generous chunks of cheese, and some soft but still edible apples that she had found in the vegetable bin. The boys had grumbled and complained about going to school but she knew they were excited to meet other children.

As Annie approached the school, she was surprised to see about twenty children of various ages playing in the snow. She hadn't realized there were so many settlers in the area. When she entered the timber building, she was enveloped in the heat from the wood stove in the centre of the room. The classroom was crammed with double oak desks and the walls lined with book-shelves. A young woman sat behind a larger desk in a corner. She looked barely twenty years old and wore her hair tied back in a severe bun, likely in an attempt to look older, Annie guessed. The teacher stood up and smiled as she greeted Annie and the children. Annie introduced herself and the boys, and the young woman identified herself as Miss Brown as she shook Annie's hand.

"Welcome to Jackpine Junction, Mrs. Kidd. I'm sure it was a bit of a shock arriving here in the middle of winter." Annie nodded, relieved to have her challenges acknowledged. "Our other seasons, though, can be quite pleasant. I hope you enjoy living here. Well, to register the children I'll need their full names and birth dates for the record."

Miss Brown entered Bobby's and Jack's names in an official-looking leather bound book using a neat cursive script. But when Annie gave Georgie's birth date, the teacher hesitated.

"I'm sorry Mrs. Kidd, but George is not quite old enough. He can come to school next September."

Georgie looked stricken and tears threatened to fall. Annie took his hand in hers and said her goodbyes to Bobby and Jack. "I'll meet you here at dismissal to make sure you can find your way back home, boys. I expect your best behaviour for Miss Brown."

Annie and Georgie reluctantly left the comfortable warmth of the school room and retraced their steps home. She coaxed a small smile from her unhappy son. "Well, I'm happy you'll be home with me. I worried I might be a little lonesome with everyone out of the house. Maybe you and I could have our own little school."

When they arrived back at the cabin, Annie hung up their coats and told Georgie to change out of his good clothes. Her hands were white with cold and her finger tips tingled in pain. Picking up an old newspaper from the box of kindling to build up the kitchen fire, she had an idea. She smoothed the paper flat and placed it on the table. Then she found a pencil stub and told Georgie that he could read the paper while she made some pies.

Georgie guffawed. "You know I can't read, Mummy!"

Annie assured him that he *could* read and printed an uppercase *"A"* and a lowercase *"a"* at the top of the front page.

"This is the word *"a"*," she said, "like *a* boy or *a* dog or *a* house. You can circle all the *"a"* words in the newspaper and then you'll be reading. When you're finished, we can count all the words that you read."

Georgie perked up and began his hunt for *"a"* words, while Annie made two apple pies. Annie watched him persevere until he found every "A" and "a" in the paper. When he said he was finished reading, Annie asked him how many words he had read.

He guessed "eighty one hundred" and Annie smiled and reassured him, "One hundred and eighty is a good guess, Georgie. I'll help you count, while the pies are baking in the oven."

They had an early lunch, and they laughed when they realized that Bobby and Jack had an extra lunch to share; Annie had forgotten to take Georgie's lunch from the canvas bag. After they had eaten, they dressed warmly for the walk to Pierre's home. Annie found a small sled used to carry firewood and lined it with an old blanket. She placed the neighbour's cooking pot in it and nestled one of the pies inside. If it turned out to be too long a walk for Georgie, she could pull him too. This time she was practical when she dressed and wore her new moose-hide mitts as well as the *mukluks*. She wrapped a thick woollen scarf around her head and made sure that Georgie was warmly bundled up as well.

The walk took longer than she had imagined and when they finally reached Pierre's house, she was exhausted and frozen. She lifted the pot and pie out of the sled and knocked at the entrance of the weathered timber cabin. Annie heard someone call out something in French and the door was opened by a short, chubby woman with a small baby in her arms. Her dark curly hair was pulled up in a messy bun, and she had kind brown eyes. She ushered Annie and Georgie into the house and quickly closed the outside door.

The house was constructed similarly to the Kidd's cabin but was much larger. Beyond the kitchen she could see a comfortable sitting room with a floor-to-ceiling fieldstone fireplace radiating heat and ambience. Two overstuffed horsehair chairs sat on either side of the hearth. Annie was uncomfortable having arrived unannounced but was relieved to see Pierre filleting fish at the kitchen table.

"Come in, come in, madam!" he called out. He introduced Annie to his wife, Marie, and their baby son, Louis.

He explained that Marie only spoke French, but that she was happy to hear that another woman had moved here. "There are twelve men to every woman at Jackpine Junction," he said, laughing.

"I'm pleased to meet you, Marie," said Annie. "I wanted to return your pot and I've made an apple pie to thank you for the wonderful meal and warm fire when we arrived."

She babbled nervously. Neither of her three languages could help her converse with the woman. Marie placed her baby in Pierre's arms, and then kissed Annie on both cheeks. She moved towards Georgie, but he hid shyly behind his mother's skirts. Marie said something in French to Pierre.

"Marie says she 'as never seen such light blonde hair before. She says your son looks like an angel."

This embarrassed Georgie; his face grew red as he clung to her skirt. Pierre explained that he had been ice-fishing, and he handed several wrapped fillets to Annie.

"Oh, Pierre, I can't possibly accept another gift."

"Madame, I 'ave 'ad much luck ice-fishin' today. I caught *beaucoup, beaucoup*. I'm 'appy to give you some."

Pierre handed Annie and Georgie mugs of an unfamiliar brew, and placed two wooden chairs close to the warmth of the kitchen stove. The tea was a welcome hot drink but it had a strong, wild odour. Annie imagined that Marie knew what plants to gather and dry for the winter. She saw Georgie's face crinkle as he sipped his tea and she quickly gave him a look to warn him not to say anything. She told Pierre and Marie that her two older boys had started school that morning and that they needed to start walking back very soon so they could meet them at dismissal. Pierre flapped a hand and shook his head.

"I have to take da 'orse and sleigh to da station for a job, and can take you, eh? Warm up while I 'itch 'im up. I'll come back in for you when I'm ready to leave."

Annie was overwhelmed by the kindness and generosity of her new neighbours. She knew that she couldn't have a conversation with Marie, while Pierre was outside, but instead she spoke in the universal actions of all mothers by cuddling and fussing over Marie's baby.

That night Annie fed her family an ambrosial meal of fresh fried fish, leftover stew and apple pie. The conversation was lively as Bobby and Jack recounted their first day at their new school.

"Miss Brown calls us Robert and John but we still like her because she doesn't shout. We have reading and arithmetic just like at our old school back home," Jack said excitedly.

Georgie proudly told the family that he was learning to read too, and Annie teased her older boys about having an extra lunch to share. Bobby frowned and looked at his mother.

"When we saw Georgie's lunch, we decided to give it to a little girl who didn't bring any food at all!"

Jim shook his head and grumbled. "I've heard about some families around here struggling but barely surviving on their farms. The land holds riches all right, but it's gold and silver for the wealthy big-shots to mine, not fertile soil for a man to farm." The children looked at him, worried. "Don't worry boys, I have steady work and you'll have enough to eat. Look how your mother magically provided a feast tonight. She even made pie!"

But Annie did wonder if their lives would be a day-to-day struggle. It was wonderful to have her family together, but what if she became pregnant again? How could she bring a baby into this harsh environment? Looking down at her lap, she discreetly wiped away a tear.

Chapter Nineteen

Annie sat at the kitchen table browsing through the day-old edition of the Toronto newspaper. The paper lessened her feelings of isolation. It was reassuring to read the news of the world. The front page was filled with reports about the Home Rule crisis in Ireland and she was grateful that the conflict was so distant. If they were still living in South Shields, Jim might have been called up because of his previous military experience. She was selfishly happy to have him to herself and away from any wars or conflicts.

She thought of the changes that this month of March had brought to her family. Thankfully, Jim had been hired for a permanent position at the railway. Annie was relieved to have the security of a steady income but she had another concern. She placed her hands on her abdomen and fought tears when she thought of this fifth pregnancy; she did not want to be old before her time like Jane and her own mother. Most of all, she feared that she would not survive another birth like Georgie's. She was jolted from her melancholy mood when the outside door suddenly opened a crack. Cold air rushed in when Jim stuck his head inside.

"Hey, Annie, put on your coat and come outside. There's something I want to show you."

He closed the door quickly, before she had a chance to answer him. She didn't really want to go out into the raw, glacial night air, but she bundled up.

Once outside, she heard Jim call, "Over here!"

She spotted him standing in a clearing in the yard and she plodded towards him, her head tucked down into her coat for warmth. She passed an enormous, snowy stack of newly felled logs. Jim had been clearing the walkway but his shovel now rested against the rough wood of the shed wall. Freezing polar gusts nibbled at her ears. She stopped a moment to pull up her collar and tied it in place with her blue woollen scarf. Her boots crunched in the snow. She felt ice crystals forming in her nose and the condensation of her breath formed a misty veil around her face. *Bloody northern winter.* She was feeling bad-tempered and only barely managed to stifle her frustrations. As she reached Jim, he wrapped his arms around her.

"Look up," he said.

When she raised her eyes to the evening sky, her bad mood evaporated instantly. Shimmering pink, white and green lights danced across the night sky.

"Oh, Jim. It's breathtaking!" They silently watched the splendorous display of light for several minutes.

"My parents saw these lights in Norway," said Annie finally. "Pappa called it a herring flash, and Mother said they were reflections from the Valkyries' armour."

Jim rested his chin on the top of her head as they gazed skyward. "My grandfather used to say that in Scotland they call them *mirrie* dancers. But Bill, my Cree friend, says that the lights are family members, who have gone to the spirit world, and they are dancing around a fire."

"I think that I like Bill's version best. I'd like to believe that this is Maggie showing us she knows where we are. What a comforting thought." She suddenly remembered the old woman's prophesy the night before they left South Shields. *She did say I would find comfort in sky lights.* A shiver ran up her back.

"I never told you about the strange old granny who came to our door the night before we left home," she said to Jim. "Maybe she was daft. Maybe not."

By late April, most of the snow had melted, and song sparrows celebrated the mornings with their lively trill. That spring, Annie and Georgie started going for regular walks in the bush on their property. The light warm breeze was fresh with the scent of new growth. The forest floor was carpeted in large, waxy lily-like flowers in white and pink. Showy wild flowers were nestled in the mulch of wet leaves from the previous autumn and Annie discovered exotic orchids growing in the forest, in the moist shady layer of pine needles. Annie recognized wintergreen and tiny wild strawberry plants in the clearing behind their house. This paradise in the bush almost made up for her suffering through the long, miserable winter.

Several robins hopped around the yard, turning their heads to listen for worms. The early May air was sweet and fresh as she staked and turned over the soil for her vegetable garden. Jim had fashioned a small spade for Georgie to dig with while Annie worked. Every once in a while she picked up an earthworm to toss over to the hungry birds. She had already ordered her seeds from a mail-order gardening catalogue; she planned to grow tomatoes and green peas as well as potatoes, carrots, onions and turnip. On impulse, she had added a package of sunflowers and one of sweet peas to her order.

She paused to rest against the shovel to ease the pain in her back, and spotted her boys returning from school. She called out and waved. But when they ran towards her, her heart skipped a beat. Their faces were covered in swollen, red welts.

"What on earth happened? Have you boys been fighting?"

Bobby laughed. "No, Ma, we haven't. Teacher says they're blackfly bites. She said she'll keep everyone inside for recess until we have a cooler day or some wind to blow them away."

"But those bites look terrible!" Annie was at a loss over what to do. Jim would know how to treat the bites but she couldn't wait until he got back from work. She hustled the boys inside and made a poultice of oatmeal and water. She applied it to their swollen bites and hoped it would give the boys some relief. She could only imagine how large these flying insects must be to inflict such damage.

When Jim came home from work, he said, "Well, I see you boys have been initiated. Those nasty blackflies are irritating pests, all right. Sometimes I put spruce gum or bacon fat on my skin to protect myself. Smoke keeps them away as well."

"I'm not going to plaster any spruce gum or bacon fat on myself, thank you!" Annie replied.

"You won't have to. I've already cut fresh spruce branches that you can light whenever you need to work outside – they create smoke. You're awful grumpy with this pregnancy, Annie." She threw an annoyed look his way. Jim shrugged his shoulders and said, "Blackflies are just a part of the North. There are so many fast-running streams and rivers here, it's an ideal breeding ground for them. If it's any consolation, they only bite during the day."

"Just when we're finally able to enjoy some warm weather we're chased inside by flying insects!" she grumbled. "What next?"

Chapter Twenty

The children heard Jim call from the yard, and all three boys scrambled out the door. Annie peered through the kitchen window and saw Jim holding the handle bars of a green, large-wheeled bicycle. She stepped outside to join them as Bobby practiced riding the bike and his brothers looked on enviously. Annie quietly said to Jim that the bike was wonderful – "but what about the cost?"

"I got it for a song, and I've arranged a newspaper delivery for Bobby. He can pick up the papers at the railway station, then bike the few miles on the new gravel road to the lumber camp. The boy should earn some decent money."

Bobby soon mastered the bike and eagerly began his newspaper route the following week. Other worries nagged Annie, though. Her body was ballooning with this pregnancy. Her legs were swollen and her hips were sore. Memories of Georgie's difficult birth haunted her as she approached the end of her term. She fretted over how she would manage with another child; the small cabin was already crowded. She felt fat and miserable and was short-tempered with the children. But most of all, she was frightened.

Her time came on an unseasonably warm, humid August night. The cabin was stifling and Annie tossed and turned trying to get comfortable enough to sleep. In the early morning hours, she felt the familiar cramping pain. When the spasms became more frequent, she touched Jim's shoulder and whispered that it was time to get the doctor. It was then, when she saw the panic in his eyes, she realized he was just as worried as she was.

After Jim threw on trousers and left the house, Annie slowly slid out of bed to wake Bobby. "The baby's coming," she told him. "I need you to get breakfast for your brothers, and take them outside to play." She saw his anxious, concerned expression, and patted his shoulder. "Don't worry, I'm going to be fine. Why don't you teach Jack to ride your bike?"

Annie abruptly turned away as a sharp pain coursed through her. When it had subsided, she climbed back into bed. Listening to her children tiptoe around the kitchen and whisper to each other, she closed her eyes and finally fell into a light slumber.

When she woke up, the house was quiet. A fierce pain surged through her. She decided to get out of bed to walk around. She grabbed the bed post and leaned into it as another cramp tore through her. When she could walk again, she went to the kitchen to get a cup of water and drank it thirstily.

Glancing out the window she could see Jack trying to ride the bicycle and Georgie tossing a ball to Bobby. Another severe pain knifed through her. She leaned over the table and clung to it for support. She tried to pace around the kitchen, trying to calm herself. *I'm fine. I've done it before. I can do this. I've managed the pain before.* Just then, she heard a small pop. Liquid spilled over her feet and puddled on the floor. She found a rag and tried to bend over to mop up the mess but a jolt of pain made her stop in agony.

Oh my God, Jim, where are you? I'm alone in this God-forsaken cabin! Bloody hell!

Suddenly the door banged open and Jim and the doctor rushed in. The two men quickly and carefully carried Annie to the bed.

The old doctor examined her. "Well, Mrs. Kidd, you've done a fine job all by yourself. One good push and I think this baby will arrive." His calm Irish brogue was enormously comforting. "There's the head. Splendid, splendid! One more push, Mrs. Kidd. There, we have a healthy little boy. He's small; about five pounds I think."

Annie lifted her head to see her new son. He had all his fingers and toes and seemed well formed, but was very tiny. His skin was a healthy pink and he was breathing well on his own. The doctor swiftly swaddled the howling baby and gently laid him on Annie's chest.

"I'm sorry that you were alone for such a long time." Jim tearfully apologized. "Oh, Annie, I, was so afraid that I might lose you this time."

Annie cried quietly, in happiness and relief. She took Jim's hand in her own and brought it to her cheek. Jim rested his other hand on the mewling infant and leaned down to kiss Annie.

After the doctor washed up and gathered his bag and hat, Jim followed him to the door and handed him his fee. Annie silently resented that they had to dip into their meagre savings. However kind and considerate the man seemed to be, she had done most of the work of birthing this baby. Before he left, though, he said how wonderful it was to help bring a child into the world instead of dealing with crushed bones or sewing up gashes. She conceded to herself, that with all the rough men around here, working, living and playing hard, it would be a pleasant change to attend to a birth of a healthy baby.

Annie changed into a clean nightgown and wrapped the baby in a freshly washed pink blanket. "I'm sorry, little one, but I was sure that you would be a girl!" After she brushed and pulled her long hair back into a neat braid, she told Jim to call in the boys to meet their new little brother. Jim opened the door and the three children spilled into the kitchen. They all spoke at once.

"He's so small!"

"Why does he have a pink blanket?"

"What's his name?"

"Are you all right, Ma?"

"He's bald!"

Jim held up his hand and said, "Enough! Give your poor mother some peace and quiet. We haven't chosen a name yet for him." He glanced at Annie. "He's so wee, he needs a manly name."

"You name him, Jim. I've only girl's names in my head now."

"Well, I've always favoured the name Harold."

"Harold is a fine name. But he's so tiny, perhaps for now we can call him Hal."

Annie felt quite weak and stayed in bed for several days with her newborn. Hal required frequent nursing but between feedings Bobby and Jack took turns rocking him, or carrying him around the kitchen to soothe him.

Annie was sitting up in bed, sipping a cup of tea and nibbling a slice of toasted bread. Georgie had climbed onto the bed to snuggle beside her and Jack was in the rocking chair with Hal contentedly nestled against his chest. Annie smiled as she heard Jack singing Jim's lullaby. Bobby was at the kitchen stove making oatmeal porridge for the family.

The calm morning was interrupted by a loud knock on the door. Bobby opened the door and there stood their neighbour, Pierre. He still wore a huge unkempt beard and was wearing a red flannel shirt despite the summer heat. His deep booming voice rang out across the kitchen.

"Madame, Jim tol' me you have a new son, 'arold. Marie, she make a little sweater and 'at for 'im, and I made a gift, too."

He reached down out of view from the doorway, and carried in a beautifully crafted pine bassinet. After he removed his boots he brought it into the bedroom and placed it on the floor by Annie's bed. Tucked inside were Marie's gifts of a soft, white crocheted baby blanket, a hand-knitted pale blue sweater and a matching bonnet.

"Oh, Pierre, this is so generous," said Annie. "The cradle is beautiful. And little Hal's brothers will be glad to see him dressed in blue. Please tell Marie thank you so much for her gifts. Will you stay for a cup of tea?"

"Oh, no t'anks, *madame*, I need to get back to da farm, but I'll take a peek at the baby. Marie will want to know all about 'im. She want annuder baby but so far we jus' 'ave Louis."

The big man clomped back into the kitchen and leaned over Jack to see Hal's tiny face. "Look at you, *petit homme*. He's very small, no? Our Louis seem big now." Just then, the baby awoke and howled. Pierre laughed. "'e may be little but 'e make up for it, eh? Well, I better get back 'ome." He relaced his boots, waved goodbye and disappeared out the door.

That evening, Hal was particularly colicky, and Annie was exhausted from lack of sleep. She was uncomfortable in the stuffy cabin. The baby's howl brought Annie to tears. She noticed Jim watching her with a worried expression on his face.

"Oh, don't mind me," she said, wiping her cheek with the back of her hand. "I'm just feeling sorry for myself, and I miss Mother. She always came to stay with us when our babies were newborn." A sob escaped. "When I look at little Hal, I remember Maggie. Marie and Pierre only have Louis. I should be thankful we have four healthy children and pray they stay that way."

Chapter Twenty-One

The following Sunday, Jim announced, "I'm taking the day off. I'll be back in half an hour and we'll be gone most of the day. Annie old girl, we'll need to bring our lunch." When he left the house Annie watched him, puzzled, as he walked down the lane.

She packed up a generous picnic, placing the food in a wicker basket to wait for Jim, outside, with the children. She heard him before she saw him. He arrived in a cloud of dust and exhaust, with the loud fanfare of an engine roar. In Annie's arms, Hal flailed and howled in protest. The automobile was dented and dusty but it was more welcome than the King of England's private carriage.

Jim stopped the car in front of the house and it wheezed and hissed in complaint. He laughed at Annie's startled expression.

"Hop in. I borrowed it for the day. We're going on an adventure."

The boys enthusiastically piled into the back and Annie tried to soothe the screaming baby as she climbed in beside Jim. They drove a few miles on a gravel road and Hal mercifully fell asleep in Annie's arms. After several more miles, Jim stopped the car in a grassy area. A clear blue lake with a fine, yellow sand beach could be seen a short distance away. A few other families were there as well, but Jim and Annie found a secluded area for themselves and spread a blanket on the sand. The boys quickly stripped to their underwear and dipped their toes in the cool, clear water. Annie watched them splash each other and test out their versions of a dog paddle. Jim removed his shirt and joined them. Impulsively, Annie pulled her skirt through her belt, took off her shoes and stockings, and walked the shoreline dipping Hal's toes in the water.

After an hour in the water, they were all ravenous and devoured Annie's lunch in minutes. Jim had to return the car for six o'clock, so by five they reluctantly gathered their possessions and climbed back into the vehicle. The day was still warm, and by the time they arrived home, they were almost completely dry. Hal had fallen asleep again in his mother's arms and Annie was content.

"That was the most wonderful day." She leaned over and kissed Jim's cheek. "Thank you. I feel renewed." She realized that she *was* coming to terms with living in the North. Even the baby seemed more settled. He was becoming less fussy now that he had discovered his own thumb. Annie hated the cold of the brutal northern winter, but the summer here proved to be pleasant and, although they were nowhere near an ocean, she was thankful to know there was water close by.

In August, Annie and the children discovered blueberries. The sandy, acidic soil provided perfect conditions for the sweet berries to thrive. The fruit was so plentiful that Annie and the boys could sit on the ground and easily fill a bucket without getting up. They started going on regular blueberry-picking excursions, and they took turns carrying Hal to keep him content. Her children ate as many berries as they put in their pails, but it made Annie smile. She made several blueberry pies over the summer and many jars of preserves.

Sometimes Bobby brought a filled basket on his paper route and sold them to the cook at the camp. One day he surprised his brother Jack. "Look what I bought with my blueberry money!" He had made enough money to buy another bicycle and so he gave his old bike to his brother.

"You are the best brother!" Jack exclaimed as he ran and jumped up on Bobby's old bike. He and Bobby took turns giving Georgie rides in the yard.

"Just wait 'til school starts up again, Jack. We can ride our bikes there and back." Bobby put his arm around Georgie's shoulders and said, "Don't you worry, Georgie. I'll give you a ride every day."

That summer Jim installed a pump in the kitchen. Annie was thrilled. "Oh, this is wonderful," she said as they stood in the kitchen. "At least until the first frost, we'll have water right in the house!" She looked out the kitchen window. "You know, except for the tomatoes, my garden has been quite successful! Maybe I can pick a few of the green tomatoes and put them on our windowsills to coax them to ripen. And I think we'll have enough root vegetables to feed us over the winter."

"You do have a gift for gardening." He joined her at the window. "Ha! Look at our boys raiding the garden. They're eating your peas and carrots."

"They think I don't know that they sneak in when I'm not looking. I won't tell them that they're good for them."

Her sweet peas had thrived; they covered the garden fence with an explosion of colour. Some animal or bird had helped itself to most of her sunflower seeds, so she ended up with only two plants. Annie recalled the day that Jim bought her a lilac shrub, which he had planted by the well. The shrub had grown over the summer and she anticipated the blossoms she would enjoy next year. As she dug up her harvest from her garden, she was already planning her garden for next summer.

Over dinners that fall and winter, they often talked about the frenzy of activity around and through Jackpine Junction. Jim heard gossip at the train station that the government had granted tender for a pulp and paper mill to be constructed, just seven miles from town.

"I can get extra work when they build a railway spur to the construction site. They need the rail to carry the heavy equipment and supplies. Then a new gravel road will be constructed to the site. Both the rail and road will pass at the edge of our property."

"That will be wonderful for your extra wages, and I won't feel so isolated with a new rail and road so close to our property."

One night, Jim returned home agitated. "You should see how many men are passing through Jackpine Junction," he said, annoyed. "There are American engineers and tradesmen from Ottawa arriving to build the pulp mill. Ukrainians, Finns and Italians are all looking for work too."

Annie said, "Let's just see how long they stay once winter comes, or when they get eaten alive by blackflies."

"I suppose. But I even saw a group of small Oriental men in funny trousers, with coal-black hair, long and plaited like girls'. A Chinese work crew - I was gobsmacked! I hear they're paying them half wages!"

"Ha!" said Annie wistfully. "To think that Pappa sailed to the Orient, and now Chinese have landed here. The world is getting smaller."

"But all these foreigners are taking away work from the real old-timers like me! It makes me angry that these outsiders, who haven't proven themselves in the North, are just taking good-paying jobs and passing through."

"Don't worry," Annie soothed. "The contractors know you're a good worker and trustworthy. They'll pick you over any unknown new man."

As Annie predicted, Jim got many extra shifts at various sites around the new mill. Often when he came home, he entertained her with local gossip and news. He said that with so many transient single men around, bootleggers had been attracted to the area to earn easy money. He said construction had slowed down numerous times when men became ill after drinking bad whiskey.

Jim returned home from a job one evening, weary and dirty, but laughing about his day.

"There have been a lot of men getting sick from this one bloke's bad booze. The mill superintendent ordered the bootlegger be brought to him, if he trespassed on mill property again. That poor bugger came back today - he got some pioneer justice, all right."

"What's that?"

"Well, they tied him to the end of a long pole and dunked him repeatedly in the river, until he near drowned. He finally agreed to stay away from town. What a sight that was, him being chased down the road looking like the drowned rat he is!"

Annie frowned. "Seems a bit brutal to me. Why didn't they call in the police to take care of him?"

"I don't feel sorry for that slimy bootlegger," said Jim. "He almost killed some of the men. Besides it would have taken a few days for the police to come to town. This way worked. They successfully ran him out of town."

Annie didn't like the idea of some men taking the law into their own hands and making up their own rules as they went along. *We need more women here to civilize them,* she thought.

A few mornings later, Annie noticed that Jim had forgotten his lunch on the table when he left for work. She knew he was busy with the many trains arriving north or heading south, so decided to bring his lunch to the station herself. It was a beautiful day for a walk; she left Bobby in charge of the others and took the path to the new train tracks that ran close to edge of their property. She knew there wouldn't be a freight train until noon so it was safe to walk beside the rails. She reached the station in twenty minutes.

Just as she stepped up onto the railway platform, she heard some large dogs barking. To her surprise she saw two Great Danes pulling a homemade cart on the tracks, galloping towards the station. The wooden cart had three wheels that fit the spur tracks and had harnesses that attached to the dogs. The strange mode of transportation stopped in front of the station, and a young man jumped out of the cart. He filled two large tin pans with water from the pump.

While the young man brought the water to his panting dogs, Jim came out carrying two mail bags, and he placed them in the cart. He helped the young man turn the cart around for the return journey to the mill.

Annie handed Jim his lunch. "What on earth was that?"

Jim laughed. "The trains to the mill site are just for freight, so they send a man to pick up the mail here every second day. That fellow was just a little inventive and figured a way to make the trip quick." He kissed her cheek. "Thanks for bringing my lunch. I wouldn't have had a spare minute to fetch it myself."

It was only three weeks later that Jim forgot his lunch once again. Annie laughed. *It's like taking care of another child*, she thought. But she welcomed the excuse to escape the house and enjoy a pleasant walk on another warm day. She left Bobby in charge and took the path to the tracks. The freight train wouldn't be travelling until early afternoon; living so close to the tracks, she knew the schedule well.

She arrived at the station just as Jim was bundling the mail for the mill site and lugging it outside. Jim greeted her but then suddenly looked down the tracks, dropped the mail bags and pushed Annie behind him. He pointed in the distance. Annie gasped. A gas speeder was hurtling down the tracks towards them. The machine screeched to a stop in front of the station. An athletic young man leaped out and announced to Jim that he was there to pick up the mail.

Jim shook his head. "Where's the other bloke with the Great Danes? And what in God's name is your hurry? Are you trying to kill yourself and take some others with you?"

The fellow laughed. "The mill just bought this gas speeder and gave me the job to pick up the mail. This baby can move. So far, I can travel the seven miles in seven and a half minutes!" Then he left as quickly as he arrived.

Annie felt the blood drain from her face, and she flopped down on the outside bench. Jim went over and took his lunch from her hands.

"What's wrong? You look like you've seen a ghost!"

"I just walked the railway tracks from our place. I knew the freight train doesn't come until after twelve o'clock. I could have been killed!"

Jim's face turned ashen. "Thank God you got here before he did! Well, we can't take that shortcut ever again. I'll tell the boys to stay well clear. That kid could easily derail going that speed!"

Annie began to shake and Jim pulled her towards him. "You're all right now. You just had a bad scare. Hold on, love. I'll get you a nice cup of tea."

Walking back home, on the road this time, Annie was still shaking. She was thankful for the time alone to pull herself together before she got home.

Chapter Twenty-Two

One evening, early in December, Jim looked out the window and remarked, "Looks like we're in for a snowstorm. I'll go out and bank the sides of the house with more snow, and bring in extra wood for you. Make sure that the boys are well-dressed when they go to school tomorrow."

The snow did not begin to fall until after the boys left for school; the blowing flakes increased in intensity over the day. Then in late afternoon it stopped snowing and the temperature plummeted.

Annie paced the floor and fretted as the weak afternoon sunlight disappeared and another dark evening set in. Jim was still at work and the boys had not come home from school yet. She listened to the wind whistle around the house exterior. The children should have been home hours before. Suddenly, she heard Mike barking and scratching at the door. She raced to open it - but the dog was alone. He continued to bark at her, and bounded down the path and back, seemingly urging her to follow.

Mike was right. She would have to go out and look for the boys, and she would have to take Hal with her. He was still a little feverish with a cold, but she had no choice. She bundled him until she could only see his eyes peeking out under all the scarves and blankets, and then she dressed herself in many layers too. Lighting a kerosene lamp, she put the baby in the sled and pulled him along the path, and then onto the road towards the school. Mike raced on ahead and disappeared.

The bush was silent, except for the crunch of her boots on the snow-covered road and the scrape of the cutters of Hal's sleigh. She felt ice crystals form on her eyelashes and frost build up on the scarf she had wrapped over her face. Suddenly the silence was broken by the howl of some animal in the bush. She shuddered, recalling her mother's stories of growing up in Norway, where wolves had often chased the cutter she was riding in. *Where is that damned dog when I need him?* She quickened her pace.

She stopped when she thought she heard voices. Listening, she identified men's voices, the higher pitch of children's and the sound of Mike's familiar deep bark. Then at the edge of the woods she saw three men pushing a snow-bound sleigh, while a fourth man guided the horse through the high drifts. Annie tried climb the snow bank edging the plowed road, but she sank up to her knees and stumbled back. Mike jumped through the drifts to greet her, almost knocking her over in his excitement.

The men looked over when they saw Annie's lamp, and she heard Georgie call out, "Mummy!" Jack, Georgie and Bobby climbed through the high snow drifts, ecstatic to see her.

When they finally reached her, Bobby breathlessly explained, "We were so cold that we all huddled under the blankets. We thought the horse knew the way home, but I guess he got confused. He pulled us through the bush and got stuck."

Jack added, "We tried really hard to push the sleigh and pull the horse but we weren't strong enough. Eddie lives close by so he ran home to get help. Mike found us and we told him to go home. We were hoping he would get you!"

The men soon freed the frightened horse and pushed the sleigh back onto the road. Everyone climbed up onto the sleigh and, within a half-hour, Annie and the children were home. The boys piled into the house in a rush to get warm and Mike followed them inside.

"Oh, all right, Mike. You deserve to stay inside tonight. Jim's going to frown on me pampering you but you were a hero tonight. Good boy!"

She undressed her sleeping baby and placed him in his cradle, and she added more wood to the fire. Within minutes of undressing, Georgie was crying from the pain in his hands and feet. There were tears in Jack and Bobby's eyes too as they planted themselves beside the stove. Their fingers and toes were deathly white. She remembered how Jim would immerse his hands in a pail of warm water when he came in after working in the cold, so she filled buckets, pans and bowls. She placed three chairs by the stove and arranged the containers of warm water for the boys. All three boys cried from the pain as their blood slowly started to circulate again. *As poor as we were back in South Shields, I never had to worry about my children freezing to death. This northern winter is brutal!*

The boys soon recovered and by the next day had bounced back to their spirited selves. Annie, however, felt increasingly despondent over the winter, in the long days alone with just a baby for company. Jim worked so many hours that she never saw him in daylight. He left the house when it was still black out and returned late in the evening after dark.

Then, in March, chicken pox swept through the school. For weeks, Annie was house-bound with her boys as they passed the illness from one to another. Luckily, Hal was somehow spared. Annie told herself that if she had to endure a fourth child with chicken pox, she would have run away from home. She wasn't sure if she meant it or not.

Chapter Twenty-Three

Annie looked out the kitchen window. The sky was pale blue and cloudless. It was a fresh April afternoon and the days were slowly lengthening with the promise of spring. She was cutting vegetables for dinner when she heard the door open, and was surprised to see Jim home early from work. One look at his face told her that something was terribly wrong.

Before she could say a word, Jim reached into his pocket and wordlessly handed her a telegram. Annie quickly opened the envelope and read.

Regret to inform Father passed away Sunday stop Memorial service when you come stop Best regards to Annie and boys stop love Mother

"I can't believe it," She held her hand to her mouth. "What a terrible shock. I'm so sorry, Jim."

Jim sat down in a kitchen chair, put his elbows on the table and sunk his face into his hands. After a minute, he looked up at Annie with red-rimmed eyes.

"I was sorting mail and I could hear the clack of the telegraph machine with a message coming through, never dreaming it was for me. The station master handed me this envelope, saying that he was sorry for my troubles. I sat down on a bench and it was a couple of minutes before I could even open it."

Annie slowly sank to a chair and said, "You've got to go back to England."

"I've been thinking about that the whole walk home. How can I manage to get to South Shields? It's impossible. We just don't have the money." She began to protest, but he said. "Dinna fash, Annie. To tell the truth, I shudder to even think about getting on another ship!"

Annie rose from her chair and went to Jim, holding his head to her chest and stroking his hair. Tears welled in her eyes; she had loved Jim's father almost as much as she had loved her own. She knew how important it was for Jim to go to his family. She also knew that they could not afford a trip to England. But she was determined that they would find a way.

Before long, Annie had a plan. "We'll borrow from the money saved to pay Alfie back. We haven't mailed it to him yet, and I know he'd understand if we were a little late. It's the only way we can get you home for that memorial."

Jim reluctantly agreed and the next day he bought his passage to England. He was fortunate to be able to arrange his travel quickly, and within two days he was gone.

In the whirlwind of the news and Jim's departure, Annie was overwhelmed with loneliness and grief, especially in the evenings when the children were asleep.

After Bobby, Jack and Georgie left for school in the mornings, she was busy with the never-ending chores in the house. Mike had taken on the duty of escorting the boys to school, and met them there when the bell rang for dismissal.

Hal, who had become an active crawler, needed constant attention. One morning he almost pulled a pot of boiling water over himself, and then he dumped the entire flour bin, covering the floor around him in thick white powder. Annie angrily picked him up and placed him roughly on her bed.

"I've had enough, Harold Kidd! Don't you dare move!" she shouted.

The little boy sobbed but stayed where he was as Annie cleaned up the mess. She soon felt ashamed of her angry reaction, and she heard him crying pitifully. She went to the bed, picked him up and took him to the rocking chair. She wiped his tears with her apron and held him closely as she rocked him.

"Ah, Hal don't cry. Mummy loves you."

He cuddled closely to her and sucked his thumb. *Poor fellow's just being a normal curious little boy.* She reminded herself how fortunate she was, thinking of Marie with only one child. *If I were only to have had one child, it would have been Maggie - and now she's gone.* She kissed the top of Hal's blond head as remorseful tears spilled down her face.

That afternoon when the children returned from school, Bobby handed her a letter that the station master had dropped off at the school. She looked at the return address and discovered that the letter was from her brother George. Without reading it, she placed it above a cupboard and fed the children their dinner. She wanted to save the letter to read that night when the children were asleep. Her nights were the loneliest and she would find some comfort in reading George's news. She had even started to allow Mike to come inside in the evening for company.

Finally, when the house was quiet and Annie had made herself a pot of tea, she brought George's letter to the table. She saw from the date that it had taken three weeks to reach her. She was thrilled to read that George was coming to Canada, and that he planned to come to New Ontario to look for work in the gold mines. The letter had taken so long to reach her that he might already have arrived!

Chapter Twenty-Four

On the fourth day after Jim left, there was a knock on the door and a familiar masculine voice called out Annie's name. She opened the door, and there, standing in her doorway, were her brothers George and Alfie. She squealed and ran to hug the two big men, then stepped back to look at them. Alfie was wearing a good quality suit with a vest, a high white collar and a tie. His dark hair was cut short at the sides and back but was stylishly long at the top. *He looks like gentry,* Annie thought, and you only saw the prosthetic hand if you knew to look. By contrast, George was dressed more casually. He had a wide masculine jaw, a straight nose and light blue eyes. When he smiled, a dimple appeared beside his mouth. His light brown hair was longish and not as meticulously styled as his brother's, but he was easily the more handsome man.

"I got the telegram from Jim about his father and his trip to England. George happened to be visiting me before he headed north, so we both decided to come see you."

"Seeing you both makes me so happy!" Annie said. "Come in, come in."

Alfie playfully punched George's shoulder as they came into the house. "George wants to make enough money to go back home and get married."

"They say there are plenty of jobs in the gold mines," Annie said. The brothers' surprise appearance made her almost giddy. "I have an idea. Why don't we all take the train to Gold Creek tomorrow for a little holiday? I'll let the boys skip a school day. They love train rides and, frankly, I need a change of scenery."

The next day, they walked to the railway station and Alfie bought everyone's tickets to Gold Creek. Annie had not ventured that far from Jackpine Junction yet, so it was an adventure for all of them. As the train pulled away, she looked out the windows and noticed how scarred the land was beside the tracks. Unsightly stumps remained where once there had been virgin forest, and many fallen trees had been left to rot. Every few miles she got a glimpse of struggling farms and homesteads. Some farms had larger areas cleared by fire, as evidenced by the charred remains.

The train ride was relatively short, and as they got closer to their destination, they passed more houses. They saw several dormitories and cottages that appeared to have been cheaply and hastily erected to house the employees of the mines. The housing seemed to reflect the transience of the workforce. Annie was pleasantly surprised, though, when they got off the train at the Gold Creek station. There were cement sidewalks on most of the streets and electrical wires threaded through the town. She saw many more homes and large bunkhouses, a hotel and a hospital. While George left to walk to the mine site and apply for a job, Alfie, Annie and the children walked to the hotel. Alfie treated Annie and the children to lunch in the dining room.

While they were finishing their meal, Annie looked up as her youngest brother entered the hotel dining room and made his way among the tables. Annie noticed how other women in the room looked at George, and she smiled. *He is quite handsome. I wonder if my Georgie will look like him when he's grown.* George appeared unaware of any admiring female eyes following his movements; Annie knew that his heart belonged to Elizabeth, back in South Shields.

"Well, they hired me on as a fireman!" George announced. "They said that my timing was perfect as they had to replace a fireman who just moved back home to Scotland. I start tomorrow!"

Annie and Alfie congratulated George on his good fortune. Annie was quietly relieved, as she hated to think of him working underground in the mines. George smiled and held up a scrap of paper. "They've given me a voucher to stay at the hotel for a couple of days until there is room for me in the bunkhouse. Here, Alfie, I've also got some coupons for some liquor. You'd better take them. I'm a slow learner when it comes to the hard stuff! I'll stick to beer and stay sober."

Annie smoothed the skirt of her good navy wool outfit. It was wonderful to be out with her brothers. She had been starved for adult company and she hated for the day to end. She looked around the hotel room filled with people and was reminded of how small her world had become in her little cabin.

Hal was squirming in Bobby's arms and she could tell the other children had reached their limit of company manners, Georgie swinging his legs back and forth under the table, Jack fidgeting. Her brother George pulled over a chair and sat down beside Annie. He rifled through his canvas bag and pulled out a small parcel and a letter.

"This is for you, Annie. Mother wanted you to have a little gift."

Annie tucked the letter into her handbag. She unwrapped the small package and found two bars of her favourite lilac soap. She laughed and reminded Alfie of their time at Mrs. Murray's boarding house.

"That was such a luxury to have a long soak in a hot tub with limitless hot water. Whenever I get feeling sorry for myself, I remember how wonderful I felt that night."

"Well," said Alfie, "why don't you take advantage of George's hotel room and treat yourself to a long hot bath? George and I can take our nephews for a walk, and we can watch the cranes and other heavy equipment."

"That would be so selfish of me, but also wonderful," Annie said. "You don't realize what a handful little Hal is. I could keep him with me, I know the older boys would love to spend time with their uncles."

"Nonsense!" said George. "I don't think little Hal will outfox us. We'll watch him, Annie. You deserve a little time to pamper yourself."

It didn't take much more coaxing to convince Annie, and she soon found herself immersed in a hot tub. She soaked for half an hour, emptied the tub, and then refilled it with more hot water. She soaked so long that her fingers wrinkled. Only reluctantly did she get out, carefully rewrapping her precious bar of soap and placing it in her handbag. She towel-dried her hair, braided it, and pinned it up. After she had dressed, she descended the stairway to the hotel dining room.

Annie chose a table close to the fireplace, bought a newspaper and ordered a pot of tea while she waited for her brothers and the children to return. It felt quite odd to be sitting alone at a dining table in the hotel. She couldn't recall another time in her life when she hadn't been surrounded by family or her children. It was strange to be so unencumbered by responsibility. She felt a little guilty to find pleasure in this gift of freedom.

What a strange woman I am, she thought. *I feel sorry for myself when I'm alone, and then here I am, happy to be by myself!*

Annie had just started to read the newspaper when her pot of tea arrived. *But it does feel lovely to be pampered.*

When Alfie, George and the children came back, the boys were eager to tell Annie about their day. "Mummy," said Georgie, "there was a huge crane and it was lifting big machines, and there was a big bulldozer making a new road. I'm going to drive bulldozers and cranes when I grow up!"

Jack added, "Uncle George bought us toffee and Hal dropped his on the road and almost put it in his mouth!"

Annie looked at her youngest child, in Alfie's arms. Hal's shirt was smeared with dirt and his lips were covered with sticky goo. He looked at his mother and whimpered, pointing to a new scrape on his hand.

George guffawed. "You didn't utter a peep when you fell. I thought you were a big boy."

Hal laughed as he looked at his uncles, and Annie joined him.

They soon had to catch the train back to Jackpine Junction. As they left George at the hotel, he promised to visit them often. Annie and the boys hugged him goodbye and little Hal gave him a sticky kiss.

Alfie would be leaving her soon as well, but rather than wallow in that sad thought, she told herself to enjoy every minute they had left.

Chapter Twenty-Five

After only travelling a few miles, the train came to a full stop. Alfie got up to ask the conductor why.

When he returned to his seat he looked perplexed. "He says there's a moose on the railway track, but the engineer was able to stop us before we hit it."

After a few minutes the train slowly began moving again. From their window, they saw a huge bull moose with enormous antlers saunter into the bush. Not much later, Annie called everyone's attention to the opposite window, where they could see a large black bear with her two cubs up in a tree, not far from the train tracks.

When Annie sat down again, Hal climbed up on her lap, stuck his thumb in his mouth and promptly fell asleep. The other boys sat glued to the windows so they wouldn't miss any other sights, but exhausted from the day's events, they were soon lulled to sleep by the movement of the train. Even Bobby, who fought to stay awake with the adults, fell asleep.

Alfie was quiet for a long time. Finally, in a deeply concerned voice, he asked his sister, "Is it a common event to see moose and bears around you?"

"That was the first live moose that I've seen. I saw a huge dead one on a neighbour's sleigh last year. I've seen a few bears but they seem to be timid creatures. The children and I saw a bear while we were picking blueberries once. I thought it was a big shaggy dog and

I chased it away by making a lot of noise banging my pot!" Annie laughed at the memory, but sobered when she saw her brother's worried expression.

"I do feel safe, Alfie. Mike is a good guard dog and I am always cautious. But I'm grateful to you and George for being such caring brothers."

Back again at Jackpine Junction, Alfie carried Georgie in his arms as they walked home from the station. When they arrived, Annie placed Hal in his crib while Alfie and Bobby got a fire going to make supper. Annie prepared a simple meal of reheated stew and toasted slices of day-old bread. She had bought a cake at the bakery in Gold Creek for their pudding. After they had eaten their dinner, she sent the boys to bed.

Knowing that Alfie had to get back to Toronto the next day, Annie suggested that they play a game of cards. She treasured every minute of adult company – especially Alfie's - and wasn't sure when she'd see her brother again. They stayed up until after midnight, playing cards, reminiscing and laughing.

"I didn't want to steal George's thunder, but I've met a wonderful girl myself. Her name's Catherine. I plan to marry her if she'll have me."

"Oh Alfie, that's great news. What's she like?"

"She's kind and beautiful, and not at all bothered that I'm missing a hand. When I see your youngsters, Annie, it makes me want to start a family too."

"Well, Catherine is lucky to have you. You'll make a wonderful father and husband." Annie triumphantly slapped a card on the table, "Ha! I beat you again!"

Alfie shook his head. "I'm not a quitter and I'm a stubborn Norwegian. We're going to keep playing until I win!"

Annie laughed for a moment but then turned serious. "You know, with three of us here in Canada now, wouldn't it be wonderful to have Mother come and stay with us? I really do miss her."

"I know that Mother is very close to you, especially since Pappa died. That would be a grand plan someday, Annie."

Early the next morning, Alfie hugged her goodbye and left for the railway station. Her brothers' visit had passed so quickly that it seemed like a dream. She was somewhat comforted when she reminded herself that George was now living and working just forty miles away.

Chapter Twenty-Six

Jim returned home a month later. He had sent Annie a telegraph telling her when he would arrive, so she decided to meet him in Jackpine Junction. As if knowing why Annie was walking to the station, Mike followed her. When Jim stepped off the train, he looked well-rested, and he had gained a few needed pounds. *His sisters must have pampered him*, she thought with a smile. She was glad that he had been able to get home, but wished that she could have gone too. Together they walked the gravel road from Jackpine Junction to their home, with Mike bounding on ahead then retracing his steps. He trotted around Jim in an unabashed display of canine happiness. Jim slung his canvas bag over one shoulder and took Annie's hand in his. It was a sunny spring day and the air was filled with birdsong.

"How was your mother?" she asked him.

"She was quieter than usual, but I know that my brother and sisters will look after her. I brought your letters to your mother."

"I'm so relieved you saw her. How is she?"

"She looked well. She sends her love to you and the boys."

Jim had some news; his father left him a small inheritance. Jane had explained to Jim that his father, Charles, had had a difficult childhood. His family became destitute and for a short period, when he was only three years old, they had lived in a workhouse in Norfolk. When Charles' mother died of consumption, he left Norfolk to live with his brother John in South Shields.

"I understand now why Da was so careful with money. He never wanted his children to experience the same hardships that he did. He must have saved every spare penny."

"He was a lovely man. I'd never have guessed that he had such a difficult childhood."

"Well, he never talked about his life in Norfolk. But this has helped us, Annie. On my return home, I stopped in to see Alfie in Toronto and repaid him. He didn't want to take the whole amount, but I insisted. I hope you don't mind, but I wanted to be free of our debt to him."

"That was the right thing to do." Annie reached up and kissed Jim's cheek. "Alfie is seeing a lovely young woman and he wants to propose. He'll need that money now. And it does feel grand for us to be debt-free!"

Annie was turning over the soil in anticipation of planting, while Hal was playing in a sand pile at the edge of the garden. It was a warm day for early June and she loved gardening. It was her reward for coping through another long, dismal winter. The appearance of tender green sprouts pushing up through the soil renewed her. She was deep in thought, planning her garden, when a large black mass, hovering over the ground in the distance, caught her attention. She put the shovel down and shaded her eyes to get a better view. The black cloud seemed to fly closer and closer.

"Oh shit! Bloody hell!" Blackflies again.

She snatched Hal from where he was playing and ran towards the house. Her panic was infectious and he began screaming. The swarm reached then before they could get inside. Annie sank to the grass and tried to protect Hal's little body, tucking her apron around him. She cringed as the tiny wings and bodies brushed against her exposed neck, arms and head. Incredibly, instead of biting, the insects flew around her and continued their journey. Confused but relieved, she decided to stay in the house for the rest of the afternoon.

That evening she told Jim about her close encounter with the hundreds of blackflies.

"I've seen those swarms before." Jim replied. "The males hatch first but they only feed on nectar. It's the females that bite."

Annie sighed and glanced down at Hal. He was on the floor, playing with wooden blocks, building a tower. He gingerly placed one block on the top but then his construction collapsed with a loud crash.

"Oh shit! Bloody hell!"

Jim looked sternly at the toddler. "Hal Kidd, what did you just say?"

Hal's lip quivered and he began to whimper. Annie went over and picked up the little boy. She looked at Jim sheepishly, "Unfortunately, Hal heard that from his own mother when we were swarmed."

"Really? Well, I'm sure I said much worse the first time I was eaten alive by blackflies. I'll cut some spruce boughs tomorrow and put them beside the garden, so we'll be prepared for them."

Hal buried his face against Annie's neck and she absently patted his back. "You're not in trouble, Hal. Those were just some bad words that we shouldn't say." She was tired of having so many challenges in her life, and was ashamed to have exposed her youngest child to such words. Just when she resolved to try to bloom where she was planted, much like the sprouts in her garden, something else would uproot her. Hal reached up and stroked her face with his small hand and snuggled his warm body against her. Though the toddler tugged Annie away from her self-pity, she couldn't help but wonder what her next trial might be, because, whatever it was, it seemed inevitable.

Chapter Twenty-Seven

Annie had brought a kitchen chair outside and was reading the newspaper while Hal played in his sand pile. Jim walked over from the wood shed and sat down on the grass. Whenever he wasn't working at the station, Jim was busy felling trees and trimming them into sixteen-foot lengths. But then he had to pay a man with a team of horses to deliver the wood to the rossing operation to remove the bark. It was heavy work with little reward. Many local men had given up and decided to clear their fields with fire.

"I've sold thirty cords of pulpwood," Jim said, "but that's my last load. There's not enough profit in it." He wiped the sweat from his brow. "Annie, I've been thinking. Now that I've been paid for that last load of wood, we have the money to get you your hot water tank."

"You're not just teasing me, are you?"

Jim shook his head. "I mean it."

"We'll have hot water whenever we want! I'll feel like a queen."

"Well, I have to admit I'd enjoy it too. Imagine taking a bath without filling and emptying pots. Anyway, I'm going into town today to spend my hard-earned pulp money."

Annie glanced up wistfully and said, "I've been thinking that we need a root cellar to store our vegetables. Do you think you could build us one over the summer? I'm sure that Bobby could help you. And what about getting a few hens this summer so we can have our own eggs? Jack and Georgie are old enough to help. Maybe Bobby can even sell some eggs on his paper route."

Jim held up his hands in protest. "Whew! Maybe I'll just go back to cutting wood!" They laughed.

Jim continued, "Actually, I was thinking about getting some hens too. I'll order about ten hens when I'm in town and pick up some wood and wire to build the henhouse."

Within two weeks, Jim had the new hot water tank hooked up to the kitchen stove and a henhouse built beside the garden. The hens arrived, and Annie soon had her own fresh eggs for cooking and baking, and many more to spare for Bobby's paper-route customers.

Over the summer, Annie watched Bobby and Jim build the new root cellar. They dug a deep hole and built wooden walls and a roof with a trap door. Then they built a shed over the roof for easy access to it in the winter.

When it was completed, Annie declared to Jim, "Just you wait and see. I'll have it filled to the brim this autumn with the vegetables from my garden!"

There was an explosion of activity at Bear Falls that summer. The new pulp mill was building a village seven miles away, just for its workers. Plans included a town park, a school, a hospital and a company store.

Many local men were anxious to get a job at the mill. It had been a tough year. The roads promised by the government still hadn't been constructed and most farms were deep in the bush, too far from existing roads. "I hear that many families are barely surviving!" Jim told Annie.

Annie envisioned the new town homes with proper plumbing and electricity. She imagined the convenience of a store close by, as well as a school and hospital. But she kept her fantasy to herself. She knew that Jim would never give up the property they owned, and she would never give up her home to move into a rented house, however grand.

At least they were safe from the war that threatened to erupt in Europe.

Chapter Twenty-Eight

Two months later, in August, Annie read in the newspaper that war was declared in Europe. The repercussions were felt in New Ontario. Suddenly, there was a huge market for newsprint and raw resources. Jim was seeing hundreds of people pass through Jackpine Junction, all looking for work at the mill or the nearby mines. There were men from the Ottawa Valley and the Maritimes, French Canadians from Quebec, Americans from New York, some Brits and Europeans too.

"Who would have thought a war so far away would have such an impact on our remote corner of the world!" said Annie. "I imagine we'll see a lot of changes around here now. I hope that some of these men bring their wives."

It wasn't long before the European war touched Annie personally. She had just latched the door to the chicken coop when she saw Jim coming home from work. He was walking alongside a tall man. Her heart skipped – it was her brother George. She put down her egg basket and ran to greet him.

"George! What a wonderful surprise. We haven't seen you for over a month. How long can you stay?"

"I'm just stopping by for a quick visit. I'll catch the train to Toronto tonight, then board a ship home." George explained that he had enough money saved so he and Elizabeth could get married. "To tell the truth though, when I have too many long, lonesome hours and some spending money, I waste it on whiskey. I never learn, do I? Elizabeth will keep me in line."

Annie felt a lump in her throat. She was happy for George, but she would miss him. She felt a pang of envy and wished that she, too, could travel to South Shields and see her mother.

"Well, I wish you every happiness. It's been lovely having you so close. Come inside and we'll have dinner before you have to catch the train. The boys are going to be thrilled to see you."

Jim added, "Congratulations, George. Annie's going to miss you something fierce. Although you're twice her size, she still thinks of you as her little brother."

"What will you do for work, George?" asked Annie.

"After we marry, we'll have a little holiday, and then I'm going to join the Royal Navy."

The boys squealed with excitement when they saw their Uncle George. After a noisy, chaotic meal of roast chicken and garden vegetables, George reached into a pocket and pulled out a bag of toffee for the children. He thanked Annie and Jim for dinner, and said he should leave to catch the train.

Everyone gathered by the door to say goodbye. Annie handed him a bag filled with sandwiches, hard-boiled eggs, biscuits and a large jar of tea.

"We wish Elizabeth all the best and we welcome her to the family. Give Mother my love. Have a safe voyage."

"Thanks for everything. I'll write you when I get to England."

He gave her a tight hug, shook Jim's hand and ruffled the boys' hair, then turned to leave. Annie tearfully watched him walk away towards the train station, and wondered if she would ever see him again.

Annie's garden provided plenty of vegetables that autumn and the children helped her fill the new root cellar. She dug up the potatoes and knocked off the excess soil, then placed them in the shade for a few hours to harden. She stored turnips, carrots, beets and onions. Annie used sand to pack the vegetables to prevent rotting. The walls of the root cellar were lined with shelves and Annie filled them with her preserves.

One morning in late October, Jack came back in after feeding the hens, his face pale.

"We've lost at least six hens! I think they froze to death."

Annie followed him back to the hen house and looked around in disbelief. Dead birds littered the coop floor. There were just four weak chickens left alive, huddled together for warmth. Although they were a food source, she pitied the ones that had slowly frozen to death.

"I suppose we can bring the live hens to the wood shed for now," she said. "We'll have to keep the dog outside until we figure out what to do." She kicked herself for not planning better. "I should have known the chickens need a heated coop for the cold weather."

Annie cleared a spot in the wood shed and the boys helped her bring in the hens. That night, when Jim went to get an armful of wood from the shed on his way in from work, Annie heard him exclaim, "What the hell?" She went out and, over the noise of the hens, told him of their loss. He shook his head.

"We should have guessed this would happen on the first hard frost," he muttered. "I'm afraid, we'll have to kill the remaining hens. I can't keep the dog in here with the chickens. We can share half the poultry meat with Pierre and Marie. They've always been generous to us."

While Jim attended to the unpleasant job with the hens, Annie pickled all of the remaining eggs and stored them in the root cellar. Tears welled up and she sniffled while she worked. When Jim came back inside to wash up, he could tell she had been crying.

"We'll be fine. Don't worry, love. You've got the root cellar filled to the brim, and although my job doesn't pay a lot, it helps to buy our necessities."

Annie nodded.

"The saddest thing, though," Jim continued, "is that we are better off than many families around. Many are still trying to manage by farming."

Annie felt a lump in her throat. *We may be better off, but what's the best of nothing? Maybe we would have been better off if we stayed in South Shields*, she thought, not for the first time.

Another long, cold, dark winter slowly passed. Annie was relieved when the snow finally melted and the warmer weather returned. That spring, their fourth in New Ontario, she noticed a strange new presence in town when she went in to pick up supplies. There were men in army uniforms all around. The army was recruiting experienced miners for the Algonquin Regiment. They needed men for tunnel and trench construction as well as men with experience in railway and explosives. It brought the distant war in France and Belgium much closer to home. She overheard the recruiters say that the unit would be made up entirely of northern Ontario men, even the commanding officer; other officers were local men from the mines and mills.

She was glad Bobby was only thirteen and that the army didn't recruit farmers. *Not that we're really a farm, but we could pass for one if we had to.* It was difficult enough knowing that her brother Jack was in the merchant marine and now George was joining the Royal Navy. *Thank goodness Jim will never get involved with this war*, she thought.

Chapter Twenty-Nine

The smell of burning wood was common now throughout the area. Jim fulfilled his obligations under the homesteader's regulations and cleared a few more acres on his land, but this time he used fire. To Annie it seemed a shame to burn the wood, but she knew it wasn't worth the work and expense to cut and sell it.

She decided to keep hens again as egg production was profitable. The previous summer, Bobby had been able to sell quite a few eggs on his paper route, and Jack and Georgie had taken good care of the birds. The boys repaired the hen house and Jim ordered another ten hens. Annie found the scratching and pecking in the hen house comforting while she worked outside. She was happy to plan and plant her vegetable garden once more, and had once again added flowers just for their beauty. Things seemed much better in the summer months. Her garden was bountiful, and she was becoming an expert on storing vegetables in the root cellar.

One day when Annie was outside working in the garden, she stood and stretched her back, then went to the lilac bush by the well and buried her nose in the blossoms. She was sure their scent nourished her soul. Jim was nearby, chopping wood to build up their supply for the winter. He smiled when he saw her and laid down his axe. She felt a little guilty for getting caught daydreaming, but he walked over and wrapped his arms around her.

"You're smiling. What are you thinking about, old girl?"

"I was just thinking how nice it is to have you home more often, even if it is because we can't sell our wood. Troubles and worries vanish this time of year."

"Aye, that they do."

The long-awaited first letter from Annie's brother George finally arrived in September. Jim brought the letter home after work one day and handed it to Annie as soon as he entered the house. Annie kissed him hello, and sat down at the kitchen table to open the envelope.

George wrote that he and Elizabeth had been married in a very small ceremony in the same church where Annie and Jim were married. He took Elizabeth for a holiday in Scotland for a couple of days and they had a grand time. He said Elizabeth had never travelled out of Shields before and he was thrilled to spoil her a bit. As promised, when they returned to South Shields, George signed on with the Royal Navy. Elizabeth was going to stay with her parents until he returned at war's end.

On a more sober note, he said he was concerned about their mother. She was late in her rent payments and her eyesight was getting worse. George had paid her rent in advance for several months before he left, but he asked Annie to write their brothers to let them know they needed to help out. George also said he was afraid their mother was going a little daft because she kept stroking her neck in what he called a strange way. Annie smiled – he still didn't know about the pearl necklace.

Jim sat down across from her and she reread the letter aloud to him.

"I wish there were some way we could bring Mother here to live with us."

"Aye, that would be grand, but we will have to wait until the end of the war. It's dangerous to cross the Atlantic now. And even if the war were to end soon, we don't have the money to bring her here."

Annie was quiet for a few minutes. She thought about writing her brothers to ask that they pool their money to pay for Mother's passage. She started to sniffle and, though she tried to hold back the tide, broke into tears.

"I'm so sorry, love," said Jim, stroking her back. "I know you two are close." But it was something more immediate that had Annie in tears. It was time to tell him.

"I'm sorry to add to our burdens. I suspect that I'm with child again." Jim was ashen-faced and silent for a moment, but then he smiled. He got up to hug her and said it was wonderful news.

"You can't fool me," said Annie. "You aren't happy about another child, are you?"

"Of course I'm pleased that you'll make me a father again."

"Well, I'm not looking forward to another pregnancy, and I can barely cope with the four boys we have. Besides, money is so tight."

"We always seem to manage, but you're right. I thought at this stage of our lives we would be settled financially. I've been thinking that maybe we would be better off if I joined the army. You'd get a regular separation allowance from the government while I was away."

Annie was silent for a second, shaking her head in disbelief, then she shouted, "No! How could you even contemplate such a thing!" Her face grew warm and her vision blurred as her eyes flooded with tears. "You're thirty-six years old and will be the father of five children. I can't believe that you'd even think of leaving me here on my own!"

Jim held her close to his chest, "Dinna fash. I was just thinking aloud and didn't mean to upset you. The promise of a steady income is quite an incentive, that's all, and I hear the Canadian army pays well. I suppose I could go to the bank and mortgage some of our land."

Annie cried out in alarm. "But this is your dream! You own land and it's paid for in full! And you know I would never agree to mortgage the house! Surely we'll manage somehow." She dried her cheeks with her apron and wondered if they really could manage.

That winter would have been very difficult without the supply of vegetables and preserves in the root cellar. Jim went hunting with Pierre and they shot a small moose whose meat they divided between the two families. There were plenty of wild rabbits around and they often had rabbit stew. One day, though, Jim told Annie that a baby had died at one of the farms deeper in the bush because the mother was so severely undernourished, she could not make enough milk for her infant. Annie felt a heavy sadness. It was little comfort to know that there were many families worse off than they were.

"Annie, I've made a decision. I feel that I have little choice. I must join the war effort. It's a solution to our money worries - and it's my duty."

"Your duty is with me and our boys!" Annie snapped. "You can't leave me and the children here on our own! I'm nine months pregnant with *your* child, for God's sake!"

"Ah, Annie, this is tearing me up." Despite Annie's reluctance, they finally had to mortgage much of the land, all except the house and five acres around it, which Jim had now arranged to put under Annie's name. Insurance, she guessed with a shudder, should he not return from the war. He knew how important it was to her that the house was free and clear. "You'll get a regular separation allowance from the government. You'll have all the security you need until I get back."

"But you won't be here. You're putting your life in danger and for what, your duty? Or is it the promise of adventure and excitement? I need you here with me and our children!"

"Annie, be reasonable. We're living hand to mouth. It's the only way. After the baby's born, I will sign my papers."

She looked at Jim, tears blurring her vision, and shook her head. Then she walked out the door.

It was an hour before she returned, still fuming and determined to convince him not to join the army and leave her. She knew all too well how many men came back with missing limbs, or who never came back at all. *This is madness*, she thought. *He'll come to his senses.*

Chapter Thirty

Annie knew from her discomfort that the baby was ready to be born. When Jim came home from the station that warm May evening, she told him to go get the doctor.

"I've had this nagging feeling all day today that something was amiss," he said. "You should have sent one of the boys to fetch me. I'll be back as fast as I can!"

He rushed out the door, shouting to Bobby to look after his brothers and see if his mother needed anything. He returned an hour later out of breath.

"The bloody doctor's in Gold Creek. We'll have to go to the hospital in Bear Falls. I borrowed a gas-powered handcar from the station. It's just out at the tracks. I phoned the hospital from the station to let them know we're coming. Bobby, you're in charge. I might not be back until morning."

Jim carried Annie the short distance to the railway spur that passed the fence line of their property. Annie normally would have balked at getting on the small wooden platform sitting on four flanged railway wheels but at this stage of her labour she was oblivious. Jim gently lifted her up to the narrow bench and climbed up beside her. He started the gas-powered engine and it came to life with a deafening roar. After a jerky start, they were soon racing down the tracks. Seeing the trees whipping by them, Annie squeezed her eyes shut and clung tightly to Jim. The trip took less than ten minutes, they were travelling so quickly.

Although Jim had said he'd notified the hospital when he borrowed the handcar, Annie was still surprised to see the doctor's Model-T Ford waiting by the track to take them the rest of the way.

At the hospital, Annie was whisked away to another room, leaving Jim pacing at the entrance. As her labour pains came closer together and grew more intense, the doctor placed a mask over her face and put her into a deep slumber.

Annie and Jim's fifth baby boy was born while Annie was unconscious and pain-free. When she woke up, she found Jim in the room with her, cradling the infant. She held her arms out. As he passed the baby to her, Jim assured her that he had all his fingers and toes and was a healthy child.

Annie gazed down into his sweet face and began to cry.

"Are you feeling any pain?" Jim asked her, his tone concerned as he kissed her cheek.

"No, I'm fine. That was the easiest birth I have ever experienced." She looked into Jim's eyes. "I just realized that now that this baby has finally arrived, you're signing up with the army, aren't you?"

Jim's eyes grew moist. "Ah Annie," he whispered, "it's the only option for us. I will wait until the end of the month before I enlist but don't worry. I won't be away long. They say this war will be over soon."

Annie swallowed an angry retort, hopefully masking her anxiety, and changed the subject. "What should we name this new baby? I have only girls' names picked out again."

"I've been thinking that if we had another boy we should name him Henry, after your father."

"Henry. I like that. Mother would be thrilled."

As she held her newborn, Annie was already worrying about how she would manage on her own. Surely she could still convince him not to sign up. Logically she understood why Jim wanted to join the war effort, but in her heart she couldn't accept it. *Bloody stubborn man! I can't believe he would actually leave me on my own, with our five children.*

Chapter Thirty-One

Annie felt lethargic in the intense July heat. The temperature had been in the nineties for days. Her hair was plastered to her scalp and her clothes held the heat against her sticky, sweaty skin. *How can one godforsaken place be so bloody cold in the winter and hot as hell in the summer?* When she last checked the thermometer on the side of the house, it had read ninety-six degrees.

Annie and the children were outside, for it was even hotter inside the house. Every surface was sticky in the heat. Hal and the baby were both fussy from a lack of sleep. She wondered if they would nap in the root cellar, if she laid an old blanket on the cooler floor there. Jack and Georgie had already discovered that the root cellar provided an escape and made regular excuses to go down.

She looked at the garden in frustration. It was bone dry due to the lack of rain for the last three weeks, and the strong, hot wind blew dust everywhere. There was a biting odour of burning wood coming from the north, and she assumed by the smoke plumes in the distance that there was a fire several miles away. Perspiration trickled from her forehead and stung her eyes. Sliding a forearm across her face, she sighed.

Jim had been stationed at Camp Borden for the past two months. She was still angry that he had chosen to go, but it was comforting to know he was not too far from them yet. As Annie headed to the house to look for an old blanket, she heard three short blasts of a train engine whistle in the distance, repeated twice – the warning signal for a bushfire. Her heart quickened with fear.

She looked down the path to the road and saw fourteen-year-old Bobby returning home from his paper route; he was pedalling his bike as fast as his legs could go. He let his bike clatter to the ground as he ran towards her, shouting.

"Ma! The bushfire is headed our way! We've got to get to the freight rail. They're picking up people and bringing them to the mill." One of Bobby's newspaper customers at the hotel in Bear Falls had told him about the train rescue, he told her as they ran to gather the other children. On the way home he had detoured by the high granite rise on the edge of town where he could see for miles, and he'd seen a huge ash cloud hovering over the bush. He described whirls of fire in the sky igniting more and more trees and brush. "Then I heard an explosion like a dynamite blast!"

By the time Annie had gathered the children and tossed blankets and a few valuables into the wheel barrow, she could see the wall of fire approaching. The wind was hot and howling. Cinders began to fall around them; heavy smoke settled over the house and made it difficult for her to breathe. She called to Jack and Georgie.

"Run with the wheelbarrow as fast as you can to the tracks!"

She picked up Hal and thrust him at Bobby. "Here son, carry Hal and run!"

Unhindered by Hal's weight, Bobby quickly outpaced his brothers. Annie lifted baby Henry into her arms and followed her boys. She tripped once, but tucked the bottom of her skirt into her waistband so she could run faster. She was relieved to see the boys had reached the train tracks. Hot cinders landed on her sleeves and skirt and she felt the sting of burns on her arms.

Beside the tracks, Annie saw a young girl, maybe eight-years-old, shielding a toddler from the flying embers. She seemed unaware that her own legs were burned black, and that her hair was singed to her scalp. Annie recognized the girl, though she didn't know her name. Her home was several miles away. *That poor girl must have run all that distance to escape the fire*, Annie thought. She heaved a dry retch, and then shouted to her children and the young girl.

"Jump into the ditch! Get as wet as you can!"

She grabbed the blankets from the wheelbarrow, soaked them and put them around the children. Then she took her good linen tablecloth, wet it as well, and used it to cover their heads. The smoke was dense and stung her eyes and throat, and she gagged at the stench of the girl's charred flesh. She covered Henry's face with her wet apron, and covered her own nose.

Annie turned and looked back into the distance as cinders rained on their house. The roof instantly caught fire and she cried as flames engulfed their home. Her vision blurred with tears.

"It's gone! Our house is gone!"

Red hot coniferous cones were tossed into the air as the updraft mushroomed and the fire advanced quickly towards them. Two Chinese men, probably from one of the lumberjack crews, jumped into the ditch beside them. One of the men cried out, "Me gonna die! Me gonna die!" His companion responded, "Me gonna die too, but me not crying!" Bobby, Jack, and Georgie started to giggle. Annie was amazed that her children were able to find a light moment in the horror around them. They quickly sobered, though, when they heard the terrified scream of a trapped workhorse, somewhere in the bush. Panic-stricken, Georgie and Jack howled and huddled closer to Annie. Hal clung to Bobby and bawled hysterically. The young girl was still holding her tiny sobbing sibling but she clung to Annie's sleeve with her other hand. Annie stared down the tracks and prayed that they would be rescued.

Chapter Thirty-Two

With his sharp hearing, Jack picked up the sound of the train whistle before Annie did. Through the heavy smoke she saw the freight train slowly chugging towards them. It seemed to take forever, but finally it squealed to a stop and everyone scrambled out of the ditch to board.

Bobby climbed into the freight car with Hal and then reached down to take Henry from Annie's arms. Jack and Georgie quickly scampered up and Annie followed after helping up the young girl with her baby sister.

Finding a small area for them in the freight car, Annie collapsed on the floor. Her heart was pounding and her arms stinging. She inspected her children, checking for injuries. Bobby had a nasty burn on one hand but the other boys seemed to have escaped without injury, other than singed hair and eyebrows. She had many small burns on her arms, but Hal and Henry were unmarked.

She looked around at the other occupants, recognizing most of them. Some people were badly burned and in pain, some temporarily blinded by the smoke and a few had injuries too horrific to look at.

Suddenly Jack shouted. "We forgot Mike!" His face turned pale and he began to sob.

"Mike's a smart dog, son," said Annie, though privately she was horrified. "He'll find a way to safety. I don't think they would have let us bring him on the train anyway."

The air in the crowded car was thick with smoke and the walls unbearably hot to the touch. Someone had tucked a shirt into a wide gap in one corner to keep the smoke out. Annie was becoming accustomed to the odour of burnt flesh around her, but she felt weak and dizzy. Her tongue was swollen and her mouth parched. Little Henry was too lethargic even to cry, and Georgie was breathing in gasps. "I'm thirsty, Mummy," he cried weakly.

"I know, poppet. I'll find some water when we get to the mill."

There was a boy Bobby's age near them, alone, gasping for air and sobbing. Annie moved towards him and touched his shoulder.

"We'll be fine now, son. We've been rescued."

The boy shook his head and cried, "My sister and grandmother are still in our house!"

Before she could stop the boy, he jumped out of the slow moving freight car. He landed on his feet and ran off frantically as if he were being chased. Annie felt helpless.

She sat back down on the floor of the freight car and tried to calm her terrified children, as the train made slow progress back to the mill, stopping often to rescue more people. On the other side of the car, one woman was cradling her young child and crying. The little boy appeared untouched by fire but Annie could see that he was dead. The woman's arms were charred and blackened. When Annie saw Pierre beside the woman, she realized with a start that it was Marie and little Louis.

"Sweet Jesus, Marie has lost her little boy," she whispered.

Annie felt suddenly light headed and her peripheral vision blackened. When she opened her eyes and saw her children gathered around her, crying, she realized she must have fainted. She sat up and reassured them.

"Don't cry. I'm fine, boys. Really, I'm fine."

She gingerly touched the back of her head and felt a goose egg developing, but was thankful that Bobby had been holding little Henry when she lost consciousness. She felt foolish for fainting and made a vow to be stronger for her boys.

She heard tormented screams from outside and looked towards the sound. To her horror she saw several wretched victims writhing on the ground, burning like pulpwood. She turned back to her children. "Close your eyes and try not look at anything until we get to the mill."

The train picked up speed and a young man in his teens leaned out of the car, panicked. "God have mercy on us," he shouted. "The railroad ties are burning now and the last freight car is on fire underneath!"

Several men told him to shut up, as the children were already frightened out of their minds. The seven-mile ride seemed to be taking a lifetime, but finally they were approaching the mill. The freight train snaked around one side of the concrete building and wheezed to a stop. It was mayhem, initially, as the crowd of people pushed their way to the exit, desperate to get off the train and find safety. Then one older man, with an authoritative voice, ordered the men to stand back and allow the women and children to get out of the stifling, smoky car first.

Annie looked back towards the fire and gasped. The three other railway tracks to the mill were blocked. One track was smothered under an inferno of collapsed cords of burning pulpwood, and there was an open container on another that she could see was filled with dynamite. *That could blow up any moment!* she thought frantically. At least thirty men were operating pumps, hoses and buckets, saturating the freight cars and explosives with river water, desperately trying to douse the flaming pulpwood.

Annie and her children were now safe from the fire, but where did that leave them? Their home and possessions were nothing but ashes. They had abandoned their wheelbarrow back in the ditch. All they had in the world were the clothes that they were wearing.

Chapter Thirty-Three

Annie guided her children to safety inside the mill. Many families were already there. Two men were at the entrance ladling out drinking water to the newly arrived evacuees. Annie made sure her children had their share, and then eased her own parched throat with several gulps. She saw Dr. Smith circulating among the fire victims, treating the most seriously injured first. Many obviously needed hospital care, but she overheard someone say that the hospital had burned to the ground. A few people were clothed only in blankets.

Annie found a nurse and asked her to look at Bobby's burned hand. The woman efficiently applied an ointment to the burn and bandaged him up. Annie could tell he was in a lot of pain, but her brave son didn't cry.

Annie noticed the schoolteacher, Miss Brown, off by herself, quietly crying into her lace handkerchief. She brought the boys over and asked if she was injured.

"Oh, I'm just being foolish. So many have lost loved ones and are badly burned, and here I am crying over my new shipment of textbooks and the lovely oak desk the trustees just purchased for me. I watched the school burn to the ground." She reached out to touch Annie's hand, "I'm happy to see that you and your children are safe."

By six o'clock, rumour was spreading quickly that the fire had changed direction and moved out of the town. But the area was still full of smoke, hot cinders and intense heat. Henry became fussy and Annie tried to nurse him, but she was so dehydrated that she had very little milk.

Around midnight, a thunderstorm broke out. Lightning flashed through the windows and sporadically lit up the interior of the mill. The downpour was a welcome respite from the earlier heat and dryness. One man who had ventured outside announced that the fire, quite unbelievably, had left the company mercantile store and the town hotel untouched. Soon after the storm ended, it was announced that food would be handed out at the company store. Annie's children had not eaten in over twelve hours, so she sent Bobby and Jack out at first light. "Go on to the store and line up for whatever food you can get."

They came back an hour later with two cans of tomatoes and a loaf of bread. Bobby borrowed a can opener from someone nearby and opened the tins. Bobby, Jack and Georgie took turns fishing for tomatoes with their fingers, careful to not lose a single drop of liquid. Annie tipped a can to Hal's mouth and he thirstily gulped the juice. Annie had to chuckle when Jack declared, "This tastes as good as Christmas dinner!"

That morning, Annie noticed that other families were venturing out of the building to check the damage. She decided to go to their property to see what remained, and she knew the boys wanted to look for Mike. She feared what she would see when they got there.

She approached Miss Brown. "Would you mind watching my three youngest at the hotel? I need to see if I can salvage anything from our farm."

The young woman readily agreed, glad to do something helpful.

Georgie complained. "But Ma, I want to look for Mike too! Can't I come with you?"

"I need you to help Miss Brown. You know that Hal doesn't always listen but he will behave for you. I promise that we won't be long."

A few minutes after Annie, Bobby and Jack left the hotel they heard a loud commotion near one of the freight cars. Annie saw one of the mill supervisors shoving and hitting a smaller Oriental man.

From all the shouting, it appeared that the labour crew was refusing to work. To Annie's shock, the bigger man shoved a protesting smaller man's face into the still-hot cinders. The labour crew still refused to work in the heat and the supervisor swore.

"God damn it, I'll show you buggers!"

Three muscular lumberjacks and the bullying supervisor forced the labour crew into a hot freight car and locked them in. Annie was so outraged that she stomped towards them. *I'm just one small woman but I can threaten to report him to the police.* She heard kicking and shouting coming from inside the freight car as the trapped men cried out, "We work! We work!"

Finally, the freight car was unlocked, just as Annie reached the supervisor, and the men tumbled out, gasping for air. Reluctantly, Annie decided not to confront the bully; she needed to conserve her energy to fight her own battles.

As she trudged along the railway tracks with Bobby and Jack, Annie was surprised to see that although some of the track had twisted grotesquely in the heat of the fire and many rail ties were burned to ashes, the railway company already had work crews repairing track. The telephone and telegraph lines were still down so she had no way of contacting Jim to let him know that they had survived the fire.

As they made their way towards home, an occasional breeze gave them a little relief, but the farther they walked, the odour of decomposing flesh became more overpowering; they choked and gasped for breath. A short distance ahead, Annie saw a pile of human remains, charred and decaying, stacked like cordwood beside the track. The boys pulled their shirts over their noses, their eyes wide with shock. She regretted having brought them with her.

A mile farther along, to her horror, she recognized the body of the boy who had jumped off the train. He and his sister had their arms around each other, their bodies fused by fire in a final embrace. They were still wet from the thunderstorm, lying beside the track and waiting for a rescue that had never came. Annie could think of nothing to say to her crying boys. She wept.

When they finally came to the ditch where they had been rescued, she found what remained of their wheelbarrow. It was a grey puddle of melted metal. Annie cried at the thought of her lost family photos. She didn't have a photo of Jim now, and she had lost all of her precious mementoes of Maggie. As they approached the remains of their home, the boys began running around and calling for Mike, kicking at columns of grey ash that had once been trees and watching the towers collapse.

All that was left of the house were the two wood stoves, now useless. She spent a fruitless half-hour sifting through the rubble, looking for anything salvageable. She then noticed that although the shed over the root cellar had burned to the ground, the cellar door was only singed.

Entering the root cellar, Annie discovered that all of her jars of preserves had exploded in the intense heat. There was broken glass everywhere. She picked through the sand to search for potatoes and carrots that were untouched by fire, but, she soon realized that they were all roasted and sprinkled with glass shards. *All of our hard work was for naught. I've no home, nor food for my children. What am I going to do?*

She climbed up out of the root cellar, and she plopped down on the ground. She was overwhelmed by a sense of fear and hopelessness. She was pulled back from her dark thoughts by the sound of Jack crying.

"I'm scared, Ma. We've looked everywhere but we can't find Mike. And where are we going to live?"

"Don't worry, son, I'm sure we can stay with Uncle Alfie for a while. When we get back to the hotel, we'll let everyone know what Mike looks like and that we're searching for him. Maybe someone rescued him. Don't give up hope. There's nothing more that we can do here now. Let's walk back to town." She hoped that she sounded more confident than she felt.

Fortunately, the bodies by the tracks had been removed while Annie and the boys were at the farm, so they were spared that horrific sight on the return trip. They entered the hotel, exhausted and dejected, and found Miss Brown and the three children; the young woman appeared to be relieved to see Annie.

"The baby was asleep most of the time, but I was happy to have George to help with Harold. He is a busy little boy. The hotel cook gave George and Harold each a piece of pie. I'm afraid that Harold's face and hands are still a bit sticky."

"Thank you. I know Hal can be a handful. And it seems that our walk was for naught. There's nothing left on our property and the boys are still looking for our dog."

"I'm so sorry. I did hear some good news though." She told Annie that the rail tracks would be repaired by the next day, and that there were several relief trains coming to take the more severely injured people to hospitals to the south. "We'll get our meals here at the hotel until then. The pulp and paper company will foot the bill. Oh, and Camp Borden is sending troops with tents and blankets. You'll see your husband."

At this news, Annie broke down, sinking to the floor and burying her face in her hands sobbing. Miss Brown and the children gathered around, but Annie could not be comforted for quite some time. The young teacher was distraught about causing Annie to cry, and she apologized repeatedly. Annie finally forced herself to stop crying; she knew she was upsetting the children. Their faces were wet with tears too.

"I'm sorry, I'm fine now. Don't cry, boys. We're going to be all right. Daddy's coming."

While Annie and the children were eating their dinner at the hotel, Annie saw Miss Brown approach her. With her was middle-aged bearded man. The young woman introduced Annie to her cousin Tom. "I've asked Tom if you and the children could stay over tonight at his home. I have a room at the hotel and I'd offer to share but it's the size of a closet."

"I'm pleased to meet you, Mrs. Kidd." Tom said in a deep voice as he held out his hand to shake hers. "I know your husband quite well. I've worked with Jim many times over the years. My wife and I would be pleased if you and the children would stay with us until you find a place to stay."

"Thank you for your kind offer, Tom, but I couldn't impose."

"I insist. We're among the fortunate few with a home untouched by the fire. We hid in our root cellar during the worst of it. We were lucky there, too – we've learned that many families did the same, but suffocated to death!"

Annie was overwhelmed by his generosity and reluctantly accepted his offer.

"Thank you. That is so kind of you." She wondered if Tom had witnessed her tears earlier and was ashamed that she had cried so openly. "It will just be a night or two. I understand that Jim will be here with the army, in a day or so."

After their meal, Annie and the children followed Tom to his home, which was just on the outskirts of town. They passed the ashes of many houses as they walked. Most of the town had been reduced to charcoal and dust; not a tree was left. When they passed the ruins of the hospital, Tom told her that the nurses had rescued every patient.

"They placed the patients on stretchers on the veranda and arranged cars to take them to safety. I heard that one nurse wanted to save her beaver coat, so she tucked it under one of the patients!"

When they approached Tom's log home, his wife, Joan, greeted them at the door with a hug and ushered Annie and her boys to a small bedroom behind the kitchen. The room had rough timber walls and one small window. The bed was simply constructed and obviously homemade. Tom's wife had tried to hide the bleakness of the room with a bright quilt on the bed and a rag rug on the floor. On a pine table Joan had placed a large bowl of water, a bar of yellow soap and a clean flannel rag. Annie wondered guiltily if Tom and Joan had given up their own bedroom.

She washed the younger boys' faces and hands and told Jack and Bobby to wash up. The water was black by the time they had finished. She had the older boys sleep across the bed so they could all fit, Hal tucked between Bobby and Georgie. She planned to sleep on the rug on the floor with the baby.

Her exhausted children quickly fell asleep, but not for long. Bobby, Jack, and Georgie whimpered with nightmares throughout the night, and she repeatedly had to calm them, sitting with them until they drifted back to sleep. She feared the horrors they had witnessed wouldn't soon fade from their young minds.

Chapter Thirty-Four

After spending two uncomfortable days in the same sweaty, singed clothing, Annie was relieved to hear that several trains were arriving from the south and other northern communities. One brought doctors, nurses, and emergency medical supplies. It also carried a hundred coffins. Thousands of pounds of food, clothing, and blankets were delivered and set up in large tents. There was also a train coming from Camp Borden, transporting three officers, two hundred tents and a hundred men. She prayed that Jim was on it.

She waited all day near the hotel hoping to hear that the military train had finally arrived. It was early evening when she thought she heard Jim's voice calling her name. Afraid it was just wishful thinking, she turned slowly. There she saw him, pale-faced and shaking with emotion, and ran into his arms.

"Thank God you're alive!" he said, his voice breaking. "There was no way of knowing, and then the first thing I saw was that stack of coffins. Jesus, you've burnt your arms! What about..."

"The children are safe," she said, laughing through her tears. "We are all fine."

She called the boys, who were just inside the hotel entrance. Bobby came out holding Hal, and Jack was carrying Henry. Georgie was close behind his older brothers. When the three older boys saw their father, they raced tearfully down the stairs and ran to him. Jim let go of Annie and gathered his children in a big hug.

Then he sent them off to play, and he led Annie to a quiet spot behind the hotel where they sat down on the back steps. She told him what she and the boys had been through over the last few days. He hung his head. "I'm sorry, so sorry that I wasn't here. I'll figure something out, Annie. I'll get you and the boys somewhere safe."

"Well, we're all alive and the family is together for now. I'm so grateful to have you here. But we had expected the military train to arrive yesterday. What happened?"

"We were forced to wait in the train for hours, stuck behind all the other relief cars. I've never known such fear in my life, not knowing for days whether you and our boys had survived." He held her tightly against his chest as if proving to himself that she was real.

"When we finally got here, I had to unload tents and supplies first, and when I was finally granted permission to leave, I went straight to our property to look for you and the boys. Of course you weren't there. I came back to town and asked everyone I met if they knew where you were. At last someone told me that any survivors could be found around the hotel or mill. Ah, Annie, my heart near stopped when I saw you on the hotel steps."

Annie knew that the family did not have a lot of time together, as Jim had to return to the temporary army headquarters at Jackpine Junction. The army was setting up shelter for survivors and searching for the missing. Luckily his unit wasn't given the gruesome task of digging shallow graves for temporary burial until bodies could be sent to their final resting places.

"I'm allowed a three-day pass to evacuate you and the bairns to Toronto. I'll send Alfie a telegraph as soon as the lines are back up."

"You can come with us?" Annie asked in disbelief.

"Aye, I'll go with you to Toronto, but I have to return here. You can stay with your brother until I find another house. The railway company is providing free transportation for evacuees to stay with friends or family elsewhere."

"Alfie won't mind us staying with him for now, and I suppose it's as good a time as any to meet his new wife. I'll certainly be happy to get the children away from all of this."

While Jim worked with his unit, Annie and the children found temporary shelter in one of the army-issue tents and continued to have their meals at the hotel. Alfie quickly telegraphed back that he was relieved Annie and the children were fine, and that he was anxiously awaiting their arrival.

Meanwhile, the tent was not such a hardship. The high temperatures and humidity were gradually replaced by warm summer weather and she enjoyed the company of other adults. The boys treated the experience like a holiday and found other children to play with during the day. In the evening, though, Annie's three older sons suffered nightmares that made them shudder and cry in their sleep.

Whenever Jim was off duty, he walked to town to spend a few hours with them. One day inside her tent, he confided to Annie, "This assignment must be worse than fighting on the Western Front. It's unpleasant work, gathering bodies. We found the remains of sixteen people who'd all suffocated in their root cellars. Yesterday, we found four families beside the river, all dead. Some were so badly burned that only fragments of their bodies could be found. What's even more difficult is that I know the families of the homesteads and farms where we found all those remains."

"My God, I can't imagine how much they suffered before they died," said Annie with a shudder. She couldn't understand why she was still alive when so many people hadn't made it. Sometimes she felt euphoric that she and the children had escaped death, but mostly she felt incredibly sad because so many lives were lost. "It's been so hard on our boys, too. They've witnessed terrible sights. I worry whether their nightmares will ever stop haunting them."

Jim pulled her to him and whispered, "Children bounce back, you'll see. I'm just grateful that you're alive. I'm so sorry that you had to face that bushfire alone." He told her that he regretted signing up, but there was nothing he could do to reverse it. If he deserted, he said he'd end up in jail, of no use to anyone. At least Annie would get a steady separation allowance while he was away. But still, her first choice would be to have him with her.

Two days later, Jim came to Annie's tent, looking shaken. He glanced around to make sure the boys were not within hearing distance, and told her in a broken voice, that the local French-Canadian settlement had tragically lost every one of its adults in the fire.

"They put their children in a rescue train, but stayed behind to try to save their homes. As the fire came closer, it seems their young priest led the fifty-six men and women to a clay-cut in a field, apparently believing that they would be sheltered. We found them all kneeling, but dead. The agonized expressions on some of their faces will be branded into my mind forever. Jesus, what a terrible sight! I'm so blessed that you and our boys were spared."

Annie shook her head. Her eyes brimmed over and she wiped away her tears with her fingers. "Those poor souls! They must have suffered unbelievably. What a horrible tragedy!"

Jim sighed and took Annie's hands in his. "I'm sorry. I wasn't thinking. I should have spared you. There *is* some good news, though. The government will give homesteaders timber to rebuild and a loan to purchase the necessities they need for a year. I guess they're worried that too many families will give up on settling in the North. We can build you a new house."

"Is it possible? I was sure we'd never own our own home again!" Annie couldn't believe it. She decided to push her luck even further. "If we rebuild, I would like to live closer to the new town. Surely we can find a suitable place when so many are leaving."

"Well, we've got until the end of October to sort everything out. You and the boys will have a good time at Alfie's, and I'll get you a new house before I have to ship out." He forced a smile. "We may be homeless for now, but we are far more fortunate than many others."

Chapter Thirty-Five

A few days before the family was to leave for Toronto, Bobby asked to be allowed to go look for Mike one last time.

"I've heard stories of animals that survived the fire. Some horses and cows found their way to the river and waited it out. Mike's smart enough to do that! I even heard that one woman found a couple of ducks and wild rabbits had followed her down the road as she ran to escape the flames. I need to look for Mike before we leave."

"All right son, but I'll go with you. I'll find someone to watch Hal and Henry."

After walking about a half-mile, Annie recognized the Methodist minister standing in front of a burnt-out farm house. There was a small, roughly built coffin beside him. The man glanced up and noticed Annie and Bobby. He called out and waved them over.

"I was asked to give the old grandmother a proper burial since the Catholic priest is still in Gold Creek. The problem is that this family also had a large dog - and the remains in this box are so unrecognizable, I'm not sure if they are the old woman or the dog!"

Annie and Bobby took part in the brief and solemn ceremony. The man bowed his head for several minutes in prayer then looked up and smiled at Annie.

"Well, if it was the grandmother," he said, "she had a decent funeral service. And if it was the dog, he had a damned good one!"

Annie glanced down to hide her smile, but not before she saw Bobby cover his with his hand.

When they finally reached their property, Bobby spent an hour roaming and calling for the dog. Annie could see how upset he was, and she coaxed him to walk with her to the junction to see Jim. As they arrived at the station, she saw the troops working around their temporary headquarters. They soon spotted Jim.

Bobby ran to his father. "I've looked and looked for Mike but can't find h-him anywhere." His voice faltered. "He... he must have died in the fire."

Jim put his arm around his son's shoulders to comfort him. "I miss Mike too. He was my best pal when you were still back in Shields. We have to count our blessings, though, because you and your brothers and your mother survived."

Bobby told his father about the strange funeral service that the Methodist minister had had them witness.

"I don't know what's funnier," Jim said with a laugh, "a grand funeral service for a dog or the minister swearing!"

When Annie and Bobby got back to town, they found Jack and Georgie in their tent. She sent the older boys to get Hal and the baby from the neighbour in the next tent. While they were gone, she and Georgie walked to a large supply tent to sort through donated clothing. Annie found an assortment for the children, even new underwear donated by stores in the south.

That night, while Hal and Henry were asleep in the tent in a nest of blankets, and the older boys were playing outside, Annie folded and sorted clothing. She heard Jim talking to Bobby before he came in. She looked up when he entered, a broad smile plastered on his face.

"I have my three-day leave and the tickets for us to travel to Toronto."

"Thank God," said Annie with a sigh. "I'll be glad to escape this devastation."

"I ran into Pierre today. He said they're leaving for good and going back to Quebec. Marie wants to be near her family. With the loss of Louis, I can hardly blame them."

"I understand, too, but I'll miss them," said Annie. "They were such good neighbours."

"Well, you'll be happy living with Alfie for a while. I have other news, though. There's an acre of land on the limits of Bear Falls. I think it'll be perfect for us."

"How did you ever find such a piece of land so quickly?"

"The owners are anxious to return to Ottawa, where they lived before. We can buy the property for a pittance and although the house has burned to the ground, the concrete basement survived the fire!"

Annie frowned. "But you have to return to Camp Borden - how can we possibly rebuild any time soon?"

"I've got it all figured out. I should be able to apply for a leave of absence. The troop ship doesn't leave until October. The commander is a local man and these are extraordinary circumstances. I'll arrange for some carpenters to help me with the construction while you and the boys stay with Alfie."

Annie was reminded that Jim would soon leave for Europe and she would be on her own again. She was frightened for herself and for him. She read the casualty lists in the newspaper regularly. Many men, she knew, never returned home.

Chapter Thirty-Six

The family approached the station platform at Jackpine Junction. Before boarding, they had to walk past the special government train car. They could see through the open door that it was luxurious, with expensive wood panelling and rich upholstered furniture. Annie was shocked at the arrogance of these privileged government men. Imagine flaunting ostentatious accommodation in the face of such loss and devastation, while the survivors lived in army-issue tents.

Jim shook his head in disgust. "The Lands and Forests minister said he couldn't understand how there could have been such a huge loss of life when there were so many lakes and rivers in the North to escape to. What a pompous ass!"

Annie shushed him because the windows and doors were open in the government car, but Jim grumbled, "I don't care if they hear me."

They boarded the train with many other families who were leaving New Ontario. The whole family had to share one bench, and the children were unusually quiet. Annie knew they were sad, but she didn't have the energy to comfort them.

As the train chugged south, she stared out the window. Some areas were still smouldering. Framed buildings that had been homes and barns were now reduced to rubble. They passed mile after mile of devastation before she finally spied green forests again.

After almost eight hours on the train, they finally arrived at Union Station. At least this ride had been quicker than their first ride north.

Carrying only fire survivors, it had not made the usual stops. Stepping onto the platform, Annie easily spotted her tall brother in the crowds. There was an attractive young woman beside him.

Alfie looked relieved as he gave Annie a tight hug and shook Jim's hand.

"God, I'm so grateful that you and the children survived! What a dreadful experience! We were so worried." He took his companion's hand in his, and beamed. "Annie, Jim, meet my beautiful wife, Catherine."

Catherine hugged Annie and warmly shook Jim's hand. "I'm sorry that you suffered such a horrid experience in that fire, but I'm so pleased that you will stay with us for a while."

Annie welcomed Catherine into the family, and introduced the children to their new aunt.

"What lovely children you have." Gesturing to her stomach she added, "You've likely noticed that Alfie and I are expecting our first child. I'm eager to have my own babies. May I hold Henry?" Annie passed the baby to her. "He's just two months old, isn't he? What a poppet. Ah, and Georgie does look like your brother George. He's a fortunate boy."

Jim slung their small bag over a shoulder and picked up Hal. They walked a short distance and climbed aboard a city streetcar. Alfie paid for their tickets before Jim could object, and they found enough seats for everyone at the back. After a brief ride, they disembarked and followed Alfie and Catherine down a city block, stopping at a handsome two-storey red-brick house. Annie admired the heavy, oak front door and the decorative stained-glass panel above it. They followed Alfie up the entrance stairs and he fumbled with some keys. He unlocked the door, entered, and flicked a switch, illuminating the inside of the home.

Inside the large foyer was an ornate hardwood staircase leading up to the second floor. To Annie's left, frosted-glass doors opened to a formal parlour, and to the right was a dining room furnished with heavy walnut furniture. There was an ornate crystal chandelier hanging over the table. *My brother must have married into a bit of wealth to have such a lovely home*, Annie mused. She was torn between envy and happiness for her brother's good fortune.

Catherine took Annie's hand and led her up the stairs. There were three doors on the second floor and they entered the first. It was a spacious bedroom with a double bed on one side, a mattress on the floor by another wall, and two canvas cots leaning against a tall mahogany wardrobe. On the double bed, Catherine had placed new nightshirts for each of the boys and a lovely nightgown with lace at the collar and wrists for Annie. Catherine apologized that the family had to share a bedroom but suggested that Henry could perhaps sleep in the master bedroom as she already had a crib set up there.

She then showed Annie the third bedroom that she and Alfie had converted into a bathroom. There was a huge claw-footed ceramic tub and, beside it, a large hot water tank. Annie was speechless.

One arm around Annie, Catherine reached up to a shelf and brought down a small package. "Rumour has it that you have a particular fondness for lilac soap."

Annie's eyes stung with tears as she thanked her host, and she joked, "My brother shouldn't tell all of my secrets."

After dinner, Annie bathed Henry. It had been a week since they all had a proper wash. She lay the sleepy baby down in the crib in Alfie and Catherine's bedroom. Then she bathed a squirming Hal, put him in his new night shirt and tucked him into the improvised mattress bed on the floor. To her surprise, Hal had fallen into a deep sleep within minutes. Georgie, Jack and Bobby each had their turns for much-needed baths. Georgie would share the mattress with Hal, and Bobby and Jack would each have their own cot. In less than an hour, all five children were sound asleep.

Annie scrubbed the tub clean and had a luxurious soak herself, day-dreaming about having her own bathroom in their new house.

That night, while lying in the double bed beside Jim, Annie listened to the children breathing softly in a sleep more contented than they'd enjoyed in months. Hal was nestled against Georgie, and noisily sucking his thumb. She had nursed Henry before she went to bed, and he had dropped off again in a satisfied slumber in Catherine's crib. With luck, she thought, he'll sleep through the night.

"I'm so tired, but I don't want to fall asleep," she said, feeling tears well up. "This time with you is a gift. I wish you didn't have to go so soon."

Jim stroked Annie's cheek, wiping away her tears with his thumb. "I'll come back to you. I promise. Remember, they keep saying that this war will be a short one. When I return, I'll find you a massive hot water tank and buy you a bar of lilac soap for every day of the year!"

Annie laughed and said, "I don't need things, Jim. Just come back to us."

Jim wrapped his arms around her but he soon fell into a deep, exhausted sleep. Annie remained awake, thinking how she felt whole when she was with him. The bedroom window was open to catch the cooler night air, and Catherine's crisp, white lace curtains fluttered in the breeze. Annie could hear the sounds of automobiles and of horseshoes striking pavement on the still-busy street below. City lights filtered into the bedroom, and she could just make out the forms of her sleeping, exhausted children.

Chapter Thirty-Seven

The next day at breakfast, Catherine leaned over and lightly touched the rough khaki of Jim's military jacket.

"Why don't you and Annie take the day for yourselves and I'll watch the boys. There's a lovely public park a short walk away, and I could pack a picnic lunch for the children."

Jim smiled. "That's a grand idea. Annie and I do have to shop for winter clothing for the bairns before I take the train back north tomorrow morning."

"Thank you, Catherine," Annie added. "I'll make up a bottle of goat's milk for the baby to tide him over until we get back."

Catherine insisted on taking Annie up to her own bedroom after breakfast. She skilfully arranged Annie's hair in a complicated bun, and lent her an attractive summer outfit in mauve. She even applied a little colour to Annie's lips and cheeks.

"You look absolutely beautiful. Who would believe that you're in your thirties, and the mother of five boys? I hope after the baby's born I can get my figure back as quickly as you did."

Annie blushed and kissed Catherine's cheek. "I've always wanted a sister and now I have a lovely one!"

As Annie came down the stairs, Jim stared at her with his mouth agape, and Alfie gave her an admiring whistle. Annie felt her face grow warm. Taking Jim's offered hand, she felt like a young woman once again, being courted by a gentleman.

While strolling downtown, Annie noticed that they received admiring glances from other pedestrians. She thought Jim looked very handsome in his uniform. Tucking her arm through his, she rested her head affectionately on his shoulder.

"It's unbelievable how normal life is here. People continue to work, laugh and shop when there's so much devastation and chaos to the north? It's hard to believe this is the same province, even the same country."

Jim looked at her. "It will be good for you and the boys to be here with Alfie and Catherine. You can forget about the North for a while, and the boys will get over their nightmares."

"What a blessing that they all had such a long, uninterrupted rest last night. I think it'll take some time before every night is like that."

"I must say, though, your brother landed on his feet when he married Catherine. There has to be some wealth in her family. That's quite the house."

"I was thinking the same," Annie laughed. "Catherine is a lovely woman inside and out. I'm so happy for Alfie. She'll soon discover how good a father he will be, too. Our boys adore him."

They walked to the Eaton's store to use their clothing vouchers; they needed to buy the boys new winter coats. Annie and Jim were in different areas in the store when Annie went to a counter to buy the clothing she had chosen. As she handed the clerk the coupons, he looked her up and down critically.

"Look sister, these vouchers are for those poor folks from the fire up north. I don't know where you got these but you won't pull a fast one on me."

Annie fumed with indignation. She knew her face must be bright red with her anger, but she didn't care. Furious, she pulled up her sleeves to reveal her burned arms.

"Where do you think I got these burns, for heaven's sake? We've lost everything. *Everything!* I have five boys to clothe for the winter and I certainly don't need to be harassed by someone who was hundreds of miles away from that fire!"

Shock registered on the clerk's face and he apologized quickly. What Annie really wanted to do was walk away, but she needed those coats. Looking down at her arms, she saw what an awful mess they looked at this stage of healing. She quickly pulled down her sleeves.

Picking up her purchases and walking away with her head in the air, she found Jim, and handed him some of the parcels to carry. She told him about her encounter with the clerk. He turned as if prepared to confront the offensive man, but she tugged him back.

"I took care of it. I've learned to choose my battles but I decided to fight that one. It's done." She smiled and changed the subject. "I have a grand idea. Let's get our portraits done on the photography floor, so we will each have a recent photo when you're overseas. You know, my greatest loss in the fire was our photos, and especially the ones of you and Maggie."

Jim shook his head sadly. "I never thought of Maggie's photos. But Ma and your mother have some pictures of her back home. We can get copies made in England and have them mailed to us." He thought for a moment. "Yes, let's get those photos taken."

Annie's spirits were lifted and minutes later, her smile was captured in the photographer's flash. They arranged to have the photos sent to Bear Falls.

They decided to have lunch at a corner restaurant that turned out to be frequented by soldiers, returned from France and Belgium. They saw men in uniform, on crutches, some with missing limbs, others bandaged or with burn scars.

"There is little difference between the casualties of the war and the fire up north. It's almost as if we left a battlefield ourselves!"

"Aye," said Jim, "I think we did. But that fire was an act of nature, not man."

Some of the other soldiers came over and asked when Jim would be shipped overseas. He explained that he'd be going over in a couple of months. He also told them about the fire, and how fortunate his wife and five children had been to survive.

When the men heard their story, they decided to pass a hat around in a collection for Annie and the children. Annie was again overwhelmed at how kind strangers could be in times of crisis.

Their day together ended too soon, and as they approached Alfie and Catherine's home, Annie stopped. Before they entered the house, she leaned into Jim's arms and kissed him.

"This day has been such a blessing. I enjoyed having you all to myself. I'll have to thank Catherine."

"Aye, it's been a gift. I'm a lucky man."

That month in Toronto was a healing balm for the children. Their nightmares came less often, and Annie was thankful they were able to experience a carefree summer.

Within two weeks of leaving, Jim wrote to say that he had bought the property on the town limits, and had received permission for a two-week leave to work on rebuilding the house. Unfortunately, all the experienced carpenters were busy on other rebuilding projects, but he managed to hire a couple of men to help him. They had cleaned up the concrete foundation of the house and built a floor over it to keep out the elements. He had the lumber to begin framing and would try to get the walls up and the roof on soon. His leave to complete the house would be in late September or early October.

Poor Jim, Annie thought. *He's been so busy, and then he'll soon be shipped out with the army.* She hated to impose on her brother and sister-in-law for another month, but they insisted that they were happy to have them. For Annie's part, she loved having the company of another woman, and she and Catherine were becoming close friends. They often took the streetcar together to an open market and bought whatever fruits or vegetables were in season.

One day, when Alfie returned home from work, Annie and Catherine were busy in the kitchen, their hair wrapped in bright silk scarves. The air was thick with the sweet aroma of peach preserves.

He laughed, "You two have enough preserves here for an army!"

The kitchen was moist with steam, and every flat surface was covered with colourful jars. Catherine's face was scarlet from the heat and Annie supposed her face must be too. She looked up at her brother and wiggled her sticky fingers, threatening to hug him. Alfie carefully kissed Catherine's cheek, then backed out of the kitchen with his arms up in surrender. The women looked at each other and laughed.

By mid-October, Annie was preparing for the return north. She often imagined their new home. She dreamed of a proper bathroom with plenty of hot water, and bedrooms upstairs for the boys. They would have electricity and maybe even a telephone. She knew that property near railway tracks was not valuable, but to her it was an insurance policy. She didn't have to explain that to Jim; he understood.

After she and the children returned to the North, Jim would be crossing the Atlantic to fight in the war. Her heart sank as she thought of the mortal danger he would soon be in. *Will he come back to me alive and unbroken?*

Chapter Thirty-Eight

It was bittersweet parting when Annie and the children left Alfie and Catherine. Alfie had hired a car to take them all to Union Station, and they waited together until it was time for Annie and the boys to board the train.

He hugged Annie, and then looked at Catherine.

"We've decided that if we have a girl, we will name her Anna, after her auntie," Catherine announced.

Annie blushed and hugged her sister-in-law, thanking her over and over again for her hospitality. The boys were very quiet, and Annie knew that her three oldest probably feared returning home, thinking of the horrors they had witnessed up north. But they smiled when their uncle handed Bobby a paper bag of sweets to share with his brothers.

They boarded, and waved at Alfie and Catherine as the train pulled out of the station.

At North Bay, the halfway point of their trip, Annie splurged on a purchased lunch for the children; she was positive there would be few treats for them for a very long time. She laughed as she watched them eagerly open their lunches. Inside each box was a chicken sandwich, an apple, a jar of lemonade and a biscuit. Her boys were in heaven.

The Jackpine Junction station had been rebuilt over the summer. The weather was noticeably cooler than in Toronto, but this time she was prepared. She pulled warm sweaters from a bag for the children and herself. Looking around, she thought how odd it was to expect to see the bright colours of autumn, and instead to see only blackened stumps all around.

As Annie placed their last piece of luggage on the wooden platform, she saw Jim coming toward them. He looked thinner, and worry lines had deepened across his forehead, but his greeting was jovial.

"Welcome home! I've borrowed a car to take us to our new property. Here, Bobby, Jack, help me load the luggage into the car."

Annie was relieved to see smiles on the older boys' faces as they anticipated a car ride. The road to Bear Falls was rough, but the boys bounced along, giggling at every bump and pothole.

When they pulled up to their new home, Annie was shocked. There was only bare framing and an unfinished roof. An army-issue tent was pitched beside the skeleton of a house.

"I'm sorry Annie," said Jim. "It was impossible to hire enough carpenters with so much construction going on in town. I've only been able to work on the house on my free evenings, with a little help from some friends. I'll finish as much as I can on my leave. It won't take long to put up the walls and roof and I've hired two men to help me."

Annie was sorely disappointed. The house was not even close to being finished. But she remained quiet, determined to hide her disappointment. Jim had tried his best, and he already had enough stress without her adding to it.

Jim bowed gallantly and, with gentlemanly airs and a smile, he offered his arm to her.

"Come, madam, and I'll give you the grand tour."

They climbed the roughly built steps to the entrance, and Jim swept his arm around to show how large the kitchen would be. "I've ordered a large cook stove to place against this wall, and over here there will be a stairway leading up to three bedrooms. This room at the back of the kitchen will be your bathroom, with - just as I promised - the biggest hot water tank in the North."

He led Annie through a large doorway. "You'll have a proper dining room here, and that room at the back will be our parlour."

"I can picture how lovely it will be, Jim. It's so much larger than any other place we've lived. Imagine!"

Bobby and Jack carried their luggage to the cellar of the house. Jim had built a trap door in the floor, and set up a ladder to reach the basement. When all their bags and boxes were stored, Annie went back outside and peeked inside the tent. Jim had laid several rough army blankets on the floor to fashion beds. She couldn't help but compare this accommodation to what they had become accustomed to in her brother's house. She wiped away a tear, and scolded herself for becoming so soft.

Standing outside, she looked around their barren yard. Autumn had arrived in the North and the brisk evening breeze promised an early frost. She wrapped her arms around herself and took a deep breath of the cool fresh air.

"I'd forgotten how pure and clean the air is here. The air in Toronto always smells of exhaust and too many people."

Jim raised an eyebrow doubtfully, and Annie grinned.

"Don't worry. I haven't turned back into a soft city girl yet." She paused. "I love how you've planned and laid out the house. You've thought of everything."

"Love, you can't fool me. I know you're disappointed that the house isn't yet finished. I'm sorry. I promise we'll only have to spend a couple of nights in the tent."

"We'll be fine, Jim." And she was really starting to believe that they would. "I'll help you. I'll have Georgie watch Hal and Henry and I'll work beside you and Bobby and Jack."

"It's getting dark. We may as well make an early night of it and get up early tomorrow morning. I'm going to teach Bobby and Jack some carpentry skills."

Inside the tent, Annie arranged a bed of blankets for her two youngest and they fell into an exhausted sleep. The three older boys soon fell asleep, too. That night the temperature dipped to freezing, but the family, sleeping so closely together, managed to stay warm.

When Annie and the children woke up in the morning there was frost on the ground. A welcome scent of coffee filtered into the tent. She peeked through the flap. Jim was standing by a campfire with a metal rack over it. He had a coffee pot bubbling and a pot of oatmeal porridge cooking. He was holding a wire fork over the fire, toasting bread and whistling a tune.

"Good morning!" Jim called. "It's time to rise and shine, boys. Come and get your breakfast."

Annie went back into the tent, and said "Bobby, take Hal out and make sure he eats. Jack and Georgie, you go get your breakfast while I nurse Henry. After you eat, Georgie, I'll need you to take care of Hal and Henry. Listen boys, you will do whatever your father asks. He needs your help." She was afraid they might grumble to Jim after having had such an easy time living with their uncle and aunt.

The children reluctantly climbed out of the tent into the cold morning air. Annie could hear Jim talking to Bobby and Jack about his work plans for the day. She was determined to help Jim too, but would have to take several breaks from the physical labour as five-month-old Henry still needed to nurse.

Within a couple of hours, Jim had Bobby and Jack working as hard as grown men. Annie was proud that her two eldest boys kept up to Jim's demands without complaint. She joined them when she could, hammering and hoisting beside Jim with such ease that he said, "I didn't know you were such a carpenter. You've been hiding special talents from me!"

Annie laughed and replied, "I didn't know either. I guess watching Pappa and my brothers build things stayed with me."

The two hired men soon arrived and the building progressed more rapidly in the days that followed. By the end of the first week, they had all of the walls up, the roof on and windows and doors installed. At least the house was now enclosed. After that, they were able to sleep inside the house, but still often woke up with their blankets stiffened with frost.

Finally, in the second week of Jim's leave, one of the wood stoves arrived by horse and wagon. The driver apologized for the delay.

"Sorry folks, these stoves have been on backorder for a while. Everyone in the North needs to replace stoves that were lost in the fire. Your larger cook stove will be in stock in a month or so I'll deliver it free for you then." The men quickly installed the stove, chimney and venting and soon had it warming the house. Jim had also ordered insulation made of oakum – twisted hemp fibre – which would be delivered in a few days, too.

In the middle of the week, they experienced the winter's first snowfall. The stove had arrived not a moment too soon.

As Jim's second week came to an end, it became apparent that he would not be able to complete their house. He worked frantically into the third week, fully knowing that he was AWOL, but determined to finish.

On the Wednesday of the third week, a soldier drove up from the base to tell Jim that if he did not report immediately, the army would send the military police. Jim asked the man to give him a minute with his wife.

He took Annie in his arms and in a hoarse voice said, "I knew that I was gambling for time. I'm so sorry. I have no choice now. We have enough money to pay to finish the house but I hate to leave you and the boys with winter coming on."

Annie wiped away her tears. "We'll be fine. Just take care of yourself." She knew from other army wives that most letters were censored by regiment officers, and that Jim wouldn't be able to tell her where he was. He had reassured her, though, that the men were issued special green envelopes once a week whose contents would not be censored by the officers, although they might be opened at general headquarters. He could write to her more personally then. "Write often," she pleaded. "I've lived through a hell here and survived, so don't sugar-coat anything for me. I need to know what's happening. I need to feel close to you."

"I'll write as soon as I get to the camp," said Jim. "If worse comes to worst, I'm sure you can go to Alfie's again."

She put her arms around him and buried her face in his shirt, inhaling his familiar scent. When she raised her head, Jim kissed her, and then pulled back to look deeply into her eyes. He told her he loved her.

He spent just a few minutes packing a bag. Outside again, he called the boys and gave each of them a hug. After kissing Annie one last time, he reluctantly got into the soldier's car and left for Camp Borden.

Bobby and Jack sobbed quietly beside her, and the younger boys clung to her skirt, bawling. Annie knew that Jim was despondent, and so was she. In fact she felt utterly abandoned. But she had to be strong. She was the sole parent responsible for five children. "Come inside, boys." Eyes welling with tears, she turned and walked slowly back to their unfinished shell of a house. The inevitable, unforgiving northern winter was quickly approaching, and they had so little protection. She shook her head and sadly wondered what was to become of them.

Chapter Thirty-Nine

After two miserable days worrying about their situation, Annie decided to swallow her pride and bring her situation to the attention of the local carpenters' union. The next Sunday afternoon, she and all five children arrived at the home of the union president. She had rehearsed in her head what she was going to say. As soon as the man answered her knock she blurted out her speech, telling him about losing their previous home and possessions in the fire, and Jim shipping out, and the house unfinished, and being alone with five children.

"I realize that the carpenters are very busy with rebuilding," she concluded breathlessly, "but I desperately need your men to help me finish my house before winter."

The man was silent for a minute, and Annie lifted her chin and stiffened her spine. She was determined not to cry if he should refuse her. Just as he was about to open his mouth, he was nudged aside by tall, thin woman.

"William, you should have invited Mrs. Kidd and her children inside. Come in to warm up and have some refreshments. Of course the local carpenters will help you, won't they, William? It's a sad world if we can't help the families of our enlisted men."

As Annie searched the man's face for signs that he might agree, his wife stepped forward and took Henry from her arms and hustled the rest of Annie's children into her kitchen, promising biscuits and milk. Finding herself alone with the man, she prepared to repeat her request, but he spoke first.

"Of course I will help you. I'll set up a work crew each day for a few hours after our regular hours during the week and rotate some men to work on Sundays." Annie barely dared to breathe. "I know your husband quite well. Jim's a good man and I'm happy to help his family."

He was true to his word. The next day, at a little after five o'clock, three carpenters arrived with the union foreman and walked around the house to assess what needed to be done. They had a short conversation outside, and soon Annie heard hammering. Each day after that, different men arrived shortly after their day shift and worked steadily for a couple of hours. On Sunday a larger work crew appeared, and by the second Sunday the exterior of the building was completed. Annie once again had her own home. It was unfurnished and hardly offered much protection from the winter freeze, but she owned it.

In Annie's first letter from Jim, he wrote that the commanding officer had torn a strip off him and said the infraction should go on his permanent record, which would mean that he would never get a promotion. But fortunately the same officer, being a man of the North too, seemed to understand Jim's reasons for not returning on time, and somehow Jim was back in the barracks as if he had never gone AWOL.

He ended his letter saying that his regiment would be going overseas within days.

In that first month after Jim left for Camp Borden, Annie and the children were uncomfortable in the house. The temperature often dipped below zero and the snow accumulated as winter settled in. The small wood-stove could not keep them warm, and Annie and the children often had to crack the frost on their blankets in the mornings when they woke up. The older boys were quite happy to go to school, which was being held in the town hall until a new school could be rebuilt. At school they could enjoy the warmth from the classroom wood stove and eat a hot lunch as well.

But Hal and baby Henry were cranky with earaches and runny noses. Annie desperately missed the food supply of her root cellar. She often had to rely on canned goods to feed the children. She heard that the local dairy cows were sick, so she switched to canned milk for the family's needs as well. She still had two wooden cases of the preserves she and Catherine had made over the summer. Each Sunday she opened a jar to treat the family. But still, she knew her boys were suffering from poor nutrition. They were often sick.

By mid-December the interior walls were insulated and the finished kitchen was now cozy with a large new stove. The carpenters had built her many generously sized cupboards for storage, along with a wooden table and benches.

One late afternoon as she sat in the kitchen, enjoying the warmth of the kitchen fire, Annie realized that, somewhere along the way, the heavy burden of worry and despair that she'd been carrying for months had been lifted. The baby was asleep in her arms, contentedly sucking his thumb, and Hal was playing quietly on the rug near the stove. Thankfully both children had recovered from their earaches and colds.

She glanced through the doorway to the right, towards the empty dining room and parlour. She knew that it would be a long time before she could afford to purchase anything for those rooms, but it didn't matter. She had swallowed her dignity and asked for help, and now she once again owned her home.

But still she pined for Jim. She prayed that he would stay safe and come back to her.

Chapter Forty

Annie fretted over how she would make her meagre funds stretch to the end of December. Christmas would come, and there was no way she could afford gifts or even a special meal for the children. Then she had an idea. She knew that the boys were still mourning the loss of their dog, so impulsively decided that she would find a puppy for them. That would be their Christmas gift. It couldn't cost much to feed, she reasoned. They could give him table scraps. She would find a small dog, one that wouldn't need to eat much.

The next day, when she picked up the mail with Hal and Henry, she asked the postmistress if she knew of any puppies available.

"Why, yes, I do, as a matter of fact. My friend Bertha has a spaniel that had a litter of pups about a month ago. I'm sure that she'd be happy to give you one. Her dog has a sweet, gentle nature. I'm afraid that the puppies are likely a mixed breed though." She continued chattering, unaware that Annie was moving to leave. "You know Bertha, don't you? She lives just one street over, in the blue stucco house with a green front door. You can't miss it. I'm sure the old gal is colour blind. Ha! Ha! Tell Bertha I'll be over to visit her on Sunday when you see her."

Annie thanked the woman, relieved to end the one-sided conversation, and decided to stroll over to Bertha's house to see the pups. A frail elderly woman opened the green door.

"Hello, are you Bertha?" Annie asked. The woman nodded and smiled. "I'm Annie Kidd, and these are my boys Hal and Henry. I heard that your dog recently had a litter. Are you trying to find homes for the pups? I'm looking for one for my children to replace the dog we lost in the fire."

"Come in, come in. I do have puppies and I'd be happy to give you one."

Annie kicked the snow off her boots and carried Hal and Henry inside. Bertha helped Hal with his hat and mittens, then took Henry so Annie could remove her boots. Hal clung to the bottom of his mother's coat as they followed the woman into her kitchen.

There was a large pine box by the cook stove and inside was a small black and white dog surrounded by four rambunctious balls of fur. Annie could see that the mother was gentle and patient, even with Hal's excited squeals as he tried to pet the puppies. She chose a tiny black pup, and cuddled his soft, warm little body against her neck.

"Ah, this little fellow is just perfect. I'd like to take him with us today, if that's all right."

"Of course dear, but I'm afraid that one is the runt and will likely remain small."

"That's why I chose him. Our last dog was the size of a small pony!" Bertha laughed, and Annie continued, "I can't thank you enough. I assure you that he will be well loved."

Bertha offered them tea, but Annie declined. "We have to be going, but feel free to stop by anytime to visit the pup." She said goodbye and tucked the puppy inside her coat for the walk home; she pulled Hal and Henry in a sleigh with her other hand.

The older boys were ecstatic. They argued over what to name him until Annie finally said, "Oh, let Hal choose a name."

The boys all looked doubtfully at Hal.

"Pick a good name, Hal, but it can't be Mike," prodded Georgie.

Hal thought very hard and then said, "Potato."

Bobby groaned and Jack and Georgie rolled onto the floor in fits of laughter. Annie saw Hal's eyes water, so quickly intervened.

"Potato is a good name, Hal, but what if we called him Spud. A spud is a potato." They all agreed and set about welcoming the newest member of the family.

Annie continued to worry over the lack of money; her separation allowance hadn't come in yet. She had given up hope that it would arrive in time for Christmas. Reluctantly she told the younger boys that Father Christmas couldn't come this year because there was too much snow. Shock registered on their faces and they began to whimper. She couldn't have felt worse. Later that afternoon, when she asked Bobby where Georgie was, he told her to look out the window. She walked over and looked out. Georgie was shovelling a path right down to the bare ground.

"Oh, no! That's for Father Christmas, isn't it?" Her voice broke. She sat heavily in a kitchen chair and covered her face with her hands.

Bobby came over and patted her back. "Don't worry, Mum. We can make something for them and say it's from Father Christmas. Besides, Spud is the best Christmas gift ever!"

Annie bundled up Hal and Henry almost every day and pulled them on a sleigh to the post office to check for mail and to drop off her letters to Jim. A few days before Christmas, there were a couple of parcels waiting for her. One package was quite large, so she had to place it on the sleigh beside Hal and make a sling from her scarf to carry Henry. Both packages came from Catherine and Alfred.

When they got home, she carried the two parcels to the empty dining room. Though it was hard to contain her curiosity, she waited until Hal and Henry had been fed and put to bed for their nap before she opened the packages. The large box, to her delight, contained a huge Christmas goose, ready for the oven. The second parcel contained English tea, a tin of toffee, homemade shortbread, and an assortment of colourful rubber balls, puzzles, children's books and brightly painted wood blocks. Tucked under the blocks, she found a bar of lilac soap. She hid the boxes in the cellar, thrilled to be able to give the boys a proper Christmas thanks to her brother and sister-in-law.

On Christmas Eve day, Bobby and Jack went out, saying they had a job to do, and took the sleigh with them. They returned several hours later, rosy-cheeked and cold, dragging an evergreen tree behind them.

"Wherever did you find a tree?" Annie laughed. "I didn't think there was a tree left standing for miles."

"A while ago I spotted some trees untouched by the fire, between the river and the bush road near the mill," Bobby replied, "Jack and I decided to keep it a secret so we could surprise you." The two boys shook the snow from the branches, pulled the tree inside and went to work setting it up in their unfurnished sitting room.

That night after dinner, they decorated the tree with homemade paper chains and pine cones. Jack and Georgie said they would look for more cones and berries the next day to add to it. Bobby made a barricade across the entrance to the dining room to keep curious little Spud out.

While the children were asleep that night, Annie sat quietly at the table and wrote a long letter to Jim, letting him know that his boys would have a proper Christmas. A wave of loneliness passed over her. The packages had reminded her of the time she had spent with Catherine and Alfie. She missed Catherine's company. Then she smiled, remembering that wonderful day she had spent with Jim in Toronto before he'd had to return to his company. She got up to place more wood in the stove for the night, and put a pot of water on a burner to make some tea.

She heard the click of Spud's claws as he came down the stairs. The puppy seemed to sense Annie's melancholic mood, and he licked her hand to comfort her, then settled at her feet. She reached down to pick up the little dog and nuzzled against his soft coat.

Chapter Forty-One

In the last days of December, the temperature plummeted to forty below. Annie and the children were stuck inside for several days. When she scratched at the frost covering the inside of her kitchen window and peered out, brilliant crystals twinkled in the high snow-banks, and the winter sun shone brightly in the pale, cloudless sky.

Feeling house-bound, she decided to walk to the post office to mail a small parcel to Jim. The school was closed for Christmas vacation, so she asked Bobby and Jack to watch their little brothers while she was out. She draped her coat, scarves and mitts over a chair in front of the stove to warm them for a few minutes, and she dressed while the boys were still at the kitchen table, eating their porridge. Henry was on a blanket on the kitchen floor, contentedly sucking his fingers as he watched his brothers.

A blast of frigid air rushed in when she cracked open the door and stepped outside. As she walked, the only sound was the crunch of her boots in the crusty snow. The air was still, and she marvelled at how the chimney smoke from nearby houses rose straight up to the sky, as if brushed with a stroke of white paint. *Winter doesn't seem such a hardship when the sun is shining*, she thought. She thought of the damp, grey, overcast winters back in England and smiled to herself, recalling how her mother used to send her brothers outside in the winter, saying "It's time to play outside and blow the stink off!" She took a deep breath of the frigid air and hurried her pace.

When she arrived at the post office, she was welcomed by the comforting smell of a wood fire crackling in the middle of the room. She stomped the snow from her boots, and walked up to the counter. The postmistress glanced up and greeted her warmly.

"Good morning," said Annie. "That certainly is a chilly morning outside, but it's quite cozy in here. Have you anything for me today?"

"Let me look. Ah, yes, here's some mail from overseas."

The woman handed her four letters. Annie thanked her, paid for her stamps, and then sat down on a wooden bench by a window. She eagerly opened the letter postmarked November twelfth, and read.

Dearest Annie,

It was smooth sailing for most of the voyage over, with only a few days of rough weather. I envy your saltwater blood. I still detest ships. There were a couple of days when almost everyone on the ship was seasick. We shipped out on October thirty-first and arrived in England on November eleventh. Training is very intensive but I feel strong and fit. I received your letter and appreciate the copy of your photo and the notes and drawings from our boys. Your picture reminds me of that wonderful day we had in Toronto. I will keep it in my Bible, in the pocket over my heart.

I wrote to Ma and received a couple of letters back saying everyone was well, except that she was a little concerned about your mother. Ma guessed that she must have moved, as there were new tenants in her place. I don't know if I will have a chance to take the train up to South Shields to check on her for you before we ship out.

I'm very thankful for the work the carpenters did to complete the house. I was sick with worry when I was forced to leave you and the bairns in a half-finished house with winter coming on.

Ma also said that she will hunt for her pictures of Maggie and get copies made for you, and mail them to Canada.

Take good care of yourself. They still say that this war won't last long, and I sincerely hope that I will be home to spend Christmas next year with you and our boys.

Love, Jim

Annie folded the letter and replaced it in its envelope, then put all the letters into her pocket. She was puzzled about why Mother had moved and wondered how she would find out where she was living.

When she returned home and stepped into her kitchen, Bobby called out, "I'm going to do my paper route now, Ma. I washed the dishes and changed Henry's nappy." He grinned at her. "Don't worry, I washed the dishes first!"

Annie chuckled as she removed her boots. "Thank you, son. Oh, if you have an extra newspaper, can you bring it home?"

Bobby nodded, dressed in several layers and quickly disappeared out the door. Annie sat down at the table with her letters, able to read quietly before the babies woke up from their nap. She put them away when Jack and Georgie came in from outside, their cheeks bright red and noses running.

Georgie was bubbling with excitement. "We played on the snow horse Bobby built us. We had fun, Mummy, but we had to come in 'cause we got so cold."

When Bobby came back, Jack and Georgie were still sitting at the table sipping their tea. "I'm back," he called out in his recently acquired deep voice. "I see you've put a scarf on your snow horse, Georgie. Maybe we should build a friend for him! Here's the paper, Ma."

Annie took the newspaper and quickly browsed the front page. The headline declared a Russo-Rumanian offensive on a one-hundred-and-eighty-six-mile front. However, more interesting to her was an article about the Governor General, the Duke of Devonshire, reviewing Canada's citizen army at Exhibition Camp in Toronto.

"Listen to this, Bobby. The Governor General told the troops from Toronto that they would get their chance in Flanders. That means your father will be fighting in France or Belgium. If we follow the newspaper reports, we might be able to trace where your Da will be."

When Bobby kneeled to remove his boots, she discreetly turned the page to read the casualty roll. She wanted proof that Jim had not been injured or killed, even though she was certain he was still training in England.

"People are acting very strange in town now," Bobby said as he hung up his coat. "Some men are swearing at other men, calling them enemies, men they worked beside for years. They read the paper about the war, and you can see it gets their blood boiling. A lot of foreigners have left town since the fire, but more are leaving town now. Some men even pick on the Chinese workers and call them enemy aliens. Even I know that China is not an enemy to Canada or Britain!"

Annie sighed. "Ah, Bobby, there are many bullies in this world and it's probably easy for them to pick on men who are smaller or look different to them. This war is bringing out the best and the worst in people."

Early in March, Annie received a letter from Jim confirming that he was now somewhere in France. He was transferred out of his battalion on January thirtieth, and then transferred once again because of his experience with the railway company. The Railway Corps would leave England on February twenty-fourth, so he would be in the field by the time she received this letter. He wrote that he still kept her photo in the pages of his Bible, which he carried in his left breast pocket over his heart.

He's on the front now! She felt both dread and fear for him. *Lord, keep Jim safe.*

That same month, Annie also received a thick letter from her brother George. When she had a quiet moment, she opened the envelope and sat down at her kitchen table to read.

February 10, 1917 HQ, Cameron Highlander Barracks, Inverness, Scotland
Dear Sister,
I now take the pleasure of writing you these few lines hoping they find you and the children in the best of health. Well, Annie, I expect that you would have had a surprise when you found out that I was in the army. All I can tell you is that it wasn't my blame that I got

discharged out of the Navy as it was the last thing I was thinking about. It was through the drink as usual. We were getting our stores aboard the ship and a case of whiskey broke open on the deck. There was nobody in charge of us at the time so we got drunk and you can guess the rest. I got it for being an uninvited guest to the Captain's whiskey. Annie, I can tell you that I am sorry I got a discharge but I knew what would happen if I took any of that stuff. Now that I am in the army I am going to see this war to the end and if I am spared to come out of it all right I am coming to New Ontario again and I am going to bring Elizabeth with me. I will let her stay with you while I go up to the gold mines again, and will send for her when I get everything fixed up.

I am sorry to give you this news. Mother was forced out of her home for lack of rent money. They were going to send her to the poor house. When they discovered she was Norwegian and nearly blind, they deported her back to Bergen! I blame our brothers as they could have looked after her. They never even wrote and told me about it so I didn't find out until two months after. When I was on leave I couldn't help her. I didn't have any money at the time. While I was down there I could have killed Jack, but he kept out of sight. The first chance I get I will have Mother live with us. Dear sister, I haven't much more to say at present so I will close.

Your loving brother, George

P.S. You might let me have Jim's address and tell me what regiment he is in, so I can drop him a few lines. Can you also send him my address as soon as you get this letter? Best respects to the children.

Annie placed George's letter on the table, and buried her face in her hands. Both Jim and George were risking their lives in this war and now her mother had been deported to Norway. She was angry that her brothers had not helped their mother and was sick with helplessness.

She stood up and paced the room as she tried to think of what to do. How could she possibly find her mother? War was going on in Europe and she was isolated in Canada's north. *Norway may as well be the moon*, she thought. She decided to write to her brothers and tell them that they needed to find their mother and bring her to Canada as soon as possible.

By the time she had written to Jim, George and her other brothers, it was seven o'clock and she hadn't fed the children their supper. She had been lost in her fury of letter writing, and realized afterwards that her children had known she was upset and were quietly playing with the puppy in the empty sitting room. She gathered her letters and placed them on a shelf, then set to work to prepare a quick meal.

Quite often, Annie would read the newspaper in the evening when her boys were asleep. The papers hinted at the conditions in France. She read of violent hand-to-hand fighting and frightful losses inflicted on the enemy. But for all the news she read, there wasn't nearly enough information given to account for all the Canadian casualties listed each day. She knew a lot of what went on overseas was going unreported. Sometimes there were reports of battles involving Canadian troops, so she had an idea where Jim was. To reassure herself that Jim was uninjured and alive, she forced herself to search the daily lists of casualties and deaths.

Every evening that she did not find his name on the casualty lists, she was reasonably sure that Jim was still alive, and hopefully unharmed. *For now.*

PART THREE

Chapter Forty-Two

The Western Front

A bitter wind, sharp as a razor, threw icy pellets against the shivering men. Jim drew his great coat closer to his chest when freezing rain drops slid down his helmet and down his back. He had only been in France for two weeks but was already immersed in an unimaginable hell. The glutinous trench mud had hardened slightly with the frost. Fluffy white snowflakes drifted down only to melt quickly in the muck. Jim and seven other men had arrived to replace those injured or killed in a recent offensive. The fields around them were littered with corpses and decomposing body parts; the dead left to decompose where they fell. Those still alive were forced to live like the rats that shared their accommodation in the dugouts. The soldiers ate, slept and defecated in the narrow trenches, open to the elements. The stench of putrefaction and human waste was only slightly alleviated by the colder weather.

"Here mate, this will warm your insides." Sam, a friendly man in his unit, passed Jim his rum ration. "I heard that we're waiting for the wind to change direction so we can launch gas canisters at the Boche before our assault."

Sam sat down near Jim and continued, taking a sip from his own rum. "This is the third postponement, for God's sake! It's hard on the nerves. Nice accommodation, though, eh?"

Jim shook his head. "It's a palace, Sam. There's nothing but mud in your food, mud in your rum, mud in your rifle, mud for a pillow."

Sam added, "Pure luxury! They're saying there's no plan to build us more permanent defences since the brass thinks the war will be over soon. Of course, they're miles away, all warm and cozy and dry by a fire sipping single malt!" He shook his head in disgust.

"Where're you from, Jim? You have a bit of an English accent, but you wear the Canadian uniform."

"I am English, but I moved to New Ontario in 1911." When Sam removed his helmet, Jim saw that he was freckled and red haired. "You look like you just got off the boat from Ireland, but you sound like a Canadian."

"Yeah, my family came to Canada half a century ago, after the potato famine. Say, you must have been in that horrible forest fire up north last summer!"

"No, I was at Camp Borden with the army. My wife and five children survived the fire, though, thank God. I came up with the army in a disaster relief train and when I got there, I didn't know if they were alive. It was a vision of hell, I thought, until I came here." Jim took another sip of his rum. "I expected that after seeing all that death and destruction up north, I'd be prepared for sights on the battlefield, but there is no comparison. At least those poor souls back home had their bodies treated with dignity." He tilted his head towards the carnage on the fields around them.

Nodding grimly, Sam said, "It's a blessing that your family survived the fire, Jim." He changed the subject to a less sombre one. "Well, we Canadians have the advantage in this colder weather. Winter in France is tropical when you remember how bloody cold our winters can be, though, granted, this wet cold goes right into your bones. I had a job as a lumberjack up north one year. Made good money, too, but I recall many days when the thermometer dipped to forty below. And then it could be hot as hell in the summer while you got eaten alive by bugs." Sam paused, "Hey, I know how I can make my fortune and win this war. We just need to bombard the Boche with blackflies!" He grinned and took another sip of rum.

Jim chuckled, then spread out his ground cape and sat down on it. "Guess I'll write a letter to my wife now, before we get the order to go over. Keep safe, Sam."

He sat down, took out his Bible, removed Annie's portrait and stared at it for a long time before beginning to write.

Dearest Annie,

I'm looking at your picture as I write this letter. I hope you and the bairns are well. I am unharmed and plan to remain that way. You may have read in the paper of the gas attacks we encountered but dinna fash, we have been issued masks. I heard that they finally handed out underwear for the poor Jocks fighting in kilts. They were getting nasty blisters in some tender areas from the gas attacks. I continue to suffer from headaches, but have all my limbs so I should not complain. The weather is colder now, although I know it's nothing compared to the winter that you're having. I dream often of a good hot cup of English tea beside our warm fire at home. The tea here is often cold by the time we get it, and it tastes vile.

Jim stopped writing. He took another sip of his rum ration and then lit a cigarette. He offered a cigarette to Sam and said, "I never smoked before coming here, but smoking calms my nerves and helps me forget my throbbing headache for a minute or two. There is no escape from those constantly exploding shells."

Jim scratched an itchy spot in his armpit. Like every other soldier on the front, his uniform was infested with lice. As bad as the blackflies and mosquitoes were in New Ontario, at least you could smoke them out or slather your skin with something for protection. There was no escape from the lice here. They lived in the seams of the men's filthy clothing, especially in the crotch, seeking heat. The only way to exterminate them was to run the flame of a candle along the seams directly.

There was a strange crunching noise nearby and Jim looked towards the sound. Three enormous rats gnawed on the exposed human leg of a corpse that lay half-buried in the wall of the trench. Jim swore, and violently threw an empty tin at the rodents to scatter them.

"My God, we're living in a graveyard!"

Sam nodded as he inhaled the smoke from his own cigarette. "We keep trying to rebury those poor buggers, but the mud continues to vomit up more bodies!"

Jim sighed, picked up his pencil again and continued writing. He struggled for a minute to think of something positive to say to Annie, but then word came that they should prepare to advance within the hour, once the chlorine gas was released against the enemy. Jim tucked his letter into his Bible and replaced it in his breast pocket.

Finally, the wind had changed direction and was blowing towards the enemy lines. On the order, the men put on their gas masks and climbed out of the trench. They advanced crater to crater, avoiding the bloated bodies in the rust-coloured ice water. There was a loud explosion in front of Jim and he dropped to the ground just as another grenade hit the soldier beside him, blasting the man's body into a mess of blood, bone and flesh.

Jim heaved and brought up his last meal.

Sam came back to Jim and urged him to get moving, adding, "Man! That was a waste of your rum ration!"

Shells exploded all around as the troops inched towards the enemy, who were firing into the gas clouds. Several unexploded cylinders were penetrated with German bullets, releasing more noxious fumes. Gas crept slowly across the field, no higher than the bottom branches of a jack pine, Jim thought.

The troops' vision was severely restricted by the gas masks as they advanced, and shells continuously cascaded around and behind them. Suddenly Jim was tossed into the air like a rag doll then punched violently into the ground. He landed on his back near the lip of a water-filled crater. He lay still for several minutes, and then rolled to his side, dizzy with pain. He patted his Bible, and Annie's photo, in thanks, thenstood and ran to catch up to the other troops.

The enemy snipers were picking off stretcher bearers and runners so they were forced to pull back. When Jim and several other men reached a large shell hole, they scrambled down for protection from enemy fire. The gas had tarnished all the brass buttons on the men's tunics. Finally the wind redirected the gas clouds and they heard the signal that it was safe to remove their masks. Jim's face was ashen and his lips blue.

Sam crawled over to Jim and shouted hoarsely, "You okay, mate? I saw you thrown into the air. I thought you'd met your maker."

"Yeah, I'm okay. My ears are ringing and my head still throbs but I'm alive. I suppose we're relatively safe here. Let's hope another shell doesn't hit the same spot as the one that made this hole."

They received orders to stay where they were until further notice. Jim's rifle was mud-caked from his fall and he tried to clean it as he waited. Echoing around them were the groans and wails of wounded men, dying or drowning in water-filled craters. Sam and Jim looked at each other sadly as they listened to men screaming for help, cursing, even calling for their mothers.

A message finally came to them that they were to hold their position overnight, and until further notice. They had not eaten in over twelve hours and Jim had lost that meal at the beginning of the battle. But he had no appetite anyway. They stayed the night in the cold wet crater, but nobody could sleep surrounded by the sounds of dying men. The next morning, the men in the trench were finally relieved by new troops. One of their replacements told them they had lost over forty percent of their men in the battle.

Jim shook his head and said to Sam, "Well that's not hard to believe. I thought we had lost more. I'm amazed that I'm still alive!"

After an improvised meal of cold tea and a hard biscuit, Jim took out his Bible and gazed again at the photo of Annie. His hands were shaking with a new tremor, but he wanted to finish his letter. He took out his pencil.

I received a letter from George and was surprised to hear that he was in the army now. I will write to him soon. I'm sorry about your mother. George told me what happened to her. Don't fret, we'll bring her to us after the war. I regret that I have not told you often enough how much I love you. Take good care of yourself.

Love to you and the children,

Jim

Chapter Forty-Three

Spring, 1917

Annie knew Jim was keeping things from her. She worried about his shaky writing. When he wrote about continuing headaches, she imagined that they must be excruciating because it was not his nature to complain about pain. She had read in the newspaper about dead covering the ground as far as the eye could see, and she could only imagine what horrors he might be experiencing. She decided that she must write to him about everyday things so he could at least envision normal life back home with his family.

She wrote to him as if they were chatting over dinner. She told him about Henry's first tooth, when he first sat up and when he started to crawl. She joked that she hadn't taught Hal any more bad words and wrote how Spud was a joyful part of the family. She wrote about little purchases she had made for the house and about her dream of having electricity in the house. She told him how well the children were doing at school, and she had the boys write, draw, and scribble messages to him.

She made Jim's favourite shortbread, and bought him English tea, and she packaged them up with her letter and with the letters and drawings from the children. She knitted several pairs of socks so that he would have dry feet. She didn't know if he had any relief for his headaches, so she added a large bottle of Aspirin.

Hal slipped quietly into the house, cradling a squirming lump inside his top as he tried to sneak past her. Annie shook her head at his antics. "What are you hiding, Hal?" He sheepishly reached inside his shirt and pulled out a tiny bedraggled kitten. The buff and white ball of fur mewed weakly.

Red-faced, he stammered. "I, I f-found him in the wood shed. Can I keep him?"

Annie placed her hand on the kitten's head and laughed as it vibrated with a loud purr.

"Oh, I suppose this little scrap won't eat much, but you have to promise to take good care of it. Here, son, let's find an old saucer and feed the poor thing."

Hal beamed and before his mother could change her mind, he hastily blurted, "I'll take real good care of him. I promise. Thank you, Mummy."

True to his word, Hal made sure that the kitten was fed and let outside when needed. It followed Hal wherever he went, eventually claiming a spot in bed beside him every evening. Hal named him Lucky. *That's an apt name for the tiny stray*, Annie thought.

Two weeks later, while washing up the breakfast dishes, Annie was suddenly interrupted by Hal's hysterical screams. Spud frantically barked and jumped at the door. She ran out the door and Bobby and Spud followed close behind.

A huge German shepherd had Hal's kitten in his jaws and was shaking the life out of it. Bobby grabbed a shovel for a weapon and furiously lunged towards the big dog. Spud's hackles were raised and he growled but he stayed a safe distance from the much-larger animal.

"Get the hell out of here! Go home!" Bobby roared.

Annie ran to Hal and gathered the sobbing little boy into her arms as the dog dropped the lifeless kitten to the ground. It growled at Bobby, aggressively baring its teeth, but then scuttled away. Bobby threw down the shovel and swore under his breath.

"That bloody cur could have bitten Hal! I recognize it, though. It's Crazy Willy's dog."

"Crazy Willy?" asked Annie.

"He's that old prospector who lives in that shack up the line. Bring Hal inside, Ma. I'll take care of this." He gestured towards the dead kitten.

Bobby came into the house an hour later. His face was pale as chalk. He glanced around the kitchen, making sure that his younger brothers were not around.

"That man's insane! I brought the kitten to show him what his dog had done in our yard, and before I knew what was happening, he snatched what was left of poor Lucky, wrapped wire around his paws, and tied the dead cat around the dog's neck!" I got out of there as fast as I could. All I wanted was for him to keep his damned animal tied up and off our property!"

Annie was speechless. She had spent the last hour consoling Hal until he finally fell into an exhausted sleep. She couldn't stop thinking of Lucky's violent death and of what could have happened to Hal. Now she was visualizing the carcass of a much-loved pet dangling another animal's neck.

Annie tried to forget the incident as best she could, and hoped the children would too. But a couple of weeks later, there was a knock at the door. When she answered, she was assaulted by the stink of unwashed body, wafting off a skinny bearded man. He was wearing filthy overalls and his hands, clutching a tattered old hat, were black with grime.

"Please ma'am, can you spare me a bit of grub? I ain't eaten in three days."

Annie tried to breathe through her mouth as her eyes watered. "Aren't you Willy, the prospector from up the line?"

"Yes, ma'am. That's me."

Ghastly memories of the kitten's demise and visions of a tortured dog flooded her thoughts. "Well, I have five hungry boys to feed and my husband is in France, fighting. And I do believe it's against the law to help a deserter."

"Oh, I ain't no deserter, ma'am. They wouldn't have me."

Small surprise there, Annie thought, but she decided that she could manage to spare a little food for the hungry old coot. "Well, just wait a minute outside, and I'll see what I can do."

She found an old pot and filled it with a generous serving of her chicken stew that was simmering on the back of the stove, then grabbed an old flour sack and tossed in two cans of beans and a tin of tomatoes. She placed a day-old loaf of her bread on top and tied the bundle into a knot.

When she opened the door again, the old man sprang up from his seat on the step. He smiled with a mouthful of rot and bowed obsequiously.

"Thank you! That's grand of you, ma'am. I appreciate it."

"You're welcome, but I'm afraid that's all I can do to help you out." She hesitated. "Do you still have your dog?'

"Not anymore! The damn thing went crazy and I had to shoot him."

At least that vicious animal's miserable, tortured life was over. She momentarily had a wicked thought of what should happen to degenerate old men.

"You know, if you're having trouble feeding yourself, perhaps you should think twice before getting another dog! You can keep the pot, Willy, but don't come back here looking for more. I can't spare it. Good day to you."

She closed the door on him and then went to the sink to scrub her hands thoroughly. *Two strays in one month is more than I can handle*, she thought.

Chapter Forty-Four

The Western Front

It was a combination insane asylum and cemetery; the dead and the living sharing the same space. Some coped by growing numb to the death and misery surrounding them. Gallows humour was common. One callous fellow, pushing past his fear of imminent death, irreverently used the exposed bone of a corpse to strike his match. A young man, about seventeen years old, had clearly gone mad - he meticulously brushed the filthy brown hair on a corpse's head that jutted out of the trench wall.

Jim was sitting on his ground cape, sipping cold tea. His stony gaze passed over the other men. We may be alive with bodies still intact, he thought, but we are all slowly losing our minds. We've already lost our humanity. Perhaps the dead are the fortunate ones, he concluded.

Sam eased himself down to the ground beside Jim. "Life is too damn cheap in this war. We all accept the risk that we could die any minute, but that poor kid should be sent home to his mother."

Jim nodded his head, and closed his eyes.

"You don't look so good, Jim. I'll see if I can find us our rum ration."

Jim was feverish and miserable. His shins were painful and every muscle in his body ached. The trench was cold and damp, but they weren't allowed to build a fire. Smoke would attract enemy assault.

Jim shivered, and his teeth chattered. Mercifully, he finally fell into a deep sleep.

He woke up being roughly jostled, strong arms picking him up from the trench floor and laying him on a stretcher. He closed his eyes, and waited to die.

When Jim became aware of his surroundings, he was on a cot in the field hospital tent. A young orderly saw that he was awake.

"Ah, good, you're back with the living. Here mate, this should cheer you up a bit." He tossed Jim a parcel. "You have a bad case of trench fever, but don't worry, the muscle pain and fever will pass. You should just enjoy your little leave."

Jim sat up cautiously and regarded the young man. He had broad shoulders, muscular arms and the rosy-cheeked health of a prairie farm boy. Jim slowly opened the parcel. In it were tea, shortbread, warm socks, and letters from Annie and his children. As he read Annie's letter, tears streamed down his face.

The empathetic orderly came back to talk to him. Jim proudly took out his Bible to show the picture of Annie.

"You are a wealthy man with such a beautiful wife - and five boys! I could make you a nice cup of hot tea if you like. Your tea would taste much better than the sewer water they call tea here."

Jim sipped his tin mug of Annie's English tea as he reread her letter, and then took out the letters and drawings from the children. There were even some scribbled pictures from Hal and Henry. He found the bottle of Aspirin at the bottom of the box.

The medic came back and whispered, "Best cover that up, mate. That Aspirin might get stolen. How are you feeling?"

"I'm feeling much better now. I still ache all over and feel feverish, but I'm on the mend thanks to my wife's well-timed parcel and your kindness. Here, take some tea for yourself. I like a man who appreciates a good cup of tea."

He held up Henry's scribbles and shook his head, "You know I barely know this little son of mine. I signed up when he was just a newborn. I wonder if he'll ever get to know his own Da."

Jim's reprieve was soon over and he was back in the trenches. His unit pushed north on orders to take control of a power station. The Germans used bombs, gas and heavy guns in retaliation and after a long, hard battle lasting several days, the tremor in Jim's hands returned.

He reached the safety of a deep shell hole and sat down beside Sam. "I seem to fall apart after the missions. I barely remember any hand-to-hand fighting. I look at those dead Germans and I can't help but think it's as if we're fighting our own brothers. They look no different."

Sam nodded. "Yeah, we're all on a slow descent to hell. I'll bet the enemy think the same about us. I once saw a dead German with the same red hair and freckles as me and my cousins. He could have been family."

The Canadian troops pushed farther north and the enemy retreated to higher ground, but both sides were cursed by high winds and freezing, torrential rain. The engineers built cork footbridges over the quicksand of carnage and mud, but if a man stepped off the improvised walkways, he would sink up to his thighs.

Jim worked laying light rails to bring the heavy artillery forward. It was dangerous work, out in the open, and through constant fire from the enemy. One night a shell landed right beside him. He froze, waiting for his death. It failed to explode. Once again, he patted the Bible in his left pocket and whispered a prayer of thanks. Like Jim, most men were superstitious. Each carried good luck charms or pictures of loved ones to ensure their survival.

Several feet ahead of Jim, a Canadian machine gunner fired his weapon. Suddenly a huge explosion cracked the air, and he staggered back a few steps after. It took Jim a second to realize the gunner's head had been blown off; blood began to pump out of his neck as he collapsed. Horrified, Jim looked away and continued to advance mechanically in the torrential rainfall.

He and his fellow soldiers walked over and around hundreds of bodies. They attacked with the fury of berserkers using machine guns, grenades and bayonets. The Canadians had earned the name *Shock Troops* for such battles. The field became a mass murder site of both enemies and allies.

Jim crawled to the safety of a captured German trench. It was well constructed, drier and better drained, but once inside, Jim was shocked to find that some of the dead enemies were little more than boys. These German troops were the same age as Bobby, or even younger. Not caring who heard him, he cried out, "This is insane! We've become animals, and for what?"

One dark, moonless evening around midnight, Jim rested on his ground sheet in a trench. For once, it was silent in the battlefields beyond. Jim searched for matches and cigarettes in his greatcoat. As he sat up, a movement in the field caught his attention. He looked hard and rubbed his eyes in disbelief. There, across the field, was a large grey, smoky mass passing over the dead. The cloud-like vision separated into several shadowy shapes. They looked strangely like floating men on horseback, patrolling and advancing towards the enemy.

Jim turned away to look at the men beside him, and the stunned expressions on their faces told him they had seen the same vision. The men were silent for a few minutes, then began to whisper. Sam reminded them about the angels of Mons, ghostly shapes on horses that were said to have appeared in the battlefield in Mons on August twenty-third, 1915, protecting the British forces from a German attack. The men all agreed that they believed in them.

"I heard about them from a respected lance corporal, who was there and actually witnessed it," Sam added.

Jim was quiet while the others discussed the visions at Mons, and then he said, "Have you ever heard of the fairy flag of Dunvegan?"

The men all looked at Jim and shook their heads, but they were eager to hear what he had to say.

"Well, on the Isle of Skye in Scotland, there's a castle called Dunvegan. It's the ancestral home of the MacLeods. They say that a MacLeod brought back a magic silk flag from the Crusades, and some say that a fairy gave it to him. Whatever its origin, the flag is very powerful. If ever a MacLeod's life is in peril, he has only to wave the flag and a host of armed spirits will come to defend and protect him. I know the fairy flag exists because my grandfather saw it when he was a young man visiting a MacLeod. The clan became impoverished after the potato famine, but they never lost Castle Dunvegan, and they still have that silk in their possession. When I first heard about the angels of Mons, I wondered if a MacLeod had been with the British troops, and had unfurled the fairy flag to summon the medieval ghost army. That would certainly explain the angels of Mons."

The men nodded their heads and looked out over the field again. They wanted to believe that they were protected by supernatural forces, but now all they saw was a vast field of murdered men.

Chapter Forty-Five

Annie came outside to investigate a commotion in the yard. Bobby called out, "Look what we found!" Jack held out a clump of earth supporting a small, struggling lilac shrub. She looked at him for a moment, and then it dawned on her that her sons had brought it from the old farm site. They were likely still searching for Mike, she realized. She didn't know how the tiny plant could possibly have survived the fire but she tenderly replanted it by her front door, anticipating the sweet aroma of lilac blossoms for many springs to come. The flowering plant had been a gift from Jim and it was all that was left from their farm.

In June, Annie finally found a buyer for her five acres of land. She had paid the mortgage fee regularly so Jim wouldn't lose his farm land to the bank, but the five acres were hers to do with as she wished. She had advertised for months on a cork board in the post office and told everyone she knew that the place was for sale. She believed she got a fair price considering there were no buildings on the site, except the remains of the root cellar. When the sale finally went through at the end of June, Annie arranged to have the new house wired for electricity. After she received her next monthly separation allowance from the army, she purchased an electric pump and had some plumbing installed in the empty bathroom. Every couple of months she made another purchase, until she had a working bathroom with a large hot water tank. The dining room and sitting room were still without furniture but she could finally have a hot bath whenever she wished. *Won't Jim be pleased with how I've managed our home?* Then she felt a pang of guilt for having these comforts to enjoy while Jim was still away living in miserable, life-threatening conditions.

She routinely scanned the newspaper for news of the Western Front, and forced herself to check the casualty list for proof that Jim was not injured or killed in action. She wrote to him twice a week, and sent parcels at least once a month. She knew he was receiving them and that he enjoyed hearing even the most trivial family news. He always wrote to thank her, though his letters were sporadic. Sometimes she wouldn't receive one for several weeks, and then she might receive two or three together. Some notes were written in his neat script, but sometimes they looked like they were written by a child, or a very old person.

In November, she received a missive written in that shaky, old-man scrawl.

Dearest Annie,

I hope this letter finds you and the children well. I had a bout of trench fever a while back but am feeling much better now. We are still fighting in this ancient battlefield. We push Fritz and he pushes back. I can hardly wait for this war to be finished. It is a little disheartening to figure out that I've been here for nine months without a break.

I have some very sad news to deliver. Please sit yourself down, dear. I'm so sorry to be the one to tell you this. I just got word that George was killed in action on October twelfth. I know what a shock this news will be to you. Try to be strong and know that your brother died a hero.

Annie had to put the letter down. Her vision was blurred by her tears and shivers went up her back. *I was being so selfish, fussing over our home, while George died. Why didn't I feel that something was wrong?*

She got up to retrieve the biscuit tin that held her treasures. A month earlier, George's wife had mailed her two photos of him in his Cameron Highlander uniform. Annie took George's photos out of the tin, lovingly touched his handsome face and cried fresh tears. George was standing tall with his left hand lightly touching an x-framed campaign chair. His regimental kilt was covered by an army-issue apron and his long, strong legs were visible above his puttees and boots. She tenderly placed the photo on the kitchen table, then picked up Jim's letter to continue reading.

I confess that I took the news hard myself. I've witnessed so much carnage in the battle field, I began to grow numb to the death all around me. I thought I had become less than human, but to lose George was a terrible blow. I was told that his death was swift and he did not suffer. You should be proud of your brother. I am so sorry to be the one to tell you of this loss.

Annie suspected that Jim had written about a swift death to spare her feelings. Jim's life was threatened every minute in this war, she knew, yet here he was protecting her from additional pain. The letter was smeared in water marks, and she knew they must be Jim's tears. She impulsively kissed the spots where his tears had fallen.

I promise that I will do everything in my power to come home to you after this war. I am heartened to hear that I may be up for a two-week pass to England in February. That would give me enough time to take the train up to Shields and see Ma. Take very good care of yourself. I wish I could be there to hold you in my arms and comfort you, and have you comfort me as well. Love to the children.
Jim

Annie dug through the old newspapers in her kindling box. At the bottom of her wood pile, miraculously saved for her, was a copy of a paper dated October thirteenth. She took the paper to the table and smoothed it out.

From the front page she learned exactly where George had died; a place called Passchendaele. She read of viscous mud, yards deep, and a drenching sheet of rain that the British troops trudged through. The attack was to begin at daybreak, but the Germans must have found out somehow. During the night, the enemy heavily shelled the British communication roads and front lines, and threw gas shells along the British forward positions while maintaining a heavy machine-gun barrage. The Germans had held strong positions along the slopes of the Passchendaele Ridge. They had concrete pillboxes and machine-gun forts, and the fire from these strongholds was incessant.

Annie wept at the horror. Why would the British army continue to advance when it was obvious the Germans were well-prepared, had the advantage of being on higher ground and obviously had prior knowledge of the British attack? *George had had no chance of survival. He was murdered.*

She went to bed angry. Not only was she angry about George, but angry at the British government for deporting the mother of one of their lost soldiers. She worried that George wouldn't have a proper burial site.

That night, she had a dream about George so vivid that she felt she could almost touch him. He told her that Jim was safe. She woke up crying, but strangely comforted.

Chapter Forty-Six

The morale among the Canadians at the front was at its lowest point. Men grumbled about their commanders being safe in the rear, while continuing to order the troops at the front to battle. Many were haunted by the number of their comrades killed since the beginning of the war.

Jim's unit continued to restore communications, roads, and railways, often working at night under fire. Once, Jim and Sam were stranded for three days with only a day's supply of food. Jim pointed out the irony of being so bloody thirsty when there was so much water all around. Everywhere they looked, there were craters filled with fetid, contaminated water. When a group of men had finally brought food and water, Jim had had to force himself to eat amid the stench of decaying bodies and the filth of the trench. The drinking water came in an old gasoline can, which gave it a peculiar taste, but Jim was desperate to quench his thirst and drank deeply.

One night, several weeks later, Jim was sheltered with a group of Canadians in a large, reasonably dry crater. They entertained each other with whispered stories of their homes back in Canada. Jim told his mates about Annie.

"My wife's just a bit of a thing, but she chased off a bear when she was picking blueberries. She said she thought it was just a big dog – and she just told him to shoo and banged her pot! But, when she first came up north, this same woman screamed like a city girl when a little field mouse ran over her shoe."

Over the course of the evening, they all tried to outdo one another with stories of wolves and bears and hardships they had overcome, back home. Later on, the men tried to get as comfortable as they could, and one by one drifted off into an exhausted sleep.

Jim had just barely fallen asleep when a tall Scottish soldier rapped him on the shoulder. Jim slapped the man's hand away and growled, "Piss off!" Feeling uncomfortable, he sat up and cursed. The kilted Cameron Highlander urged him to get up and follow. Jim looked closely at his face and swore again - it was his brother-in-law.

"Jesus, George, it's good to see you!" he cried in relief. "I heard you were killed in October."

George put his finger to his lips and turned, signalling again for him to follow. Jim climbed out of the slippery shell hole and cautiously crawled behind George. They travelled several hundred feet to another large crater and lowered themselves to the bottom. When Jim reached the muddy floor of the hole, he found a spot to lay his ground cape and turned back towards his wife's youngest brother. He wasn't there. Puzzled, Jim called several times for George but there was no reply. Suddenly he heard heavy shelling coming from the enemy, so kept his head down. The firing continued throughout the night and through the next day.

Finally, under the cover of the night sky, Jim crawled out of the hole and returned to the crater he had been in before George found him. To his horror, every man with whom he had shared stories and rum the night before was dead, half-buried in the muck of the shell hole. He saw Sam's red hair in among the mangled bodies. His face grew pale.

"Oh God," he moaned. "Why should I have survived?" He knew in his head that George had died at Passchendaele, but his heart told him that his brother-in-law had saved him. Jim pulled Sam's body out of the mud and fetid water, swearing with the effort, and dragged him to a groundsheet. "I won't leave you here, mate. I'll take care of you." He mechanically gathered all the nametags for identification and searched pockets for letters and photos. He stopped at last at Sam's body and broke down and cried uncontrollably. It took a half-hour before he had the mental strength to move on.

He slung Sam's body over his shoulder and slowly walked the two miles back through the battlefield to the command post. He almost wished that a sniper would train his sites on him, and end his pain. He reverently placed Sam's body beside a tent, insisting that his friend's remains be treated with respect and that he be given a proper burial.

Jim had planned to keep the story of the ghost of his brother-in-law private, but did not anticipate the heavy questioning he received. He broke down in tears several times recounting the death of Sam and the others, and finally he reluctantly told of the ghost that saved him. The officer shook his head, patted Jim on the shoulder and said, "You've been hallucinating from lack of food, soldier. Go back to the cook tent and get yourself a bowl of hot stew and some tea."

On the way to the cook tent, Jim had to stop and kneel down on the ground. He could not keep his body from shaking. He buried his head in his hands and wept for the senseless loss of his mates, especially for his friend Sam and, once again, for his brother-in-law.

Over the next few weeks there were subtle changes in the war as new conscripts arrived from Canada. There were fresh American soldiers as well; the States had finally entered the war. The addition of robust, strong troops was a great advantage now and the Germans were pushed back towards Belgium. Morale was boosted, and men were getting their long-promised passes to Britain.

Jim finally received notice that he'd been granted his two-week leave to *Old Blighty*, the slang the men used for England. The welcome news lifted his spirits; it also helped to have a bath and be issued a new uniform. His old uniform was filthy, torn, and crawling with lice. Jim eagerly anticipated the short crossing to England, then a train ride north, back to the sanity of his mother's home in South Shields. Hoping his leave would not be postponed yet again, he celebrated with a mug of rum-laced tea.

Chapter Forty-Seven

The war had caused many changes in Bear Falls. When the government brought in conscription, Annie heard that some men disappeared into the bush. The story was that they didn't view the war as their battle and that some did not feel any allegiance to Britain. Sixteen-year-old Bobby came back from the hotel one evening, quite excited with a story about a local Irishman.

"They say that he refused to report to duty when he received his draft orders. He was at the hotel, and said he would not wear a khaki uniform until Ireland was free. Two military police came in and arrested him!"

Annie shook her head and was torn between thinking these dodgers to be unpatriotic cowards, and envying their wives, who would know that their husbands would remain alive and unharmed. These men were guaranteed to be with their wives at the end of the war.

Later that month, she read in the Toronto paper that the Irishman from Bear Falls had been court-martialled and sentenced to two years in the penitentiary. *He's a lucky man,* she couldn't help thinking. *He knows he'll still be alive when his two years are up. He's in a safer place than Jim.*

While taking her latest letters from Jim to reread at the kitchen table, Annie noticed that one envelope had unfamiliar writing and she realized she had accidently been given someone else's mail.

Mrs. Sarah Smith, Mile 225, New Ontario. Annie decided it was probably easiest for her to deliver the letter herself. She had heard there was a young English woman who had just moved into a house not far away, and Annie was keen to meet her. She decided to give Sarah her letter the next day.

Sarah Smith's husband was also overseas with the Canadian army, and she and Annie became fast friends. Sarah was from Cumberland, had strawberry-blonde hair and freckles and was not much taller than Annie. She began coming over to Annie's house regularly when the older boys were at school. Sarah did not have any children, and she loved to fuss over Hal and Henry. The women enjoyed each other's company, and Annie was often reminded of the lovely time she had had with Catherine in Toronto.

In mid-February, however, a week passed without Annie seeing her new friend. Annie grew concerned. When Bobby, Jack and Georgie left for school one Friday, she bundled up Hal and Henry and walked the short distance to Sarah's house. She knocked at Sarah's door but there was no answer, so she entered, calling out Sarah's name.

The house was dark, and almost as cold as the outdoors. The fire was out in the kitchen stove. Annie called to Sarah again as she walked through the kitchen to the back bedroom. There she found Sarah curled into a ball on the bed.

"Are you sick, Sarah?" Annie asked.

Sarah shook her head. Her face was mottled and streaked with tears. Annie sat down on the bed and stroked her friend's back. Sarah had a letter crumpled in her hand.

"Has something happened to your husband?" Annie asked.

Sarah handed Annie the note and Annie reluctantly flattened the piece of paper on her lap to read it. It was an official letter, reporting that Sarah's separation allowance would be stopped temporarily as her husband was being treated for V.D. in the General Hospital in Etaples, France.

"Sarah, he's just ill or injured. If you're short of money you know I'll help you."

Sarah shook her head and sobbed. "Annie, he has V.D. I can never forgive him. He has abused my trust; he totally betrayed me. I'm going south to Toronto to stay with my sister until I figure out what to do. I know this: our marriage is over."

Annie was stunned by Sarah's outburst. She also felt foolish for not knowing what V.D. was and was hesitant to ask her devastated friend. She convinced Sarah to come home with her and stay until she was ready to go to her sister's.

Sarah stayed with Annie for a week, and Annie helped her pack her belongings. They had a tearful farewell at the train station, and both women promised to write.

Annie was lonesome with Sarah gone; she missed her friendship and company. She received a letter from her the following week, in which she let Annie know that she had arrived safely at her sister's home. After that, Annie wrote regularly, but didn't hear from Sarah again.

A month after Sarah had left the North, a letter was finally delivered to Annie. She didn't recognize the writing, and tore open the envelope. The enclosed note was from Sarah's sister. She wrote that she regretted to inform Annie that Sarah had passed away.

Annie sat down hard on the bench in the post office. She felt the blood drain from her face, and for a minute she was quite still. Then she summoned the courage to finish reading. The note said that Sarah had been despondent about the end of her marriage, and was inconsolable. Sarah's sister did not give the cause of death, but it was not hard to conclude that Sarah had committed suicide.

Annie felt a lump in her throat. *Oh, Sarah, I'm so sorry,* she thought. *I should have helped you somehow. This terrible war has wasted one more young life.*

Annie still didn't understand why Sarah would have taken her own life. Surely a husband's illness did not warrant such an end to a marriage and suicide. She decided to consult a woman with whom she was acquainted at church. Mrs. Mitchell was a nurse who would be able to answer her questions, Annie reasoned. The next Sunday, after church services, Annie invited her over for tea the following day.

Mrs. Mitchell arrived promptly at ten o'clock Monday morning as arranged. The woman was tall and had a matronly figure, and her dark hair was pulled back into two neat braids pinned around her head. The two women made a casual conversation for a few minutes before Annie told her about Sarah, and asked her directly what V.D. was.

Mrs. Mitchell quickly swallowed her mouthful of tea, and looked at Annie. She was quiet for a few moments.

"I'm sorry to be blunt dear, but V.D. is a disease that infects a man's private parts, causing much pain and inflammation. A man becomes infected with this disease if he has had sexual relations with a woman who is already infected, most likely a prostitute. The treatment to cure it is almost as horrible as the disease. Patients are injected with arsenic and mercury, and their lesions are rubbed with iodine or mercurial ointment."

Annie felt the blood drain from her face as Mrs. Mitchell studied her.

"Don't be too condemning of Sarah's husband. This war has taken our men away from the civilized world and dumped them into a brutality we can only imagine. The men assume they will die at any moment, and even the most faithful man can weaken at temptation while on leave. I'm sorry I didn't get to speak to Sarah before she left. I blame the officer who sent her that letter. Her death is on his hands. I'll be surprised if her husband survives the war when he hears of her passing. I wonder how many other women received such letters and acted as she did." She continued that she had acquaintances in the higher ranks of the military, and that she planned to address the issue promptly.

While Mrs. Mitchell fumed with outrage, Annie was still coming to terms with the nurse's description of the disease. She was shocked at the information, and embarrassed when she realized how naive she had been. She finally understood why Sarah had been so devastated.

God, she thought. *What an innocent I was before this war!*

Chapter Forty-Eight

England
Spring, 1918

The crossing to England was quick and uneventful, and Jim arrived in London more than ready for his hard-earned fourteen-day leave. He had been in France and Belgium for a year without reprieve, and was nearly a broken man.

As soon as he arrived, he found a pub filled with other soldiers, quaffed a pint of Guinness, bought another, and ordered fish and chips. His dinner came wrapped in a newspaper; he peeled away the paper and inhaled the salty, greasy smell. This simple meal was nothing less than restorative, and when he was finished, he sat back for a few minutes to watch the other patrons. Some men tried to include him in their conversations when they saw his uniform, but he didn't respond. They finally shook their heads and left him alone.

After he had satiated himself, Jim walked to the railroad station, bought a return ticket to Newcastle, and boarded the train. The sound and movement of the train lulled him to sleep. He was surprised when a conductor woke him at the Newcastle stop.

He stepped off the train and began the long walk to his mother's house, but within five minutes an elderly man with an impressive handlebar moustache stopped his car. He leaned out the window, asked Jim where he was off to, and offered to drive him to South Shields.

"I see that you're on leave. Hop in. I have a son myself, fighting in Belgium now, and I would want someone to offer him a ride, too. I lost two of my boys in Ypres." The old gentleman's eyes grew moist.

Jim thanked the man and offered his condolences, but then fell silent. The older man seemed to sense that Jim didn't want conversation and allowed him a quiet ride for the remainder of the trip. He stopped his car a few streets away from Jane's home and wished Jim good fortune.

Jim bought a small bouquet of flowers from a little girl at the corner. He quickened his pace as he approached the house, and when he came up to the doorway, he called out to his mother.

Jane threw open the door and wept, hugging him tightly, then stood back to get a good look. He could tell she was shocked by his appearance. He knew he had lost a lot of weight, but at least he was considerably cleaner that he'd been just a few days before. For a couple of hours, Jim allowed his mother to fuss over him and serve him his favourite foods. But finally he said, "I'm sorry, but I'm just tuckered out, Ma. I need to catch up on some sleep."

He woke up two days later.

Jane was visibly relieved when he emerged from the bedroom. "I was so worried an' I stayed by your cot tuh make sure ye were still breathin'. Then ye tossed an' cried out so that I was afraid to wake ye. I borrowed clothes from Charlie fo' ye, so I could clean your uniform. I put a hot iron on the seams tuh kill the lice!"

"Thanks, Ma. Sorry to worry you." He chuckled, "If you thought this uniform needed cleaning, you would have fainted at the sight of my old one!"

"Never fainted a day in me life I'll have ye know!"

One day, when he was sitting at the kitchen table sipping tea and enjoying a large piece of cake, a lump of coal shifted suddenly in Jane's fireplace and fell in the grate with a loud bang. Jim ducked and dropped his mug, which crashed to the floor and shattered, scattering broken shards and tea.

Jane looked at his white face and trembling body and said, "Oh, hinny." She held his head to her chest as she had when he was a boy.

The two weeks passed quickly, filled with visits from Jim's sisters and their children, each trying to outdo the other with treats for Jim. On the day he was to leave for the train to London, he said his goodbyes to his mother.

"Thank you, Ma. You restored me. I truly believe that this leave saved me from insanity. But now I don't know how I can face a return to the front. Maybe I would have been better off staying in France."

"Dinna say that, Jim. The war will be over soon an' ye'll be back tuh Annie before ye know it."

Jim returned the hug and kisses, bid her another goodbye, promised to write, and then reluctantly turned to leave.

It didn't take long for the memory of that pleasant time in South Shields to fade. Jim was soon returned to the front, working above the trenches, repairing lines damaged from shelling. He helped lay light rail to the front so the tons of rations and ammunition could be brought forward each day.

In March, they began constructing a rear defence trench system with over a hundred miles of trenches in total. The hard labour helped Jim; being so physically exhausted at the end of each day encouraged a deeper sleep, and helped him to forget his misery.

That spring almost everyone had bronchitis. Jim had to regularly put down his shovel and cough, often coughing until he felt weak. There was a frenzy of activity in spite of the fact that so many men were ill. The troops dug hundreds of kilometres of trenches, positioning barbed wire, laying telephone cables and burying water mains in preparation for an offensive attack.

One evening, Jim was resting in a dugout that was supported by some scrounged steel. He had wrapped himself in a blanket as well as his coat, to keep out the icy fingers of a frigid wind. He felt revived after a meal of lukewarm stew and a strong brew of cool tea fortified with rum, so he pulled a few sheets of paper from of his greatcoat pocket. As was his custom, he gazed at Annie's picture before he began to write his letter. He told her he'd heard that the German troops were malnourished and living on black bread and meatless sausages, which he hoped wasn't just propaganda. He told her that much of his work now was similar to the jobs he had had when he first came to New Ontario, laying miles and miles of broad-gauge track.

Jim stopped writing, put down his pencil, and reread his letter. He realized that he was recording sanitized, bland events that were completely separated from his reality. Like every other soldier in the war, he knew that any bullet could be destined to hit him. He could die with his most important words unspoken. He picked up his pencil again, but this time he expressed his love for Annie, his plans for their future and his dreams for their children. When he finished, he folded the letter and placed it in his Bible beside Annie's photo. That night, he fell into a dreamless, healing slumber.

Chapter Forty-Nine

Late one evening, near the end of March - when the boys were asleep and the house quiet - Annie grabbed her coat and called to Spud to come for a little walk. She slipped out the door. Her footprints crunched on the snowy path. The air was fresh and clear with a promising hint of warmer weather to come. Spud pranced around her, and rolled playfully in the snow.

There seemed to be electricity in the atmosphere and Annie raised her head to look at the stars. She was met with a vision of red, violet and green lights, dancing and shimmering across the sky. She was mesmerized for several minutes as she gazed at the swirling coloured ribbons undulating across the star-lit evening sky. She was comforted by the memory of watching the Northern Lights with Jim.

Although the extreme winter temperatures in New Ontario persisted, the days were getting longer and Annie was eager to start planning her new vegetable garden. She had already mailed her order for seed catalogues and sketched out her gardening plans in her head. She knew now from experience what plants would grow in the short summer season and which root crops were the best, and she planned to get some topsoil and manure to build up her new garden. *Oh, to feed the children fresh food again!* She thought. *Not to mention the money I'll save.*

In his last letter, Jim had said he was in Belgium. She tried to read between the lines as he never complained or gave many details of his life in the field, but his writing was very shaky again and this worried her.

She wrote telling him about the children and the latest northern news, to let him know everything was fine at home. She never mentioned any money concerns or told him when one of their sons was ill or misbehaving. She often wished that she could have travelled to England to spend time with him when he'd been on leave, but she was grateful that Jim's mother and sisters had treated him so well when he was there.

Annie tried to make the children's lives as normal as she possibly could and was busy during the day with chores and caring for her two youngest, while Bobby, Jack, and Georgie were at school. It was in the evening when the house was quiet and the children asleep that she missed Jim the most.

Her hopes for an early spring were soon dashed, however. A few days later, a cruel winter storm blew in from the east. The snow accumulated to incredible heights. To add to Annie's disappointment, the temperature then plummeted. Thankfully, the extra insulation from the snow packed against the house and a good supply of firewood kept the family cozy. House-bound for a couple of days, the children managed to entertain themselves; the older boys found a deck of cards and Georgie helped Hal and Henry build structures with their wooden blocks.

Annie knew there was something bothering Bobby. She patiently waited him out. Finally, he hesitantly spoke to her. "Ma, I want to start earning a wage. I know there are positions open at the mill. I'm ready to quit school and get a job."

Annie looked at her eldest boy and realized that at sixteen years of age, he was almost a man. She knew she had burdened him with many adult responsibilities since Jim had left.

"Yes, son," she said with a sigh, "I suppose it's time. And the extra income will certainly help."

Bobby looked at his mother, not believing what he'd heard. Then he wrapped her in a tight hug. "Thanks, Ma."

"You'll need to properly apply for a position, and ask for letters of reference from the high school principal and the minister and perhaps even the hotel manager. They can all attest to your good character. You want to aim high, son, and get an apprenticeship for a trade. They'll probably make you a broke hustler in the paper mill for the first bit, but that's how you'll prove you're a good, honest worker."

The following day after the roads were plowed and the boys had shovelled the walkway, Annie left Hal and Henry with Jack and Georgie and walked with Bobby to visit the principal, the minister and the hotel manager. All three men readily agreed to write a letter of recommendation for Bobby. It was public knowledge that the mill needed to replace employees who had enlisted or been drafted; the newsprint business was thriving during the war. Bobby made an appointment for an interview, and before the end of the week, he was hired.

On his first pay day, he handed his wages to his mother. She was proud of him and could see that he was pleased with himself. It was a relief to have more money coming in as well. She put half of Bobby's wages into a bank account for him and used half to support the family's needs. She and Bobby both wrote letters to Jim to tell him the good news. She wondered if her other sons would be young men as well before their father returned. She shuddered. *If he returns.*

Chapter Fifty

Thoughts of her mother's situation continued to haunt Annie. She was determined to find out where she was and somehow bring her to Canada, but she didn't know how to accomplish it. Although Annie understood Norwegian, she couldn't write a formal letter of inquiry to authorities in Norway. This problem nagged at her. She knew there were some Norwegian immigrants in the North, but she needed someone who could properly compose a letter.

One Sunday, after church services, she approached the school principal to explain her problem and asked him if he knew of any Norwegian teachers she might ask.

"Why, as a matter of fact, I do. There's a high school mathematics teacher in Gold Creek. His name is Lars Nilsen. The poor man is blind in one eye, so he wasn't drafted into the military. Write to him in care of the school in Gold Creek and he'll be sure to receive your letter."

Annie wrote to Mr. Nilsen, explaining her need to locate her mother and requesting his help to write a letter to the correct authorities in Bergen. To her delight, Mr. Nilsen replied within a week and said he would be pleased to help. He wrote that he had many contacts in Bergen and was confident that they could find Annie's mother, although it would likely take some time, because of the war. He regularly visited a distant cousin in Bear Falls and would be in town soon.

Lars Nilsen arrived at Annie's door, two weeks later, as arranged. He was a handsome young man in spite of the cloudy eye. He had thick, light brown hair and was as tall as her brothers.

After a few words, she unconsciously switched to speaking in Norwegian. She was surprised how easily the language came back to her. She had invited Lars to stay for dinner and she planned to prepare a few of her mother's Norwegian recipes. Over the afternoon, she told him the whole story of what had happened to her mother and of her own plans to bring her mother home to care for her.

"I think it should be simple enough to locate your mother. I have an uncle who's a lawyer in Bergen. He'll know which authorities we would need to contact."

While Annie finished her preparations for dinner, the young man composed the letter at the kitchen table. Annie was pleasantly surprised that her boys were quiet and shy in the company of a stranger and careful in their table manners. After dinner, Lars thanked Annie for a lovely meal and promised to mail the letter the next day.

"I'm sorry that I cannot pay you, but I'm happy to cook dinner for you anytime."

"A good meal is priceless, most especially good Norwegian fare. I'll contact you when I receive any information about your mother. Thank you, Annie, and I wish you and your children a good night."

After the younger boys were in bed, Bobby joined his mother at the table. Bobby was old enough to remember his grandmother fondly and he looked forward to seeing her again.

"I can help you convert the parlour into a bedroom for Granny Larsen. I'll buy a new bed for her, with my savings."

"What a grand idea, Bobby." The parlour would be perfect; Annie's mother wouldn't have to climb any stairs. "There's no need to spend any of your savings, though, son. Your uncles will help us with expenses when we bring your grandmother here."

After Bobby went upstairs to bed, Annie wrote a long letter to Jim to tell him of the events of the day and her plans for her mother. She knew it could take several months to find her and arrange for her travel. It might even take years if the war continued. It was disheartening to imagine the war lasting another year or longer. Her dearest wish would be to have Jim back home with her again and to bring her mother over, too.

Miraculously, within two months, Lars Nilsen had located Annie's mother. In June, Annie received a letter from her, scribed in unfamiliar handwriting. She was almost blind now, so had dictated a letter to Lars's contact in Bergen. Annie read it with anticipation.

> *My dearest daughter Annie,*
>
> *I could not possibly be happier. I can hardly believe that you found me. A lawyer named Jen Nilsen located me here and arranged for a lovely young woman to write this letter for me. I'm afraid that I can barely see but otherwise am in good health. How lucky I am to have a daughter who wants me to live with her. I realize that travel is impossible until the end of the war, but I have waited this long, and can wait a bit longer.*
>
> *Annie, life has been hard these last few years. When I could not pay for my room in South Shields, they sent me to the poor house. It was humiliating. My pearl necklace was stolen there. I suspect the matron. That necklace was to be your inheritance and now it's gone. It was our connection to your Pappa and I'm so sorry that I can't give it to you.*
>
> *They soon discovered that I was born in Norway and they promptly deported me, so here I am.*
>
> *Well, I will look to the future now. I am anxious to see my grandsons. Does Georgie still look like our George? And I have several new grandchildren to meet! Tell Hal and Henry that their Granny loves them. I am looking forward to seeing Alfie's little girl, Anna, too. How rich I am, with all my grandchildren! God willing, I will see you all again soon.*
>
> *Love from Mother*

Annie was angry over the loss of the pearl necklace; her mother had received so much comfort wearing it. It added insult to injury that the mother of a lost British soldier could be robbed and deported. Annie froze. *Oh my God, Mother doesn't know about George.* How she wished that she could be with her mother now.

When Annie sat down to write, she decided not to tell her about George yet. It would be kinder to tell her in person. She was conscious that a stranger would have to read her letter to her mother, so at first, she was cautious in her words. Then she remembered that beautiful letter from Jim, when he wrote from his heart, not caring what a censor might read.

Dear Mother,

I am ecstatic that I have found you at last. I have made such wonderful plans for you when you come. I will have a bedroom set up for you downstairs and will do everything in my power to make up for all your troubles. Your wee Bobby is a grown working man now. He has a good job in the paper mill and I imagine that Jack will soon want to work there too. I am enclosing two photos for you. The one of Jim and me was taken in Toronto just before Jim went overseas. The picture of our five boys was taken quite recently. I'm sure that you will see a huge change in Bobby, Jack and Georgie.

Jim is fighting in Belgium now. It has been lonely without him and I'm sorry that he's missing Henry's babyhood. Our youngest child was just two months old when Jim left for the army. Bobby is very eager to have you with us, and I often overhear Jack and Georgie telling their little brothers about you.

I have missed you so much since we moved to Canada and will count the days until we see each other again. I have given your address to Alfie so you will be receiving a letter from him soon. Stay well, Mother. The boys and I send you our love.

Annie

The next time Lars visited Annie, he stayed again for a special Norwegian dinner that Annie had prepared. She thanked him again and again for finding her mother. After their meal, she declared, "I'm so happy, Lars. We should have a celebration!"

In the top corner of a cupboard Annie had a small bottle of single-malt scotch that Alfie had sent up for Jim, months ago. She brought a chair over to the cupboard and reached up to get the bottle. The boys had retired upstairs, even Bobby, likely bored from the Norwegian conversations that he did not understand. Hal and Henry had been asleep for an hour and Lars had stayed on and entertained Annie with stories about Norway.

As she handed him a glass of the amber liquid, she asked, "Did you ever see the Northern Lights in Norway? Are they the same as what we see here in the North?"

"Oh yes, they are just as beautiful. My parents always said they were reflections from Valkyries' armour."

Annie smiled, and took a sip of scotch. "Oh!" She coughed and then laughed in embarrassment as her eyes watered. "I suppose single-malt scotch is an acquired taste!" She put the glass down on the table. "Those are the same stories I grew up with, but I never saw the Northern Lights until I came here."

It was so wonderful to be in the company of another adult. They chatted late into the night, and then Lars said he'd better leave before the cousin he was staying with gave up on him and locked the door. Before he left, Lars thanked Annie for the lovely meal and company, and then he leaned down and kissed her.

Annie blushed and quickly said good night, closing the door after him. *Whatever will the neighbours think?* Lars was very nice, but she hoped he didn't think she had been inviting that kiss. She didn't want to give him the wrong impression. Without his help, though, she wouldn't be looking forward to having her mother with her again.

She decided that the next time he visited, she'd keep Bobby in the room and they'd speak in English.

Chapter Fifty-One

Annie placed the newspaper on the kitchen table and sat down. The afternoon sunshine streamed into the room and a warm, June breeze drifted in through the open window. She had spent a pleasant day planting her garden while Henry and Hal played in a sand pile in the yard. Both little boys were now sound asleep upstairs, tuckered out after their games in the fresh air. Annie had just a half-hour to browse through the paper, before Jack and Georgie returned from school.

She read on the front page that conscripted men were bringing the Canadians to full fighting force again. The Americans had finally joined the Allies. It was predicted that the war would end soon but Annie was skeptical of such opinions; an early end to the war had been assumed erroneously many times before. She folded the paper, stood up and looked around the kitchen. Her bread looked ready to bake, so she picked up the pans from the counter. Just as she placed her loaves in the oven, she was startled by the front door suddenly opening.

"You're home early, son!" she said to Bobby.

Bobby put his lunch pail on the counter and hung up his cap. "I don't feel well, Ma, so the boss sent me home early. I have a vicious headache. I'm just going to lie down for a while.. Don't bother to wake me for dinner." He handed his mother two letters. "I stopped by the post office."

Annie put her hand to his forehead. "You're burning up! Go on upstairs and try to rest. I'll catch Hal and Henry when they wake up from their nap, so they won't bother you."

She watched him slowly climb the stairs. Bobby was seventeen years old now and taller than his father. He had a muscular build; his thick hair had darkened to a deep brown but his blue eyes were still the same shade as Jim's. She watched him go. In his illness he appeared more boy than man again.

Annie looked down at the letters in her hand. One thin envelope was from Gold Creek and there was a thick letter from Jim. She saw that the mail from Jim was in one of his special green envelopes, so she knew that it was likely uncensored and more personal. She'd save that as a special treat to enjoy later in the evening.

Annie sat down at the kitchen table and opened the thin envelope. It was a short note from Lars Nilsen. She had not heard from him for several weeks, but was relieved that he had written instead of visiting. She knew that she would feel quite uncomfortable in his company after their last meeting.

Dear Mrs. Kidd - Annie, if I may be so bold,

I write this note with my most sincere apologies for my behaviour when I last left your home. I can only say that the alcohol must have impaired my judgment. I would never want to offend you and will not trouble you again with my presence. I do wish to continue to work to bring your mother to Canada. I did not write earlier as I have been very ill with influenza and am presently at home with a bout of pneumonia. I will contact authorities in Bergen for information on immigration to Canada and notify you by mail of any new developments.

Humbly,
Lars Nilsen

Annie's face grew warm as she remembered her last meeting with Lars. She crushed the note and put it in the stove fire. She did not blame the poor man entirely but was relieved that she would not see him again in the near future. She sincerely regretted her judgment in offering him a glass of scotch.

Hearing Hal call out from upstairs, she put Jim's precious green envelope on a shelf and hurried upstairs, not wanting the little boys to disturb Bobby.

Jack and Georgie were in the kitchen when she came back down. Jack helped himself to a large slice of cheese, then announced that he was going to deliver the newspapers and left as quickly as he had arrived.

Annie asked Georgie to watch Hal and Henry while she went back upstairs to check on Bobby.

Georgie looked at her in confusion. "Why's he home now?"

"He came home from work early. He's got a fever and a headache."

Georgie nodded, then he sat on the floor to play with the younger ones. Annie watched her two towheaded boys giggle and tackle their patient big brother.

"Hal and Henry! Play quietly! Bobby is sick and trying to sleep."

Annie didn't have time to read Jim's letter until after nine o'clock that evening. The boys were sleeping soundly by then, and the house was quiet. Bobby had slept through dinner. Though he seemed to be fevered whenever she checked him, she knew sleep would be healing. She had been looking forward to reading Jim's note and treasured this quiet time for herself. Sitting in her rocking chair by the kitchen fire, she removed the pages from the green envelope.

Dearest Annie,

I hope this letter finds you and the children well. It is hard to believe that I've been overseas for such a long time. It saddens me that I have missed our Henry's babyhood. I thought of him on his birthday and was shocked when I realized that he's two years old now. Poor lad doesn't even know his Da.

Thank you for the photo of our five boys. I hardly recognize them, they have grown so. I can't imagine that Hal is a four-year-old now. I remember that we thought that maybe the only job for him when he grew up would be a jockey. He was so tiny. I guess we won't need to arrange riding lessons for him after all! Imagine our Bobby a working man now. Jack looks like a twin to Bobby and Georgie looks more Larsen than Kidd. He'll soon be taller than his brothers. You've done a grand job raising our boys, Annie.

I assure you that I am well. I wouldn't have believed it myself, after my leave earlier in the year, but my nerves are a lot steadier. I didn't think that I could face the front again after having two weeks leave in England. We have been training very hard this last month; however we do have time for some sports and rest. I had my first bath in two months and boy did that feel good!

We are training for something and I suppose they will let us know when the time comes. Some of the blokes, who have been here since the beginning of the war, give the new conscripts a hard time, but we are all glad to be at full strength once again. The worst part of the training exercises is that we have to wear our gas masks at all times. It's hard to see with them on and you can't help but sweat under all that rubber.

I'm in good spirits, though. One day when the big-wigs were here, I saw our ace pilot Billy Bishop demonstrate his flying stunts. I don't know what keeps him in the air. He was flying upside down and making figure eights. The RAF patrolled the skies during the display to protect us (more likely protecting the brass) from any possible enemy planes and bombs. What a grand show.

Annie, I can write you at present about what I've experienced these past few months, now that I've survived with my body intact. If anything has been blacked out then you know that my green envelope caught the censor in England. The German offensive was very strong when I returned to the front after my leave. They were aiming to defeat us before the Americans came in force. Nearly everyone had bronchitis then, including me (don't worry, I'm in good health now).

The weather is quite cold because of the wind and the dampness everywhere. I'd much prefer the dry cold of a New Ontario winter. You're always wet here in the winter months and it makes for miserable conditions. We dug hundreds of miles of trenches and *laid miles of barbed wire to fortify our defences. Gas is used in every battle on both sides, but the Germans are sending over a nasty one. This mustard gas stays in low areas for days and blisters any of our exposed skin. It is yellowish brown and has a sharp mustard smell. I saw men with massive blisters filled with yellow fluid. Our respirators protect our faces and lungs, but the gas settles on any exposed skin and soaks into our clothes. It remains for weeks in the snow and frozen mud, and then vaporizes when the sun comes up. We lost many men who died in agony after exposure to this gas. I did get gassed, but was able to remove my clothes soon enough and wash off with a pail of water. Luckily for me, my blisters were not severe, compared to what some other poor blokes suffered. One fellow I knew quite well jumped into a shell crater to seek cover from fire. He didn't have his respirator on. Mustard gas had settled in that hole and he was blinded. His lungs bled and he died a few days later. I no longer know how many of my mates have died here. I've lost count. The only good thing about the gas is that it has exterminated many of the trench rats. I tell you all this Annie, after the fact, and to reassure you that I am fine and in much improved spirits since March.*

Annie's reading was interrupted when she heard a shout. She put Jim's letter on a shelf to finish reading later, then she climbed the stairs to Bobby's and Jack's bedroom. Bobby was tossing and turning and his face was wet with perspiration. Annie placed her hand on his forehead; he was burning up. She hushed him like a baby until he calmed down and she remained beside his bed for most of the night. At times he coughed so continuously that she had to help him sit up for relief.

In the morning, Bobby was still suffering with a high fever and persistent cough. As soon as Jack was awake, Annie sent him to find the doctor. Before she made breakfast, she and Georgie carried her mattress down the stairs to set up a bed for Bobby in the empty dining room. By the time she had the bed made up, and bowls of breakfast porridge set on the kitchen table, Jack had returned.

"The doctor will stop by after his hospital rounds, probably by eleven this morning."

"Thank you, son. Come help me bring Bobby downstairs."

They climbed the stairs to Bobby's bedroom and helped him out of bed and onto his feet. They supported him as he weakly managed the steps down. By the time they got him to the dining room, he was coughing profusely and he collapsed on the mattress.

"I'll bring you some tea, Bobby. The doctor's coming later this morning and hopefully he will give you some medication." She affectionately laid her hand on his cheek, then covered him with a light blanket.

"It looks like a lovely day outside," she said to Jack and Georgie. "Take Hal and Henry out to play, after you finish your breakfast, and try not to be too noisy. I don't want you boys to bother Bobby."

When the doctor arrived, Annie took him to her improvised sickroom. Dr. Miller was in his seventies, barrel-chested and brusque, but he had the reputation of being trustworthy and competent. After looking in Bobby's throat and pressing his fingers to his neck he placed a thermometer in his mouth, then listened to his chest.

"I don't believe Bobby has pneumonia, but he does have a temperature of 104. Your son has influenza, Mrs. Kidd. They're calling it the Spanish flu. Send Jack to my office later today and I will have medication prepared."

As the doctor left the sickroom, he said, "I don't mean to alarm you, Mrs. Kidd, but if he starts to cough blood, bring him to the hospital immediately. We don't want to fool around with this. It is a particularly virulent disease. Five people in Blackspruce Bay died on the same day last week. Those poor people are trying to live the old ways by hunting and trapping. It's a hard life and losing so many to influenza makes it harder. It's good that you have Bobby in here, separate from your other children. Send Jack to me, if Bobby gets worse. Good luck and good day to you, Mrs. Kidd."

Bobby was seriously ill for several days, but he did not develop pneumonia, and to Annie's relief, he slowly began to recover. By the following Sunday, Annie felt that her eldest was well enough that she could leave him for a couple of hours. She left Jack at home with Bobby and took her younger sons with her to church. After the church service, she sought out Bobby's supervisor from the mill. The man was in his sixties and had a weathered face and a head of thick white hair.

"Thank you for sending Bobby home when you did. He was quite ill for a while, but thankfully he did not get pneumonia and is now recovering."

"He's a good lad, Mrs. Kidd, and a reliable worker. I'm glad he's on the mend. It's a nasty bug, that one. Don't let him worry about his job. We'll see him when he's well again. "

As Annie was saying goodbye, the school principal approached her."Mrs. Kidd, how is Bobby? I heard he had the flu."

Annie assured him that although he had been quite ill, Bobby was recovering now.

"That's good to hear. He's a fine boy. That's a wicked illness that's going around. I heard that thirty-seven people died in Gold Creek. I'm sure you heard about Lars Nilsen."

Annie froze. "What do you mean?"

"He died. I'm sorry, I thought you knew."

"You must be mistaken. I just had a letter from him last week!"

"I'm afraid it is true. I'm sorry to be the bearer of sad news. I know that he has been considerably helpful to you in your search for your mother. The poor man died of pneumonia. His family's in Norway and he died alone. Dreadful!"

"I- I can't believe that he's gone," Annie stammered. "What a terrible shame." Flustered, she muttered, "I must get my children home, and see to Bobby. Good afternoon."

She quickly turned away as her eyes filled with tears. She was sorry for the death of the young man, but she felt a rush of guilt; perhaps if she hadn't invited Lars Nilsen to her home, Bobby would not have caught the Spanish flu.

The flu left Bobby weaker and thinner, but eventually he felt well enough to return to work. When he came home after his first day back at work, he told his mother that the Spanish flu had spread throughout the town.

"There are over two hundred cases in town and all the schools and churches in the North will be closed to prevent it from spreading further. Apparently there are so many deaths in the North that there's a shortage of coffins. Victims are being buried in trenches in the cemeteries."

Annie was sure he was thinking the same as she. It could have been him buried in a trench.

Annie shook her head. "Haven't we been punished enough? People here are still mourning for family lost in the fire, and now this. It was frightening when you were so sick, Bobby. We are fortunate that you are healthy again. Dr. Miller says that since you've had the Spanish flu, you won't get sick with it again. At least that's comforting."

Chapter Fifty-Two

Unfortunately, a week later, Jack and Georgie fell ill. Both boys had severe headaches and high fevers. Bobby helped Annie bring two mattresses down to the empty dining room and she once again set up a sick-room. She was exhausted caring for her two rambunctious little boys and now seeing to Jack and Georgie's needs. When Bobby went to work that next day, she was on her own and overwhelmed. In spite of the fee, Annie did not hesitate to arrange to have the doctor come again.

At one o'clock, there was a loud knock at Annie's door. When she answered, a tall young man introduced himself as Dr. Hughes.

"I've just moved to the North, Mrs. Kidd, and I'm in partnership with Dr. Miller. I understand that you have two lads who are ill."

"Welcome to town, Dr. Hughes. Thank you for coming. I do have two very sick sons. I've kept them separate from my younger children. Follow me."

She led the doctor to her sick-room and watched as he examined fourteen-year-old Jack. The doctor then turned to examine Georgie, and when he listened to Georgie's chest, he swore in Welsh. Annie anxiously asked the doctor, in Welsh, what was wrong. Dr. Hughes' face grew red.

"I apologize, Mrs. Kidd. I've been reprimanded for swearing in the past, so now I use my childhood language. Until now, I've been undetected. I'm sorry to say, George has pneumonia. We must watch him carefully. Both boys have influenza. I'll stop by tomorrow to check on them. Here is some medication for them and the instructions." He handed her the bottle and a scrap of paper.

Leaving the sick-room, the doctor noticed Hal and Henry playing on the floor.

"You have your hands full with two sick boys and two very young children. I know of a fine girl who could help you with your little boys while you're caring for Jack and George."

"Is that so?" Annie had never thought of hiring help, but she loved the idea.

"She's from a large family and has considerable experience in caring for youngsters. I believe that she's fourteen or fifteen years old. She wouldn't require much payment if you give her a couple of meals each day. Would you like me to stop by her home and ask her to come over?"

"Oh, yes, Dr. Hughes, thank you. I'm weary to the bone. I could really use an extra pair of hands."

"Very well then, I'll speak to her. Her name is Yvonne." He paused awkwardly, blinking his kind grey eyes. "And I apologize again for my language. You taught me a good lesson to not make assumptions. Are you Welsh?"

"No, but I attended school in Cardiff when I was a young girl. Don't worry." She smiled. "You reminded me of a time when I thought I was swearing undetected, but I got caught, too. I thought I had forgotten my Welsh over the years, but apparently I remembered some words!"

"Well, I'd best be on my way. I shall see you tomorrow."

"Dr. Hughes, before you go, I have a question. Ever since Bobby became so ill, and now that Jack and Georgie are sick, I've been worrying that I brought this sickness into my house. I invited someone from Gold Creek here, and that person died last month."

"Oh no, dear woman, this Spanish influenza spreads much quicker than that. Your eldest son likely caught it at the mill. The pulp and paper mill has people in and out from many parts of Canada and America, as well as men returning from overseas. It could have come from anywhere. Ease your mind. You could not have brought it home."

Two hours later, there was a tentative knock at the door. Annie opened it to the pale face and thin frame of a young girl. Annie immediately felt pity for her; obviously the child did not get enough to eat. She had a thick wave of black hair and large green eyes fringed with long lashes. Annie thought she would be a beauty, if she gained some weight.

"You must be Yvonne. Come in."

The girl answered in a soft voice, "Hello, Mrs. Kidd. Dr. Hughes said you needed someone to take care of your youngsters." Yvonne looked as though she were ready to run away or burst into tears.

The girl was painfully shy, and Annie worried that the arrangement wouldn't work. She changed her mind quickly, though, when she introduced Yvonne to Hal and Henry. Yvonne knelt down to speak to the little boys. Henry, who was normally leery of strangers, allowed her to pick him up.

"Yvonne, there's soup on the stove and a fresh loaf of bread on the counter. There's also a block of cheese in the ice box. Give Henry and Hal their lunch and help yourself. Henry still needs some help feeding, especially with the soup. I'll just be in the next room with Jack and Georgie."

Annie went back to the sick-room but peeked into the kitchen now and then. Yvonne was efficient and patient with the children, with a ready smile on her face. After she fed the little boys, she demolished her own bowl of soup in seconds.

Annie returned to the kitchen. "I made too much soup and Jack and Georgie have lost their appetites with this flu. Have another bowl, dear, and help yourself to the bread and cheese. It's a fine day outside. After your lunch, you can take the boys out to play in the sand by the garden or take them for a wagon ride."

"Thank you Mrs. Kidd, but I can clean or do anything else for you, too."

"No, dear, I just need you to watch my little boys while Jack and Georgie are sick. I really appreciate you taking care of them. I'll call you in when I have dinner ready."

Yvonne's eyes filled with tears. "I'm sorry. I'm not upset. You and Dr. Hughes are very kind to me. I promise to take good care of Hal and Henry."

While Yvonne and the little boys were outside, both Jack's and Georgie's temperatures spiked. Annie could feel the heat radiating off of them. She recalled her desperation and anxiety those many years ago, when Maggie was fevered. Annie cooled their foreheads with wet flannels and tried to get them to drink a little water.

Georgie's cough worsened and he complained of chest pain. His breathing was laboured. He was eleven years old now and although he was tall for his age, he still had a cherubic face. His hair was light blond and his nose was spattered with freckles. She pressed her hand affectionately to his flushed cheek.

Bobby came home from work at his usual time. The room was filled with the tantalizing aroma of a chicken baking in the oven. The two little boys were at the table with Yvonne contentedly eating apple slices. Annie introduced Bobby to Yvonne, explaining how she had come to be helping them. Bobby blushed and nodded to Yvonne, then went upstairs to change out of his work clothes.

As Yvonne washed Hal and Henry's faces and hands after their snack, she offered, "Next time, Mrs. Kidd, I'd be happy to make dinner while I watch your boys."

"Yes, I think that would be better. Georgie seems to be getting much worse now."

When Hal and Henry were asleep for the night, Yvonne set out to leave for home. Annie hugged the young girl.

"Thank you so much, Yvonne. You've been a great help to me today. You are so good with the children. I'll see you tomorrow morning about eight o'clock then."

Yvonne's whole face lit up. "I've had a wonderful day, Mrs. Kidd. See you tomorrow."

Annie smiled to herself as she watched Yvonne almost skip down the street. When she returned to the sickroom, Bobby offered to sit with Jack and Georgie for a few hours.

"I'm not tired, Ma. You go up and have a nap. I'll wake you if either one gets worse."

Exhausted, Annie whispered, "Thank you, son."

Once upstairs, she fell onto her bed fully dressed. She was asleep in seconds and slept for three hours. She awoke to the worrisome bark of continuous coughing from downstairs.

She wearily stood up and checked Hal and Henry. Henry was sucking his thumb. His chubby cheeks were pink from his outside play. Hal was snuggled beside his brother and breathing heavily in a deep sleep. Annie adjusted their blankets; how angelic her two little boys looked while sleeping. Then she braced herself to return to the sick-room.

Jack was sleeping soundly, but Bobby had Georgie sitting up, and was patting his back. Bobby looked at his mother relieved.

"Poor Georgie's having trouble breathing."

"I'll take over now, son. You have work tomorrow. I had a lovely rest, so don't worry. You go up to bed."

After Bobby left, Annie checked Jack to be assured he was sleeping peacefully. *Jack looks so much like Bobby,* Annie thought; *he's the mirror image of his older brother at fourteen.* She adjusted his blanket, then turned her attention to Georgie.

Annie was alarmed by how much his illness had progressed. She sat on the edge of his bed, and ran her fingers through his hair. He looked at her with tears in his eyes and asked in a hoarse voice, "Am I going to die, Mummy?"

She fought to stop her own tears, and said in as calm a voice as she could muster. "No, Georgie, of course not! You just try to rest and I'll stay right here beside you."

Georgie's fever remained high throughout the night, as he coughed and struggled to breathe. Annie tried to push aside memories of Maggie's illness as she nursed her two sons. She was so frightened that her hands shook and her eyes repeatedly filled with tears. Feeling helpless, she stood up often and paced the room. Through her tears Annie spoke silently to her father. *Oh, Pappa, I can't lose another child. This illness is so frightening!*

Eventually, she felt calmer. Georgie was still gasping for breath, but Annie felt the strength and support of her father's love. She rolled up a blanket to prop Georgie up and help him breathe easier, and then she went over to Jack's bed to check on him. He opened his eyes and Annie whispered to him.

"How are you feeling now, Jack?"

"My headache is gone but I'm hungry, Ma. Can I have some soup?"

"I'll warm up some for you right away," Annie replied with great relief. "Why don't I fill the tub and put some fresh sheets on your bed while you have a bath. That will make you feel better."

"Thanks, Ma. How's Georgie?" Jack looked over at his brother.

"I think his pneumonia is worse, Dr. Hughes is coming in the morning, thank God. I'm so relieved that you're feeling better, Jack. I'll come to help you walk to the bathroom when I have the tub full. You'll still be feeling weak for a while yet."

The next morning, Yvonne arrived at seven-thirty. She brought Hal and Henry downstairs and made breakfast for them. Bobby came into the kitchen, ate his breakfast quietly, and made his lunch. He tiptoed into the sick-room and looked relieved when he saw Jack sleeping peacefully. Georgie still looked very ill and Bobby glanced anxiously at his mother.

"Poor Georgie, is he coughing up blood?"

Annie nodded and whispered back, "I'll be glad to see Dr. Hughes this morning. At least Jack seems to have improved."

Annie saw how worried Bobby was when he said goodbye and left for work. She stayed with Jack and Georgie, and listened to the cheerful banter between Yvonne and Hal in the kitchen. Later, she heard the door open and close, when Yvonne took the little boys outside after breakfast.

Dr. Hughes had arrived at about nine o'clock. He examined both boys and shook his head when he listened to Georgie's chest. Back in the kitchen he quietly spoke to Annie.

"Jack has improved. He'll be a little weak yet. Just make sure he gets plenty of liquids. But Mrs. Kidd, I'm going to take George to the hospital. His pneumonia is much worse and I'm quite concerned. I'll take him in my car right now. I'll make sure the nurses let you see him any time."

Dr. Hughes went back to Georgie's bed and lifted the boy into his arms. Annie grabbed a pillow and blanket and followed the doctor to his car. She placed the pillow on the back seat and cried as the doctor gently laid Georgie down. Annie covered Georgie with the blanket and kissed his cheek.

"I'll come to the hospital, son, as soon as I can. You are going to get better now, Georgie. Dr. Hughes will take good care of you."

Georgie looked frightened; his eyes filled with tears. Annie closed the car door and watched as the car pulled away and disappeared down the road. She stood frozen on the same spot for several minutes trying to compose herself. A hot summer breeze blew around her and she wondered how the sun could shine on such a dreadful day. She heard Yvonne's steps in the gravel road and she turned around. Yvonne was holding the boys' hands.

"Mrs. Kidd, I can take care of Jack and still watch Hal and Henry. I'm used to caring for my brothers and sisters. You should go to the hospital. I'll even stay overnight if you want."

Annie wiped away her tears with her apron and replied in a broken voice, "Thank you, Yvonne. You're right. Maybe if I'm with him, he'll fight harder. If I lost my Georgie, Yvonne, I just couldn't bear it."

"Don't worry about anything here. I'll take care of your boys until Bobby gets home. If he wants me to stay over to watch Jack tonight, I will. I can just run back home to let my parents know. If they're concerned about me being alone in a house of boys, I'll bring my sister or brother back with me."

"You've thought of everything, dear. I'm so grateful that Dr. Hughes sent you to me. Bobby will probably want to come to the hospital too, when he gets home. I've plenty of eggs and bacon in the icebox and you'll find cans of food in the cupboard over the counter." She impulsively gave the girl a warm hug. "Thank you, Yvonne."

Annie quickly changed her clothes. She gave Henry a quick hug and kneeled down to kiss Hal goodbye. Neither little boy fussed as she left; they were happy under Yvonne's care. She briskly walked the mile to the school, which had been converted to an influenza hospital. By the time she reached the building she was overheated from her walk in the summer sunshine. She climbed the concrete stairs and pulled open the heavy wooden door at the entrance and was greeted by a volunteer, who handed her a mask and directed her to the largest classroom on the next floor. Annie's shoes clicked on the hardwood floor as she walked down the long hallway. She slowly climbed the stairs to the second floor. It was odd to see beds filling rooms of blackboards and bookshelves. She passed through the doorway of Georgie's ward and saw many cots arranged in rows; every bed held a sick child. The nurses had set up a station in the cloakroom and filled it with bedding and supplies. Annie searched the room and finally found Georgie in a bed in the middle-row. A nurse was taking his temperature when Annie introduced herself.

"Dr. Hughes said I could stay with Georgie. If there's anything I can do to help with his care, just tell me."

The nurse looked kindly at Annie and replied, "I'm glad to see you, Mrs. Kidd. He's frightened and it'll be reassuring for him to have his mother beside him. We're trying to get Georgie to drink some fluids, so perhaps you can get him to sip a little water. I'll bring a chair over for you."

Georgie momentarily opened his eyes and gave Annie a weak smile. She glanced around the ward and heard a cacophony of coughs, moans and sobs. She loosened the collar of her dress; the room was stifling. Annie marvelled at how quickly the smell of chalk dust had been replaced by the sharp antiseptic odour of a hospital ward. She imagined that she could also smell the children's fear. As Annie stayed beside Georgie throughout the day, he often opened his eyes in a panic. When he saw her, and she assured him that she would stay with him, his expression would soften and he'd close his eyes again.

At eight o'clock that night, Dr. Hughes came to the bedside.

"Mrs. Kidd, go home. You'll end up getting sick yourself. We have nurses here throughout the night and they'll call me if Georgie is in distress. I imagine you haven't eaten all day either."

Annie's eyes welled with tears. She struggled to steady her voice. "Dr. Hughes, I lost my first child, my only daughter, in 1902, to measles. I still have a huge hole in my heart. Georgie is named after my youngest brother, and he died in battle last year, at Passchendaele. My husband is in Belgium now and I worry every day about him. I cannot lose Georgie. I truly believe that if my son knows that I'm right here beside him, he'll fight harder."

The doctor patted Annie's shoulder. "I'd never underestimate the power of a mother's love. I'll get one of our volunteers to bring you a meal."

Soon after Dr. Hughes left, Bobby appeared.

"You look exhausted, Ma. Do you want to go home for a rest and I'll stay beside Georgie? Everything is fine at home. Yvonne is quite organized and she's patient with those little monkeys. She made dinner, and brought back her older brother to stay the night with her. Her brother is with Jack now, and Yvonne is upstairs in Hal and Henry's room. I can stay with Georgie."

"No, son. Thank you for offering, but Georgie is so sick, I don't want to leave him. I'm glad you asked Yvonne to stay. You have to go to work tomorrow. If Georgie improves, then I'll go home for a bit tomorrow evening, while you sit with him here. I'm glad Jack is feeling better, because I don't know how I could have managed."

Bobby stayed for another hour before returning home and promising to come again the next day after his shift.

Annie dozed in the chair beside Georgie's bed, and in the early morning hours she was suddenly awakened when she felt his arm fall over her knee. She sat up and looked anxiously at her son, taking his hand into her own. He mouthed the words "I love you, Mummy." She felt a huge lump in her throat and fought her tears.

"I love you very much too, Georgie. You need to fight hard and get better, son."

He smiled weakly at her and closed his eyes. He lay stock-still and Annie held her breath, remaining as motionless as her son. Then she forced herself to put a hand on his chest, not sure whether she could feel a weak heartbeat. She put her ear to his nose and mouth and remembered that old crone's prediction back in Shields the night before they left for Canada. True to the prediction, Annie had crossed water and battled fire. Did fighting disease and death mean she was going to lose

Georgie? Was she being punished for loving this boy maybe a little more than his brothers? Just then, she felt her cheek caressed by a brief weak exhalation.

"Oh, thank God. I need you to stay with me Georgie. Don't you dare give up!"

She remained awake for the rest of the night, watching him closely. A nurse came by to take his temperature at about four in the morning, and whispered, "Mrs. Kidd, it looks like his fever has broken! Dr. Hughes will be pleased when he comes on his rounds."

When the doctor came by at seven o'clock, he said, "It looks like George is over the crisis. I believe he will recuperate, but it may be a slow process. His heart and lungs have been weakened, but he has youth on his side, as well as a determined mother."

That evening, when Bobby came into the hospital after his shift, Annie decided that she could go home for a while. Dr. Hughes said he should check Jack again and offered to give her a ride home in his car. She readily accepted.

"Thank you once again, Dr. Hughes. It will take me a while to pay you for all your services but I assure you I will. I'm so weary; I was not looking forward to the walk home. I'd appreciate the ride."

The doctor followed her out and opened the passenger door for her. She slid into the seat and fell asleep before he even started the ignition, waking only when the car stopped in front of her house. She was mortified.

"I'm so sorry. I can't believe that I fell asleep in your car!"

"Don't worry. I'm pleased you were at peace and could nap. Let's go in and see how Jack is doing. I'm sure Yvonne has managed the house and your boys quite well."

They entered the house and were welcomed by the warm, teasing aroma of baking bread. The counters and table were scrubbed clean and the kitchen floor had been mopped. There was a vegetable stew bubbling away on the stove top. Annie felt a surge of love for the slip of a girl who had so recently come into their lives.

Yvonne was in the sick-room, taking away dishes from Jack. He was sitting up in bed with Spud curled up in a ball warming his feet.

"How are you feeling, son? You're looking much better. I see that Yvonne has been taking good care of you." She turned to the girl. "Dinner smells wonderful! You are doing a fine job of managing the house." Yvonne's face reddened. Annie looked again at Jack with relief. "Indeed, you have become a pampered gentleman!" she teased.

Jack laughed weakly, then spoke in a raspy voice. "I am feeling better, Ma, but... how is Georgie?"

"We think the worst is over now. He may be in the hospital for a while yet, but he has improved. Dr. Hughes wants to check you. Come along, Yvonne. Let's have a cup of tea and I'd love a dish of your stew. It smells delicious and I'm famished."

Annie went upstairs to check her sleeping little boys, and then changed her clothes. By the time she came back down, Yvonne had the table set with three bowls of stew and was at the counter slicing thick wedges of her warm homemade bread. Dr. Hughes looked up sheepishly from the table.

"I'm afraid I have invited myself for dinner, Mrs. Kidd. My bachelor meals are pitiful. I'll have to take a deduction off my bill to repay for this hearty meal. You know I just might hire Yvonne and make her my own housekeeper, once George is well!"

Yvonne blushed and lowered her head, but smiled at the compliment.

The doctor looked at Annie and said, "Seriously, Mrs. Kidd, you must get some rest after your dinner. I'm going back to the hospital after I eat and will keep a close eye on George."

Annie consented. "Yes, I'll follow the doctor's orders this time. I'll have a nap after dinner."

Bobby visited Georgie and Annie, in the children's ward, every day after work. He soon reported to Annie that Jack was well enough to get to the table for his meals and sleep upstairs in their bedroom. He reassured his mother that everything was well taken care of at home.

One day Annie teased him about having a pretty girl around the house. Bobby blushed crimson and guffawed, "Ma, Yvonne's just a kid. She's not much older than Jack!"

Georgie seemed to be slowly improving and Annie was eager to bring him home from the hospital. Over the next two weeks, she watched in horror as sheets were pulled over other little bodies and cots wheeled out of the ward. At least ten children had passed away while Georgie was in the hospital. The smell of the disinfectants permeated her hair and clothing, and the summer heat collected and stagnated in the ward. Windows were kept wide open to catch any errant breeze. Annie was becoming accustomed to the odours and the heat, but was haunted by the coughing and crying of so many ill children. She watched as despair and exhaustion wore away at the nurses and doctors.

At the end of the second week of Georgie's hospital confinement, Dr. Hughes came to examine him while on his regular rounds. The doctor looked extremely tired. He had dark circles under his eyes, and his forehead seemed permanently creased in worry; it seemed he had aged in the short time since she met him. He approached Georgie's bed, listened to the boy's chest, and nodded.

"Well, Mrs. Kidd, I believe that Georgie has recuperated sufficiently enough to return home. He will still need a lot of time to rest, and I'll have to monitor his heart and lungs for several months. It would be good for him to sit outside by your garden for a few hours on each warm day, but he must not do anything strenuous for a couple of weeks or even longer."

He grinned and said some words in Welsh. Annie knew it was a wish for good fortune. He placed his large hand on Georgie's shoulder and said, "You are blessed, Georgie. I wasn't sure you could pull through, but I'm pleased to see that I was proven wrong. Mrs. Kidd, I have to make a few house calls near your house. I can drive you and George home tonight."

That afternoon, when Bobby stopped by the hospital after work, Annie told him the good news.

Bobby's face lit up. "We'll have to have a proper celebration for you, Georgie. Are you feeling better now?"

Georgie beamed and replied, "Yes, and I really want to get out of here. Tell Spud, and Jack and Hal and Henry, that I'm coming home."

"I will, Sport," said Bobby. "See you tonight."

When Dr. Hughes' car pulled up and parked outside the Kidd's home, Georgie was greeted like royalty. Yvonne was on the door step holding Hal's hand and carrying Henry on her hip. Bobby and Jack were outside too and they all cheered and clapped as Georgie came out of the car. Georgie's pale face lit up with a huge smile. There was a sign pinned to the front door that read "Welcome home, Georgie!" He was still quite weak, so Dr. Hughes picked him up and carried him into the house, placing him gently in the rocking chair. In the centre of the kitchen table, there was a chocolate cake.

"Vonny made a cake for you, Georgie!" Hal announced. "Me and Henry helped." He looked at the doctor and said, "You can have a piece of cake too, mister."

Dr. Hughes laughed and replied, "I have to attend to another patient but I will certainly return for a piece of cake. Thank you."

Annie wished that Jim was with them to help celebrate Georgie's recovery. With a start, she realized that Jim didn't even know how close they had come to losing another child.

Chapter Fifty-Three

Belgium
November, 1918

The shells fired from enemy dugouts were a continuous threat to the troops. The men had to wear their gas masks throughout the early evening, even when it was pouring rain. Wrapped in his ground cape, Jim shivered and listened to his own breath rattling in and out of his respirator.

When the cold wind abruptly changed directions, Jim anxiously looked towards the signal post. The flag announced that it was safe to remove gas masks and he quickly pulled his off, mopped away the moisture from his forehead and sighed with relief.

At midnight, orders came to advance. Jim's unit began the assembly of a prefabricated bridge to the other side of the canal. They placed light rails parallel to the waterway and a large pivot that allowed the bridge to swivel across.

"Damn, I hate working out here in the open!" complained a man working beside Jim. They were straddling a large metal shaft.

"We might as well have targets painted on our backs! General Currie's probably sitting beside a warm fireplace right now while we risk our lives."

Jim grunted, then said, "Aye, and likely after a big meal of roast beef and Yorkshire pudding."

As soon as the pivot was assembled, Jim and about thirty other soldiers stood on one end to provide the heavy load needed, to allow the bridge to lift and swing across to the other side. Jim watched the horses cross, straining as they dragged the heavy guns. Suddenly the night lit up in an explosion of machine-gun fire and the horses collapsed on the bridge. The Allied gunners quickly retaliated with a heavy bombardment, aimed in the direction of the enemy machine-gun nest.

Jim quickly jumped down to a rocky ledge in the wall of the canal, and heard a loud thud and splash below him. One of the horses had toppled off the crossing. Soon other horses followed as soldiers pushed the dead animals over into the water. The men pulled and pushed the loads of weapons to the opposite side. Jim cautiously climbed back up the slimy stone wall and continued the construction work with his division. Within four hours, they had three prefabricated spans in place.

When the final overpass was completed, the remaining heavy guns were rolled across to the opposite side. Waves of Canadian troops surged forward and began a massive assault on the enemy. Jim and his unit followed in the rear. The night sky was illuminated from the continuous detonation of weapons, and throughout the battle there was no escape from the deafening whine of shells and intense explosions. Jim's head throbbed and his ears rang.

The army pushed on through Belgium. Jim's company continued with the construction of cork bridges and rafts, so that the army and heavy artillery could cross the rivers. They worked under cover of the dark to avoid detection by enemy snipers. Jim grew more and more exhausted from the heavy labour and continual marching as they chased the retreating Germans through Belgium.

Emaciated horses were worked to death, often flogged while pulling heavy loads of artillery in the advance. It was common to march past hundreds of dead horses rotting in the mud. During the weeks of fighting in the cold, unrelenting rainfall, the men were never dry. They marched past the gruesome sight of corpses littering both sides of the road. Some men collected souvenirs from the

German bodies until one soldier was killed when he set off explosives booby-trapped to a corpse. There were dirty tricks on both sides. In retaliation, knowing that the German soldiers were starving, a few men threw can after can of bully beef at the enemy trenches; they waited for the men to rush to grab the tins, then threw hand grenades at the hungry German troops.

While chasing the retreating Germans, the Allies were treated as liberators by the civilians as they marched from village to village. People lined the roads and cheered them on. Some handed the men flowers and even pressed previously hidden bottles of wine on them. The troops saw how extremely malnourished and thin the Belgian villagers were, and often gave some of their rations to the children.

When they stopped at one small village, Jim finally had a break from duty, and took the time to write a letter to his wife.

Dearest Annie,

At last I have the time to write you, and I pray that this letter finds you and the boys well. Finally we are able to sleep in houses instead of trenches. What luxury. Apparently the Germans told the civilians that Canadians were wild colonials who would rape and murder them! What nonsense.

We may be liberators but at a huge cost. I've lost too many mates and seen too much death. I'm tired to the core and just want to get home.

Tonight I am sitting at a table in a kitchen belonging to a kind elderly couple. I've shared my food with them and they've allowed me to sleep in their spare bed tonight. I showed them your picture and the photo of our boys. I have no idea what they said but it sounded like a compliment to my family.

I hear rumours of armistice but we are still ordered to continue through towards Mons. We are all in a foul mood and there is a lot of cursing and swearing. I have made it this far, and I pray that I will survive this war and soon be home with you and our sons. I miss you.

Your loving husband,
Jim

At the end of the following day, Jim was in an abandoned barn, with several other men. The building was to be their billet for the night. The stone and wood structure was dusty and permeated with an odour of manure from the animals that once slept there, but it had a solid roof and provided dry shelter.

Letters were picked up and new mail delivered to the men. Jim was handed a thick envelope from Annie. He sat down on the straw-covered floor and opened it.

Dear Jim,

I hope that this note finds you well. We have had a very trying time this last month, but I assure you that we are all healthy now. Bobby was very ill with Spanish influenza, but he soon recovered and is now back to work. Then Jack and Georgie came down with the flu. Jack recovered fairly quickly, but our Georgie was deathly ill. He had to spend a long time in the hospital. I thought we were going to lose him, Jim, he was that ill. He had a severe case of pneumonia and I think I bullied him to fight for his life. I could not bear to lose another child, and I know it to be the same for you.

Jim stopped reading; he closed his eyes and swore. He touched the pocket over his heart, which held his precious family photos and Bible. Then he continued reading. Georgie was home now but still quite weak. His heart and lungs were stressed. Annie assured him that she had enough money for the hospital bills. She wrote that the flu had hit the North quite hard, and that there had been many deaths. She was thankful that Hal and Henry remained healthy. As he was reading, several pages slipped down to his lap. He picked them up and discovered notes from Bobby, Jack, and Georgie, a picture drawn by Hal with a carefully printed *Daddy,* and some scribbles from Henry. Jim read the letters from his sons, then folded them and replaced them in the envelope. He took out his photos and stared at the picture of his children. A young man from Nova Scotia sat beside Jim and handed him his rum ration.

"I hope that was not bad news from home, Jim. You look a little shaken."

Jim took the rum and poured a few splashes of it into his tin cup of tea. "No, Ben, everything is fine. It's just very difficult being so far away from my family. My wife wrote to tell me that three of our boys were sick with the Spanish flu. We almost lost one son, but thankfully he's recuperating at home now."

"That's one nasty disease going around. Perfectly healthy men go to bed one day and they're dead the next. I heard this Spanish flu is spreading all over the world now." Ben shook his head. "Did you hear that General Currie has ordered us to take Mons from the Germans? After the terrible losses we've suffered in battle these last months, why is he volunteering the Canadians for this one? I hear that the German army is starving and losing the will to fight; their allies are all surrendering. This war is almost over. Nobody wants to be the last soldier killed, but I guess Currie wants the glory. What do we care about reputations as liberators? I just want to come out of this alive!"

Most of the men in the barn joined in the conversation and cursed Currie for his drive to win what could be the last battle of the war. The next night, however, they followed orders and marched over Belgian fields towards Mons, passing abandoned German guns and helmets. Jim felt very vulnerable marching overland for miles. There were many areas around them that could conceal an enemy sniper; he was used to the security of trenches and craters. When they were within sight of the town, the army stopped and waited for further orders.

Late that night, the Canadians encircled the town. Scouts had reported that most of the German machine gunners were in the southeast section of Mons, so the army entered the town from the south, west and northwest just after midnight.

Jim crept along the rain-soaked cobblestone streets, with all of his senses on high alert. A cloud cover shrouded the town in a ghostly haze. Jim heard explosions of gunfire to the south and slipped into a doorway, aiming his rifle towards the street.

He saw a flash of light and heard the staccato of gunfire coming from an upper-storey window across the street. With lightning speed, a Canadian sniper returned the gunfire. As Jim cautiously looked around, he saw a fellow soldier, collapsed on the ancient stones of the street. He ran to the injured man, grabbed him by his tunic, and dragged him to the safety of the door recess.

The injured man's eyes were open and he muttered, "Thanks, pal. I think Tom got the bugger. I'll get up in a minute. I'm having trouble seeing out of my left eye, but I think I'm all right."

Jim could see that a bullet had entered one side of the soldier's temple and exited the other side, yet miraculously he had survived. Jim helped the man struggle up to lean against the heavy wooden door.

"Stay here, mate, and I'll see if I can get help. You've been shot in the head."

The injured man gingerly put his hand to his head, looked at the blood on his fingers, and crumpled to the steps in a faint. Jim recognized one of their runners coming towards him and yelled.

"Get this man to a medic. He needs help now!"

Jim saw that the injured soldier was breathing fairly regularly and would soon be attended to by a medic. Reassured, he advanced farther into the town. The heavy fighting continued through the night.

The battle was over by seven o'clock that morning. The last of the Germans in Mons had surrendered or been killed, and, a few hours later, Jim heard the news that all hostilities would cease at eleven o'clock.

A Canadian runner raced into Mons and shouted, "The Armistice has been signed!"

Several soldiers ran through the cobblestone streets, banging on doors and windows and shouting that the war was over. Jim watched families slowly emerge from their cellars. They were thin and bedraggled, but spirited as they surrounded their liberators. The Canadian Highlanders further stirred emotions when they marched their pipe bands through the town. Jim found himself surrounded by ecstatic civilians as they crowded and cheered. The troops were back-slapped, kissed and given small gifts of biscuits and bits of ribbon. The sound of the deadly gunfire of those early morning hours was now replaced with the joyous ring of church bells and the rousing call of the pipes. The town clock added to the noisy celebrations as it clanged eleven times.

Jim smiled weakly and detached himself from the crowd. He slipped into a deserted alleyway and pulled out the photo of Annie. Emotion broke his voice as he whispered, "I'm coming home, Annie. I'm coming home."

Chapter Fifty-Four

Bobby burst through the front door and shouted, "Ma, the war is over! The news is all around town. Everyone is cheering and celebrating! Listen, you can hear all the church bells ringing." He gave his mother a hug and added, "This means Da is coming home!"

Annie was afraid to believe it. "I thought this day would never come. It's been a long two years without your father."

"It will be grand to have him back home. And Ma, now we can buy the ticket for Gran! We can start to fix up her bedroom in the parlour."

Annie regarded her eldest son affectionately. It made her heart glad that he fondly remembered his grandmother and was eager to see her again.

"You're right, son. I'm just as excited as you are to think that we will soon have them both here with us. We can be busy making plans for your grandmother while we wait to hear from your Da. In fact, I'll write to the ticket agents in Toronto today."

The following day, Jack came home with three newspapers and handed them to Annie. "They printed up three editions of the paper yesterday!"

Annie looked over the headlines. "Oh, boys, the war is really is over. I was afraid to believe it!"

She knew from Jim's last letter that he had been heading for Mons, so an article about Canadian troops capturing Mons as the last act of the war caught her attention. She read that Mons had been taken from the Germans shortly before dawn. She tried to suppress her worry about Jim being in this last battle. She would not know if he had survived it until she received a letter. She took the newspapers upstairs to her bedroom to privately check the lists of casualties in all three papers. She turned to the page that named the wounded and dead, and ran her finger down the list; thankfully she did not find Jim's name.

Annie decided to focus all her energies on plans to get her mother to Canada. That afternoon, she wrote out a cheque for the enormous amount of one hundred and ten dollars and forty-five cents to A.F. Webster and Sons. She wrote the address in Toronto on the envelope and asked Bobby to mail it, knowing he would want to.

Annie still did not receive mail from Jim the following week, nor thankfully a telegraph bearing bad news. Bobby brought home a letter from A. F. Webster and Sons, however, and she wasted no time in tearing the envelope open. Inside she found a receipt and a short note.

Mrs. J. Kidd,
Bear Falls, Ont.
Dear Mrs. Kidd,
We duly received your letter of the 12th enclosing a check for $110.45 for passage for Mrs. Larsen from Bergen to Toronto. We have sent the ticket forward as requested, and now enclose a receipt for the same.
Yours truly,
A.F. Webster and Sons
Steamship Ticket Agents

She found a salmon-pink slip of paper enclosed; it was the receipt for transportation for one adult from Bergen to Toronto, marked *paid in full*. Annie held the paper to her chest and closed her eyes. *It is finally becoming a reality. Mother will come to live with us now.* She had arranged for Mother's transportation in early May because she thought that the ocean would be calmer than in the winter, and it would also involve a shorter train ride to Toronto because the seaway would be open. Annie and Alfie had already planned that their mother would stay a month with him in Toronto, and then take the train north to Annie in June.

Early in December, Annie finally received a letter from Jim. It had taken several weeks to reach her but she was reassured by the date on the envelope that he had survived the battle at Mons. She sat down on the familiar bench by the window in the post office, her vision blurred with sudden tears. Trying to calm herself, she took off her hat and unbuttoned her coat. Inhaling deeply, she opened the envelope and began to read.

Dearest Annie,

It does not seem real to me yet, but I will finally be returning home. I'm sure you have read in the papers how we were in Mons the same morning of the ceasefire. I can't help but resent that we suffered more casualties when we could have just waited. You likely saw a picture of Currie perched on his horse saluting us in Mons main square. I suppose it is possible that I am somewhere in the photo. Old soldiers like me followed the orders, but we were angry to have to risk our lives one more time when the end of the war was so close. I should be happy that I survived, but can't help but feel guilty that I am still alive when so many others perished.

I will be shipped to England sometime in January. We all want to leave now, but we have to wait until decisions are made. You must forgive me for my melancholy mood. I think I'll improve once I'm back on English soil. We've been marching for miles and I am weary. I know that I need to be thankful for all I have. I often wonder why I'm still here, but I just have to pull out your photo and the picture of our five boys - then I'm determined to get home. Take very good care of yourself and give my love to the boys. I will write again when I get to Eat Apples (our slang for Etaples) and will hopefully know by then when I will be shipped home.

All my love, your husband, Jim

Annie refolded the letter and tucked it into her pocket. She dried her eyes with her mitten, and stood up to button her coat and arrange her scarf before she left the warmth of the post office. She opened the heavy wooden door and braced herself for the sharp tingle of freezing air on her forehead and cheeks. Large snowflakes clung to her hat and coat as she walked, trudging through the soft snowdrifts accumulating on the road. The strong, cold wind increased in intensity. Annie was relieved when she finally climbed the front steps to her house.

Once inside, she quickly closed the front door behind her and stomped her boots on the mat to loosen the snow. Georgie was sitting on the floor near the kitchen stove, keeping Hal and Henry laughing by building wood block towers and purposely toppling his creations. Georgie was pale and thin, but much stronger now. Annie felt a catch in her throat as she looked at him.

Jack was stirring soup at the stove and looked over to his mother. "I have lunch almost ready now. Did we have any mail?"

"Yes, we did get a letter from your Da. He is fine, and just waiting for a ship to take him to England. Oh, boys, I can hardly believe that he's finally coming home!"

Chapter Fifty-Five

Jim got off the military train at Etaples. It was his fourth time in this small fishing port on the coast of France since 1917, and he hoped it was his last. The town was a railroad centre, convenient to the Allies, and had a huge concentration of military camps and hospitals. There were miles and miles of army-issued tents arranged precisely in regimental units throughout the pine trees. He was directed to a large round canvas shelter, about five hundred yards from the sandy seashore. He was to share it with eighteen other men and did not look forward to sleeping on the hard wooden floor. The one luxury, however, was the opportunity to take a hot shower in one of the converted factories.

For several days Jim was detailed to burial duty while he waited for his transportation to England. Spanish flu was a final lethal insult to many men who had survived poison gas and shrapnel during the war, only to be killed after it was over, by a virus. Each day sick men were placed in cots at the front end of the influenza tents. As their illness progressed, they were moved towards the other end of the tent, then finally to a deathbed. Men coughed up blood, and suffered through uncontrolled hemorrhaging. Their faces took a bluish tinge as they slowly suffocated. The mortally ill patients were removed from that end of the tent when they died, and quickly buried. Jim was humbly reminded of how close they came to losing Georgie to this deadly illness.

When Jim finally heard that he would leave for England on January sixteenth, he wrote to Annie.

My dear wife Annie,

Hallelujah, I have word that I will leave for England on the sixteenth. It has been a long wait to get back to Old Blighty. Camp here has not been too uncomfortable but our meals are monotonous. We get bacon, bread, jam, tea and cheese for almost every meal. The odd time they ship over some beef, we finally get our fill. Your mother would have wondered why they didn't feed us fish when we are right here at a fishing port. I can imagine how she'd scold those in charge of our rations! It will be wonderful for you to have your mother near you again. I know you have sorely missed her.

I have stayed well and avoided catching the Spanish flu so far. We have lost a shocking number of men to this deadly disease. I've watched many men suffer through it and I can't help but think of our three boys who were just as sick. It is a miracle that they survived. I guess the boys here just don't have their own mothers to help them pull through.

I believe that I will be in Surrey, at Witley Camp, when we get to England, and I hope that I will get the time to go up to South Shields to visit Mother before leaving for Canada. I heard that we get two weeks leave once we complete our documentation, and I expect to be in England for a month. Perhaps I'll be home by the end of February. I'll be counting the hours until I have you in my arms again. I miss our boys and send them my love. I will write again when I get to Surrey.

Love, Jim

Jim arrived in the tin city of Witley Military Camp, in Surrey, on January sixteenth as planned. When he found his assigned building and entered, he was greeted by a disgruntled soldier.

"Not another man for here. We're bloody crowded as it is! Welcome, mate, to a drafty corner of the floor. The coal's scarce, the hut's cold, we've thin, miserly blankets and horrible rations. It's a right pleasant spot of heaven, it is." He sighed, "I've been here a month and still no hope of sailing home. I get a promise, and then the sailing is cancelled. Then just today, I heard that some fresh conscripts - who didn't even finish training nor see a battle - got to go home ahead of me! I've been in the war since 1916, and I get treated like this!"

Another man butted in, "Give over, Bill. This poor bloke has just come over from Mons. Give him a break."

Bill was a tall, thin man with a receding hairline. He leaned on a cane for support and said to Jim, "Sorry, mate. I'm just frustrated about missing another ship home."

Jim replied, "No offence taken, Bill. I've grown a thick hide." He reached into his canvas sack and pulled out a box of Annie's baking.

"Here, have some of my wife's shortbread. Maybe it'll sweeten your mood."

Jim stayed at Witley Camp for two weeks. Bill was right, it was miserable accommodation. When the men received orders to report to Knotty Ash Camp, near Liverpool, none were sorry to leave Witley. It was a long, cold march through Reading, Birmingham, and Rhyl, and the men suffered more discomfort in the steady wet drizzle, but they were heartened to be getting closer to the Liverpool port, their gateway home.

Jim had delayed writing to Annie for a couple of weeks because he wanted to give her his sailing date. Now he sat down on his cot, searched through his bag for paper and, began a letter.

Dear Annie,

I've been here near Liverpool for over two weeks now. I'm sorry to say that I still don't have a sailing date yet. They try to keep us busy with drill and sports but we all just want to get home. I have filled out over a dozen documents now, answering tedious questions. I will have my discharge medical soon, then I will have two weeks off and can take the train north to visit Mother.

At present I am quite miserable with a very swollen, painful jaw. I took advantage of the free dental services offered to us here before demobilization and had three molars extracted at one time and without any pain killers! Had I known that it would involve such

torture during and after the operations I would not have agreed to it!
The plan, apparently, is to get all our documentation completed
here before we ship out, so we can get home all the quicker once we
are on Canadian soil. I do know that I will be on a ship that will take
troops to Halifax, and then we will take the train to Toronto.

Even though they split up our northern regiment once we arrived
in England, the men from the North will be a group again as we head
home. There are men here in camp from many towns of New
Ontario, so I'm pretty sure that we will be travelling together.

This military camp that I'm in now is American. It's a small city
of hastily erected huts with serviceable streets and sidewalks. Some
Americans in the camp have only been in England for eight months,
and I met a few who were here for just nine days. It's very difficult to
be civil when I still have the mud of the Western Front on my boots,
but then again I just want to forget the war. I've been having
nightmares. Although my body is here, my mind is still in the
battlefield. I won't report that when I have my medical because it
may delay my departure. But hopefully once I'm home again I'll be
able to escape the war memories.

I hope to see you in February, but I'll let you know when my
sailing date is as soon as the army decides to tell me. I send my love
to you and our boys.

Your husband, Jim

Jim mailed his letter, and then joined some mates for a pint.
While enjoying his beer at a table with other men from Canada, one
soldier elbowed him.

"I suppose we had better enjoy our alcohol while we can. I hear
that Canada is still dry, thanks to the Women's Christian Temperance
Union. It makes no sense to dole out rum rations on the front and
expect us to be happy with abstinence once we get back home!"

Jim shook his head and replied, "I hadn't thought of that. It makes
this beer taste all the better right now!"

On the following day, Jim had the medical examination that was
required before his discharge. A simple three-letter word, *fit,* would be

his ticket to get home. Jim breathed a sigh of relief when he read it in his documents. He filed his application for his war service gratuity and was pleased to see that as a married man with his length of service, he qualified for five hundred dollars. He had all his documents ready for demobilization and just had to wait to be assigned a ship. The delay was further complicated with many strikes by dock workers, police officers and railway employees throughout England.

As soon as Jim was granted his two-week leave, however, he immediately walked to the Liverpool railway station to purchase a return ticket to South Shields. It was overcast and cold; it had snowed a little the previous day and grey mush covered the road. Jim marched briskly to the station, content to be alone. He avoided eye contact with anyone he passed, unable to tolerate idle conversation with strangers. It began to drizzle as he approached the railway station, so he ran the last few steps.

Jim bounded up the stairs and entered the waiting room. He noticed one booth without a line up and walked over. He curtly requested his ticket to avoid any pointless chatter, and purchased a ride on the first available train going north. He found an empty bench in the waiting room and sat down to wait. Jim glanced around nervously, feeling disconnected from the other passengers. He was emotionally numb and felt like an old man, in spite of the fact that he was still in his thirties.

After a few minutes, one of the conductors called out, "All aboard!" Jim slowly rose from the bench and walked mechanically to the tracks, then got onto the passenger car. He found a seat at the back and sat down beside a window. He looked out at the grey, wet landscape. The weather would not be any warmer or drier in South Shields, but he would soon find the comfort and peace he craved, in his mother's home. The train slowly pulled away, then picked up speed as it chugged north. Jim closed his eyes and soon fell into his first dreamless sleep in months.

Chapter Fifty-Six

"It looks perfect, Bobby."

Annie and her eldest son were in the parlour. The new furniture had just been delivered and arranged. Annie put her hands on her hips as she surveyed the bedroom. She admired the white, enamelled iron bedstead and the ash bureau and wardrobe, both stained a rich mahogany colour. The afternoon sun filtered through the white lace curtains and gave the room a warm glow. The walls were painted a subdued yellow and a framed print of an English cottage hung over the bed. A large fern spread out over a wicker stand under the window.

"Now we just have to wait for your Granny to get here."

The moment she heard Jack come in the front door she called out, "I'm in the parlour."

He answered, "I picked up the mail, Ma, - there's a letter from Da." He walked into the room, whistled in appreciation at his mother's handiwork, and handed her the mail. Georgie had followed Jack, and he looked at the letter with anticipation.

"Hurry and open it Ma! What does Da say?"

Annie smiled at Georgie and sat down on the bed as she opened the envelope. She quickly read the note.

"Good news, boys. Your Da is sailing on the *Celtic* on March tenth! He should be in Halifax about a week later. The men from New Ontario are sailing with the Fourth Canadian Rifles from Toronto, so we should be able to track him in the Toronto newspaper. He says he'll wire us when he arrives in Halifax and again from Toronto when he knows which train he's taking home." Annie looked at her sons. "Your father will be here in a week!" She stood up and hugged them. They cheered loudly and their boisterous noise travelled to the upper floor, waking Hal and Henry. Bobby laughed when he heard Henry call out.

"Sorry, Ma. I'll go bring them downstairs."

When Bobby carried the two little boys into the newly furnished downstairs bedroom, Hal's eyes opened wide as he looked around.

"Oh, it's gorgeous!"

His older brothers laughed at his choice of words, but Annie picked him up and said, "Thank you, Hal. I think it's gorgeous too."

The family moved into the kitchen when Annie said their dinner was likely ready. Bobby looked back towards the bedroom.

"I'd better make some kind of door or barrier to keep Spud and the little guys out of there. We want to keep it nice for Gran."

On March eighteenth, Jack came in the door and announced, "I just picked up my newspapers, Ma, and the station master handed me a telegram for you. It has to be from Da."

Annie tore open the envelope and read aloud, "Arrived in Halifax stop train arrives in Toronto tomorrow stop love Jim." She turned excitedly to Jack. "Oh, thank God. Your father's in Canada! He'll be home very soon! Jack, you must get me a copy of the newspaper tomorrow as soon as they're delivered to the station. They'll likely write about the *Celtic* arriving because most of the men are from Toronto."

She found herself wandering aimlessly around the house all day, and silently cursed the delay in getting the news from Toronto. When Jack finally handed her the newspaper, Annie immediately sat down at the kitchen table to read it. The paper reported that the *Celtic* had docked in Halifax and it was expected that the eighteen hundred troops would reach Union Station on the evening of March nineteenth. Toronto was planning events to welcome the men home. Annie was overjoyed when she saw that the newspaper had published the names of all the men who sailed on the *Celtic*. She ran her finger down the list and stopped when she came to *James Kidd, Bear Falls.*

"Look, boys! Your father's name is printed right here in the paper! It says the troops will arrive in Toronto at about eight o'clock tonight." She expected he wouldn't get home for another day or two because of demobilization paperwork.. "Oh, I wish we could be at Union Station to meet the train. He said he'd wire us when he knows when his train will get to Jackpine Junction."

The boys all crowded around the paper. Henry cried, "Me too!" Annie picked him up and showed him where it read *James Kidd*.

Two days later, Annie was just clearing the breakfast table when Jack burst through the front door and shouted. "The wire is here, Ma!"

Annie dried her hands on her apron and took the envelope from Jack. She quickly tore it open. She took out the single sheet of paper and read out loud, "Arriving today Jackpine Junction 8:00 p.m. stop See you tonight stop love Jim."

Annie's heart started beating rapidly and she felt weak; she sank to a chair and reread the message to herself. Jack and Georgie hopped around the kitchen in excitement, making a great ruckus; Hal and Henry joined in.

They spent the day tidying the house, and Annie prepared Jim's favourite meal of roast beef and Yorkshire pudding, with apple pie for dessert. The boys all had baths and put on clean clothes. Annie gave the boys a snack since they would be having a late dinner, then searched through cupboards and drawers until she finally found her last bar of lilac soap.

"I'll be in the bathroom. Don't disturb me unless the house is on fire or there's blood and broken bones!"

She indulged herself and had a long bath. When she finally emerged, she sat in front of the kitchen stove to dry her hair. Henry climbed up onto her lap and lay his head against her chest. "You smell nice, Mummy." Annie cuddled her youngest child and kissed the top of his head.

At seven-thirty, they bundled up in layers of winter clothing and left the house. It was a clear, cold evening and the night sky sparkled with starlight. Bobby had borrowed a neighbour's horse and sleigh and was waiting outside for them. Annie handed Henry up to Bobby, and helped Hal climb up. The two little boys snuggled between Annie and Bobby, while Jack and Georgie settled in the back.

Bobby flicked the reins and the horse jolted the sleigh and trotted down the road. The horse had bells attached to his harness. Annie thought the joyful jingle seemed appropriate for their happy excursion, as they travelled the road to Jackpine Junction.

Hal looked up at the stars and cried, "Oh! Oh!" Then Henry looked up and repeated, "Oh! Oh!"

"What is it, boys?" Annie asked.

"The little stars are peeping to see if we are sleeping!" Hal cried.

Henry climbed onto his mother's lap, closed his eyes and put his thumb in his mouth. Annie's smiled as she thought of the lullaby Jim first sang to Maggie. Jim had never had a chance to sing it to Henry, but she had made a point of singing it to her youngest sons each evening.

"Don't worry, poppet. The stars know this is a special night for us."

The horse guided them to the station and stopped out front. Bobby stepped down to cover thehorse's back with a blanket to keep it warm while they waited for the train. Jack and Georgie jumped off the sleigh and Annie helped Hal and Henry down. The light from the station windows spilled over the snow and light standards illuminated the tracks. Annie took Hal and Henry inside the station and sat them on a bench. There was a warm wood fire burning in a large stove in the waiting room. Several other families were chattering excitedly while they waited for the train to arrive. Annie loosened the children's coats and removed their hats and scarves. She glanced up at the large clock on the wall.

"Your Da will be here in ten minutes, boys. That's not a long time to wait at all. You can look out the window that way and you'll see a big light when the train comes."

Hal and Henry squealed when they first spotted the headlight of the train engine. Annie buttoned up their coats and put on their hats, scarves and mittens, and they all walked out to the platform.

"Wait beside Bobby," she told Jack and Georgie. "and be sure to hold Hal's and Henry's hands tightly!"

The evening air was crisp when the train pulled into the junction and hissed to a stop. A cloud of condensation shrouded the tracks.

Inside the second car, Jim picked up his bag and put on his new hat. The passenger beside him looked out the window and said, "March twenty-first is the spring equinox, but apparently we're still in deep winter in here."

Jim nodded. "It does look like the dead of winter, but I feel warm inside. I'm home at last."

He was wearing the new wool suit and winter coat that he had just purchased in Toronto with his thirty-five dollar clothing allowance from the army. He patted the breast pocket that held his back-pay bonus, and followed two other passengers out the door and down the steps to the platform.

There were five or six passengers getting off the train at Jackpine Junction and Annie eagerly watched as the men stepped off the steps of the passenger car. At first she didn't recognize her husband. He was wearing a long, smart, wool coat and a bowler hat. He looked quite the gentleman, she thought, and gasped when the wind blew his hat off of his head. His thick hair was snow white.

She called out his name and he looked in her direction. He answered huskily, "Annie!"

She ran into his embrace and kissed him, then looked deeply into those familiar blue eyes. She brushed away his tears and her own.

"Welcome home, Jim. It's been a long two and a half years."

Jim kissed her again and held her tightly against him before he said, "It's been a hell of a long way back to Bear Falls."

He looked over Annie's shoulder and asked in a rough voice, "Where are the bairns?"

Annie took Jim's hand and leaned into him as they walked off the platform towards their boys.

Bobby led his brothers to their father. Jim stopped and gasped, "My God Bobby, you've grown into a man. Come here, son."

Bobby's face lit up and he gave his father a bear hug. Jack and Georgie followed and put their arms around Jim. Hal and Henry shyly stayed behind and held hands.

Jim knelt down to look into their little faces.

"Do you not remember your own father, boys?"

Hal and Henry both stepped away from him and Annie saw the hurt register on Jim's face. She suggested to their two youngest sons, "Why not shake hands with Daddy?" They allowed Jim to take their small hands in his.

As the family walked towards the horse and sleigh, Annie laughed suddenly, "Look up, Jim."

There, in the evening sky, a shimmering curtain of light swirled and tumbled. Jim looked up at the ribbons of green, pink and violet, and whispered, "My God! How could I have forgotten such a grand sight?"

He wrapped his arms around Annie and held her close, proudly looking around at his boys.

"I'm a lucky man. I'm finally home."

Annie shared the bench on the sleigh with Bobby and Jim; she felt surrounded by love as her husband affectionately pulled her closer to him. Their eldest son steered the horse homeward while the two youngest boys sat in back, cuddled between Jack and Georgie. She glanced up at the Northern Lights dancing in the evening sky and thought of Maggie. She silently included her little girl in their family reunion.

My life has changed incredibly since that horrifying bushfire, especially with Jim away at war for so long. They had lost everything in the flames, except their lives, and Annie thanked God every day that they had been spared the loss of another child. It had been a challenging time, managing alone with five children, and worrying about Jim. *But, I've become a stronger, more independent woman because of all that.*

Annie was impatient to get home and show Jim all she had accomplished in their new home. He would only remember the unheated shell from years ago, she thought. She anticipated his reactions, even though she had described each new purchase in her many letters to him. She could barely wait until he actually saw the electric lights that were wired throughout the house, the new bathroom with its large, hot water tank, and the bedroom set up for Mother, who would be arriving in just three months. She had left the light on in the kitchen and knew the room was warm and inviting, filled with the aroma of the roast beef, Yorkshire pudding and apple pie, waiting to welcome them home.

She devoured Jim with her eyes. Her heart was full of happiness. *He's home! Owning a house is not the most important thing after all. Home is where we're all together and finally, we really are!* It was going to take her a little time to get used to Jim's white hair, but he came back to her whole, unlike so many other men. She worried about the tremor in his hands and wondered how difficult it was going to be for him to readjust to a normal home life, after witnessing all that carnage in the battlefields. Perhaps it would be difficult for her at first, too. *Yes*, she thought, *I'm a different person now as well, but we have all of our tomorrows together. May we be blessed with many tomorrows.*

Author's Notes

Northern Ontario or "New Ontario" was developed through the hard work of countless politicians, financiers, engineers, prospectors, miners and labourers. The North was already rich in native culture and natural beauty before these men arrived. They discovered and exploited the precious metals and natural resources in the boreal forests, and created "New Ontario". My main character is a woman who, along with other wives, sisters and mothers, helped give "New Ontario" a soul. I wanted to put flesh on the bones of those early pioneers and let them live again. I have changed the names of towns and created characters because my novel is not a documentation of statistics, facts or numbers, but a human story.

I found several books that helped me in my research. An invaluable community-formation study of Northeastern Ontario is *Changing Places* by Kerry M. Abel. *Killer in the Bush: The Great Fires of Northeastern Ontario* by Michael Barnes is a fascinating history of the many huge bushfires that occurred in the same time frame as my novel. Tim Cook's historical book, *Shock Troops*, gives insight to the horrific WW1 experiences of many men, some from New Ontario. An interesting memoir of life in Northeastern Ontario in its early years is *Northern Doctor* by C.H. Smylie M.D. and several of the colourful anecdotes that I have included in my story were found in *The Broke Hustler* and the *Pulp and Paper Magazine* archives. Most interesting are oral histories from first-hand experiences; my uncle, Charles Johnson, often entertained his children, nieces and nephews with his colourful memories of life as it was when north-eastern Ontario was known as New Ontario.

Jim's lullaby was handed down from generation to generation in my family. I discovered that it is a common lullaby in north-eastern England and along the Scottish borders, but it appears that the section familiar to me originates from a song written by Lucine Finch in 1899, "Here Comes the Sandman."

"Come You Not From Newcastle" was a poem written by Bishop Thomas Percy in 1868, set to music by John Pyke Hullah in 1884, and published in *Hullah's Song Book*.

There are several people who guided me and advised me while writing and editing this story. Thank you to Karen Connelly and the Humber School for Writers, Alison Latta, and a special thank you to Jess Shulman.

CPSIA information can be obtained at www.ICGtesting.com
Printed in the USA
LVOW07s0916210116

471244LV00005B/231/P